CROWS AT TWILIGHT

An Omnibus of Tales

by

GREGORY MILLER

**Illustrations by
John Randall York**

West Arcadia Press

ISBN 10: 0615897479
ISBN 13: 987-0615897479

West Arcadia Press
gmillerwriter@gmail.com

First West Arcadia Press printing:
October 2013

Scaring the Crows: 21 Tales for Noon or Midnight was originally published by StoneGarden.net Publishing in May 2009. Reprinted with permission.

On the Edge of Twilight: 22 Tales to Follow You Home was originally published by StoneGarden.net Publishing in August 2012. Reprinted with permission.

Cover and interior art by John Randall York

Praise for Gregory Miller and his books:

"Gregory Miller is a fresh new talent with a great future."
—Ray Bradbury

"Miller's prose has a luminous clarity rarely seen in a postmodern age where mysterious opacity is often touted as a virtue...He addresses the reader in a poetic language that is translucent, heartfelt, and wise."
—Roderick Clark, Editor/Publisher of *Rosebud Magazine*

"The small town life depicted in *The Uncanny Valley* is in many ways familiar and comfortable territory, but each story demonstrates that something unnatural lurks beneath the surface. As the stories coalesce to form a larger narrative, the perversity builds...On its own, each individual anecdote is merely curious; as a collective, they become morbidly sinister."
—*Booksellers Without Borders*

"Miller's intriguing premise and incredibly creative stories had me completely enthralled...One of the best eerie books I've read."
—*Book Matters*, reviewing *The Uncanny Valley: Tales from a Lost Town*

"[*The Uncanny Valley*] is an inspired and original idea, breathing fresh life into a popular and revered genre."
—Novelist and critic Daniel Cann

"Gregory Miller's tales in *Scaring the Crows* are wonderfully dark, wonderfully various, and wonderfully wrought."
—Brad Strickland, award-winning author of the *Grimoire* series.

"*Scaring the Crows* is a delightful collection. The stories are chock full of heart and description, and you're left amazed that you could grow so attached to the quirky and often quite likeable characters in such bite-sized works."
—*Hawleyville Reviews*

"It's easy to imagine [*Scaring the Crows*] being done by one of the old greats…This book is a treat."
—*Book Reviews Weekly*

"Miller's prose is unique in that it's both straightforward and elegant. The combination makes the stories powerful regardless of their length and ensures that the endings, one of the author's fortes, have an impact on readers. The range of subject matter in this collection is only matched by the skill with which the author blends nostalgia, humor and the uncanny. "
—*Buzzy Mag*, reviewing *On the Edge of Twilight*

In Memory of Ray Bradbury:
Mentor,
Teacher,
Friend,
with "love to the end of the 21st century"

And for Zee,
always and forever my Big Sis

Table of Contents
from
Scaring the Crows

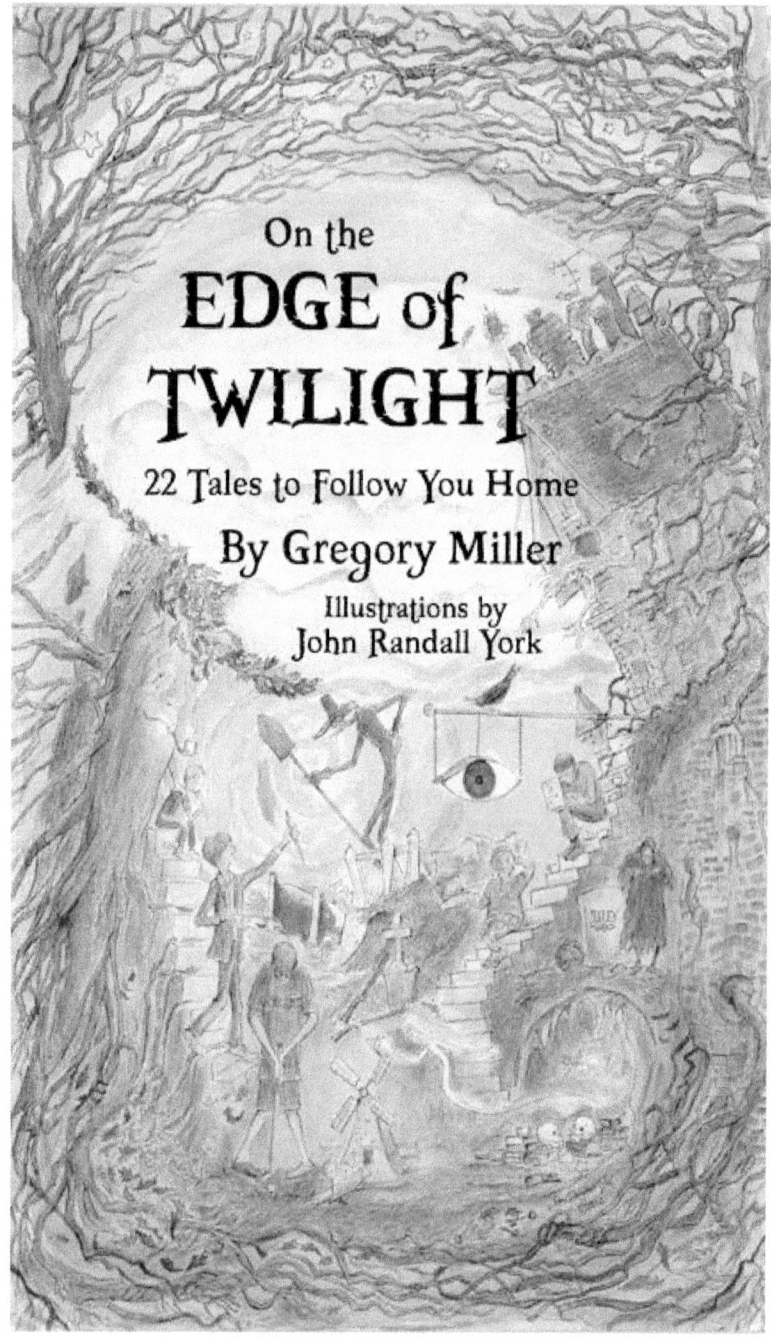

On the
EDGE of
TWILIGHT

22 Tales to Follow You Home

By Gregory Miller

Illustrations by
John Randall York

Table of Contents
from
On the Edge of Twilight

Scaring the Crows

Edith Krepps had given up on men years ago, and now avoided them with a passion that bordered on obsession. Too many abuses, insults, lies and disappointments had left her barren of optimism for future relationships and possessive of a distrust and hatred for virility that gained ground with every passing day.

Anger, she constantly reminded herself. *I'm* angry. *I have a* right *to be angry*. And so she was.

Yet intermingled with her anger, at first subtly, then all too obviously, was something else.

She fought it heart, soul and mind. She reasoned against it. She raved at it. But as the flame of her anger burned more brightly, so also did...fear. Men scared her. *Terrified* her. Intellectually, she had come to understand her own inherent strength. She was self-sufficient, autonomous, and resourceful. She had a good brain on her shoulders and a strong body to support it. But she was...she was...

Oh, God. *Fear*ful.

Pittsburgh, home all her life, became unlivable. The close city streets contained too much to prey on her nerves. The source of her fear was everywhere: stopping by her walk with the mail, processing her groceries at the store, handing her change on the toll roads...

Even Edith's Family Diner, her one claim to critical and commercial success, had become an emotional liability. Dodging three dozen fears a block, she arrived at work every morning a frazzled, anxious wreck. Once there, she spent the rest of the day serving her apprehensions meatloaf, chicken and biscuits, corn soup, coleslaw, and burgers.

Have there always been this many *in here?* she wondered one day, surveying the patrons as her waitresses moved among them. Stifled by testosterone, Adam's apples, Y-chrome voice boxes and splayed-legged posturing, she closed up early that night, sold out, and retired at the age of forty-seven to the suburbs.

The suburbs, however, turned out no better than the city. Paternal households hemmed Edith in, keeping her up nights. Since the neighborhood rules precluded mailboxes, every morning the mailman *came to the door* and jammed letters through a slot. Once every few months a meter man prowled the bushes in the back yard.

Even Edith's nervous tics developed twitches. She began grinding her teeth in her sleep.

Then one day she noticed an ad in the paper for a rental house just an hour away, on the edge of a tiny town called Still Creek, population 1207. It was a fading town, dying because the coalmines were closed, the men who worked them having black dust-coughed themselves into early graves decades before.

It was a quiet town. Isolated.

Perfect.

The house, and old Victorian, was large. It stood on the other side of a hill at the end of Still Creek's last street. Beyond it, before it, and on both sides? Corn fields. The mailbox was at the end of a dirt lane over two hundred yards from the house.

Also perfect.

She rented a moving van, loaded everything up herself, drove it to Still Creek, unloaded everything herself, took a brief look round the property, locked the door tight, and basked in the absence of clammy hands, creeping flesh, pounding heart, and nauseous stomach.

Life, for the first time in several years, was finally good.

*****

The feeling was like a wet, ice-cold finger twisting in her ear.

In the back yard garden, Edith looked up sharply, pulling off her dirt-caked gloves and letting them fall in the lettuce.

She stood up slowly, peering carefully at the unshuttered house, the dustbowl driveway.

Nothing.

Nothing at all but the dread, three months gone but now returned, seethed through her veins in numbing pulses.

She turned with a gasp in a quick, tight half-circle, eyeing everything.

Knee-high corn stalks rustled in a warm, gentle breeze.

The weathervane rooster atop the house twisted, creaking, to face east.

A man was standing in the field, staring at her.

Even as she screamed, Edith took in his patched blue jean overalls, his red and black checkered shirt, his frayed rope belt and black-knit gloves. Her eyes moved up his body, dilated pupils capturing his tattered, wide-brimmed straw hat, his lolling neck, his mottled...

She squinted in the sun and took a step closer, then two, three, ten.

A man? Clothes rippling in the wind but no body movement? Arms spread messianically against a wooden pole?

A man? Straw sticking out of the shirt? A ceramic jack o' lantern for a head?

The scarecrow grinned at her stupidly. Edith breathed a long, shaky sigh of relief.

But where had it come from? It hadn't been there yesterday, or even earlier that morning, and she hadn't been away from the house all day. Edith had made it clear to her landlady, Mrs. Amos, that *no one* was to set foot on the property without prior warning via telephone. No one had called, and beyond that, she should have seen a work truck or heard the pounding of the scarecrow post as it was knocked into the earth.

She went back inside and called Mrs. Amos, but her son answered instead.

"She's in Florida for the next six weeks. Needs the time off and doesn't want bothered. Her blood pressure, you know. What can I do for you?"

But Edith, gasping for air, her very bones chilled, had already slammed the phone down with a heavy *clunk.*

Fine, then. The police!...But in this district? Men, all of them...

Trespasser or no, she would have to make do alone.

*****

As the green fields of rustling corn ripened, yellow shocks and seedling strands waving in hot, late-morning summer wind, Edith woke unrefreshed, unfulfilled by sleep, bothered by the lingering obsessions of one AM, two AM, three AM, four. There had been no sign of any outsiders on her property since the appearance of the scarecrow, but the nagging sense of insecurity still plagued her.

Why? she demanded. *No one in the house, no one on the property. No one in* sight.

But...

But there was, really.

After the sixteenth restless night had passed, at last, into pale morning, Edith went downstairs and made a pot of strong hazelnut coffee. As she ground the beans she happened to glance out the kitchen window, her gaze quickly drawn to the ragged effigy splayed upright in the field beyond the yard.

She shivered, then slowly looked down at her gooseflesh, pressed a hand to her quivering, bloodless lips, and tapped a finger to the racing pulse in her clammy wrist.

"Ridiculous!" she proclaimed. "Beyond ridiculous!"

Really? Is it really?

The scarecrow's clothes, build, presence. Her clacking teeth, cold veins, burning trepidation. The looming sense of dread. The unfounded, pervasive sense of constant invasion; of being watched, scrutinized...

A scarecrow? Yes.

Only a scarecrow?

"Only a scarecrow, yes...but male."

Ignore it, she thought. *Ignore.* To be afraid of the living is one thing. That fear, however irrational, had a foundation in her life. To be afraid of the dead? A little more abstract, but she could understand it. But fear of dried corn stalks and an old farmer's hand-me-downs? That was a fear that needed to be put down, knocked away, cast off and forgotten. Killed.

Go on out, now. Ignore it. Go tend the garden.

"Damn it," said Edith a week later, peering from behind lace curtains at the dead plants gone back to dust.

*****

It was the following day, in the calm, humid warmth following a brief summer storm, that Edith noticed the change.

The scarecrow was gone.

Gone! Knowing it was in the field was bad enough. Somehow, not knowing where it was struck her as far worse.

Taken? Knocked off the pole by wind? Battered down by rain?

She went to her bedroom on the second floor and looked out the window. Peering down from that angle she could see the empty bamboo pole clearly. Straw hands, wet cloth and a ceramic pumpkin skull lay in a tangle several feet away among the corn stalks.

"Fine," she assured herself. "That's fine."

But the next day wasn't so fine.

"If I didn't know better," Edith said, looking out the window for the two-dozenth time in as many hours. She closed her mouth with a clatter of enamel.

Days passed.

An inch. A foot. A yard. Ever so slowly, but without a doubt, the scarecrow was closing in on the house.

"A trick of the light," Edith said. "Wind. An animal. Kids."

At first she believed it, yet the sunlight and moonlight were steady and played no tricks. The air was muggy and calm. There was no evidence of dogs or other large animals on her property. Besides, what animal would return night after night to nudge, prod, pull—just enough to scare? Teenagers? They never bothered her, preferring the intrigue of woods or the troubles of parties far out in the countryside to the boring, cultivated fields around her end of town.

The chair dragged up from the kitchen became a fixture by her bedroom window. In turn, so did Edith. Downstairs existed in dimness and dark, the curtains pulled across the windows, the doors latched, bolted, and reinforced by stools lodged firmly under knobs. She wanted to leave town but could not; beyond Still Creek prowled fears she could not face. Even the progress of the straw man scared her less than them.

It did, however, scare her very, very much.

September came, autumn on its heels. The scarecrow reached the edge of the cornfield.

That morning, waking from a short, troubled doze in her chair, Edith's tired, glazed eyes slowly focused. She leaned toward the frost-paned window, found the subject of her constant attention, and stared at it for a long moment before jumping up, skin seething with shock-sweat.

Colin!

A high school boyfriend came crashing into her mind, dredged up from deep, lost years: his thick neck, wrestler's arms, and close-cropped brown hair; his strangely high-pitched giggle when they watched *All in the Family* on Tuesday nights; his haughty stride, ridiculous posturing, and constant primping; his overbearing smile when he announced that, yes, he *was* too good for her now, it *was* time to move on, his parents *didn't* approve, she came from the *wrong side of the tracks*; and last but not least, the way he'd swung his Number 28 Martinsville

Mariners varsity jacket over his right shoulder as he'd walked away from her for the last time.

"Now how," she asked the scarecrow, "did you get that?"

Instead of the red and black woolen shirt, the scarecrow now sported a tight-fitting denim Martinsville Mariners varsity jacket, Number 28.

She took two Quaaludes and slept for twelve hours.

When Edith woke up, she sighed with relief. The jacket was gone, the old weather-stained shirt back in place. It was the same—

"Wait. Wait."

Penny loafers.

"Bernard Renfrew." A no-show at Senior Prom. But the day before that horrible night, he'd left those shoes at her house, part of a rented tuxedo outfit that had been used to charm and impress—not her, but a close friend instead. She had fed them to Flower, her pure-bred German Shepherd. Now they adorned the scarecrow's husk feet.

And the scarecrow itself was unquestionably closer.

From then on, every time she turned away, slept, ate, scratched herself over the next few days and nights, the scarecrow gained ground...and not only that, *changed.*

David Palchak. Nick Miller. Lloyd Stackhouse.

It reached through the last corn stalks, face down, arms splayed out before it, its left wrist sporting a gold Rolex that gave Edith shudders of memory.

Ryan Nelson. Wallace Goodwin. Jason Knapik.

It lay among tomato husks in the abandoned garden, a thin silver necklace she had bought for Brian Caldwell, the first man who ever punched her in the face, around its corn stock neck.

Stuart Baumgarten. Peter Wendell. Marty Bainbridge.

It sat propped against the peeling red picnic table under the maple tree, a gold and amber ring lodged on a twisted, dried-grass finger that dredged up memories of a high-society penthouse, two defense attorneys, and drugged drinks.

Lester Ringwold. Richard Brummet. Burt Winger.

It slumped six feet from the back porch door, and on its grinning, hollow head a dark smudge in the shape of her ex-husband's birthmark reminded her of three years she had spent the previous decade trying desperately to forget...

Palpitations plagued her.

Blood thudded in bright red ears.

Breathing grew difficult.

Then, finally, *finally*:

"Enough!"

After days of watching, silent, hungry, scared, Edith leapt to her feet. "Pitiful. *Pitiful!* You're a failed businessman now! Your second wife left you! Your son hates you! Six months in jail for a third DUI! *How did that feel?* You're nothing! Broken! *You're nothing at all!"*

Triumphant, she grinned. Then, still smiling, she let darkness come. Her eyes rolled back in her head, the world went muddy, and her body ran like water to the floor.

*****

Numberless hours of dreamless rest plus something Edith couldn't later put into words rose to nullify seventy-two hours of sleepless vigil and left her feeling oddly refreshed as cold night fell, veiling the house and yard in long shadows.

Words fell from her lips: "He was the last." Again: "He was the last."

She got unsteadily to her feet, leaned against the chair for support, and pressed the fingertips of her right hand to the cool glass of the window.

She looked out.

The scarecrow was gone.

Taking a deep breath, running a hand through her matted tangle of hair, Edith stood, head cocked, listening intently to the sighing of the house. The tension of her weight creaked the floor timbers. A pine branch scratched gently against the tin gutter pipe on the roof.

Down below, in the dark, something rustled.

Edith went to the edge of the stairs and peered into the black.

"You were a hundred and one people, and now all that's left is…you. That's my bet."

The darkness listened.

Edith hesitated a moment, then started downstairs.

The hallway was murk, the arched entryway to the living room a yawning mouth. In the living room, something whispered too softly to be understood.

Creaking across the old wooden floor beams, feeling the way carefully in her blindness, Edith paused at the entryway.

"One by one I relived my failures through your clothes, my pains through your face. You tested me, and…I survived. I *survived*." She sounded surprised, and realized she was. She was also very calm. "And what's left is…what? Straw and stick, corn cob and grass. Leaf and wire. Am I right?"

The silence was noncommittal.

"No, more than that, of course. You walk. You watch. You wait. But harmless. Defenseless. Easily burnt, broken, withered. Easily mildewed and rotted. More than that, very cold. And, perhaps…lonely?"

The assent came, and it was a corn-shuck voice, a reedy rasp that spoke around the fumblings of field insects and clods of cool mud.

"I must admit," she continued, "it has been a *very* long time since I last had a man in my home—of *any* kind," she added hastily. "I'd like to take it slow. Maybe we could just talk?"

Yes, the voice said, talking would be fine. *Just* fine. Come in. Sit down.

"Oh yes," Edith said, stepping into the living room's pregnant dark.

She felt her way to the couch and sat down at one end. She could feel the weight of something else on the other. She cleared her throat.

"I think maybe we should have a little light. That's only proper. A little light?" she asked.

Yes.

"Okay," she said, and flicked a switch.

Edith looked at what was sitting beside her on the couch…and *winked*.

Big Plans

He laid his new tie and freshly pressed shirt on the dresser. He took his sports coat from the closet and whisked it down before giving his new loafers a final polish.

"Ben," said Cathy, looking sleepily over at him from the bed.

"What, hon?"

"It's five in the morning. Your interview isn't until nine and it only takes an hour to get to the city."

"You never know about Pittsburgh traffic," said Ben, adjusting his tie. "And there's construction on 76. How's the hair? I think Ross cut it too short."

"Fine as always."

He ran his fingers through it, unconvinced.

"Now how is it?"

Cathy rolled her eyes. "*Still* fine, as always. I should get up and make you breakfast."

"No, not a chance. I didn't mean to wake you up. Go back to sleep."

She shook her head. "This is an important day. You need to eat."

"I can make myself something."

"You need something more than just *cereal*."

Downstairs in the kitchen, Cathy tended the bacon while Ben stared out the window, a folded *Still Creek Gazette* untouched by his elbow.

"You don't need to be nervous," she said, forking the bacon onto a paper towel and blotting the grease. "You said you already got the job. It's just a formality."

"I know. But the superintendent will be there. I've never met her before. And both principals this time. And the head of the English department. And there *are* two other candidates. If I blow it, they're waiting in the wings."

"That won't happen."

Cathy handed over Ben's breakfast and took a seat beside him.

"Tell me again what we'll do with the money," she said.

Ben sipped his coffee and allowed a smile. "We'll pay off all our loans. We'll sell the house and move to North Hills, just ten minutes from the heart of the city. We'll see shows and eat at a different restaurant every Saturday night. Then we'll find three, maybe four restaurants that we really like and we'll only go to those. The waiters and waitresses will learn our names. We'll be regulars. And every Christmas, our families will drive out from the country and we'll take them to Pine Forest to see the light display—the biggest in Pennsylvania. And I'll teach thirty years' worth of students, and attend seminars downtown every summer. And you'll become head librarian at Carnegie University, or maybe Pitt. And every August before school starts up again we'll fly somewhere different for vacation."

Cathy smiled. "Every time you say it, you add something new. There's no need to *fly* somewhere for vacation every year. Driving is just fine."

Ben shook his head. "Well, maybe *sometimes* we'll drive. But I'm sick of Harrisburg and Gettysburg and Baltimore and Washington D.C. I want Los Angeles and Chicago and Denver and Seattle. I want London and Paris and Rome!"

"You've got egg on your tie."

Ben sighed and brushed it off.

Cathy kissed his cheek as he stood to go. "Drive safe. Take deep breaths. Pop a mint before you start to talk. And watch out for that nervous twitch. Remember that, and you'll do *fine*."

Two hours later, she picked up the telephone with a tremulous hand.

"I did fine," Ben told her.

*****

She walked the three blocks to Stockton's Grocery and spent twenty-two dollars before returning home laden with brown paper bags. She spent half an hour on the phone.

The small house they had shared for three years quickly filled with family and friends. There was a steady hum of life like bees in a hive, all bustle and work and business and laughter. Good smells wafted out from the kitchen and balloons bumped the ceiling in the dining room. Warmth saturated the living room, fogging the windows and holding back the cold outside.

"There's so much else we'll be able to do," Cathy told her mother. "So many new opportunities. So many new chances."

Her mother kneaded piecrust in a tin pan and smiled without looking up.

"Big fish in a small pond, is that it? And Pittsburgh's the ocean?"

Cathy nodded. "No more debt. No more small, crowded rooms and second-hand furniture. No more leaky ceiling or rusted-out shed. All our lives, and now we're moving out. That's how it should be. That's how it's supposed to happen."

"It's awful far."

She gazed at her mother for a long time. "Not so far. You and Daddy will come visit and spent weekends with us."

Her mother smiled again. Still, she did not look up. "Yes," she said, and patted her hand. "Yes, that will be fine. It's a wonderful chance. We're all very proud of you."

Shortly before six, they heard the driveway stones crunch under Ben's car, and everyone fell silent.

"Here he comes," Cathy whispered. The house hummed with hidden life.

As they waited, she looked around at the still, expectant faces. She smiled. Then, unexpectedly, the smile fell away, but it came back when Ben unlocked the door and stepped inside.

The wind had flushed his cheeks and blown his hair into a mess of bangs. His eyes, so often red and tired at the end of the day, now twinkled. The tilt of his mouth spoke of triumph. Before he could take another step, a benign flood of people bore him up and into the house.

"Congratulations!" everyone cried. "Congratulations!"

And when, an hour later, the phone rang and Ben answered it, no one thought to ask who it was. Well into the evening they celebrated. Cake and ice cream and beer and songs. Stories and future plans. Back-slaps and bear hugs. Ben stayed in the middle of it all, laughing loudest, telling the tallest tales, eating and drinking and accepting all good wishes with a toothy smile. And if he looked a little tired now and then, who could blame him? It had been a long day.

When the last of the friends left with the last of the family, they shut the door and stared at the litter scattered about the empty house. The smile fell from Ben's face along with his color. His shoulders slumped. Cathy watched as he trudged up the stairs without another word, and it was only then that she remembered the phone call and realized what it meant.

*****

He lay in the dark on the bed, above the blankets, shoes still on. Outside, wind beat against the frost-rimmed windowpanes and shook the eaves. The air felt thin and cold. The night was thick.

Cathy crossed over to the bed and stared down at the darker shadow of her husband. She could hear his breathing. It was even but hard.

She sat down beside him and did not speak.

"It was an issue of clearances," he said at last. "That DUI when I was 21. They didn't know about that. I didn't even think to mention it. Here it doesn't matter so much, but there it does. I'll never be a teacher in the city."

More breathing in the darkness. Cathy's respiration found Ben's rhythm and joined it, chest pacing chest.

"There will be other jobs," she said. "Other opportunities."

"Not like that one," he replied. "Not like that."

She lay back on the bed, hair nestled beneath her head on the pillow. The mattress ebbed and flowed with their breathing, a living thing.

"I wanted to give us something we never had before," Ben said softly.

"I know. But then again, I'm not as upset as I thought I would be. Strange."

A sharp movement, and Cathy knew Ben had sat up and was looking at her.

"Tell me," he said slowly, "what we would have done with all that money."

Her eyes adjusted to the darkness and she stared up at the ceiling slats. "We would have paid off our loans," she began slowly. "Then we would have sold our house here and moved to North Hills, just ten minutes from the heart of the city. We would have seen shows and eaten at a different restaurant every Saturday night."

Ben was very quiet beside her, still looking at her through the dark. She could see him faintly now.

She continued, "Then we would have grown lonely and wondered why we had decided to move. We would have missed our family and friends. We would have missed the walks around town that we had once thought we would never miss. We would have invited everyone over for Christmas, but it wouldn't have been the same. And each year fewer and fewer people would have come. And so, after ten years, we would have moved back here, to this town that's small but *not* dying, and I would have taken my old job back as the Still Creek Elementary School's assistant librarian, and you would have taken your old job back as a Still Creek High School English teacher. And we would have been content at long last."

She felt the bed creak as Ben lay back down. A hand found hers.

A gust of wind rattled the storm windows, bringing with it a spray of late-season ice that clattered against the glass and aluminum siding.

Inside, the room had grown very warm.

Cathy sat up and flicked on the light. She stood quietly at the edge of the bed.

"Please get up," she said.

"What?"

"Get up. Put on your coat."

Ben got up, looked around the room, looked into her face, then went to the closet and took out his coat and put it on. He sensed, rather than knew, that now was not the time for questions.

"Follow me," she said.

Cathy went ahead of him, down the stairs, and, after hesitating, he followed.

As they reached the front door she opened it and said, "Outside."

"What?"

"Just step out."

Ben stepped out the door and she followed, shutting it behind them. They were out in the night.

"What are we doing?" he asked.

"Why, it's March 17."

"That date," he said. "It's very familiar."

Cathy nodded. "Three years ago today, we moved into this house. Here." She handed him a key.

He looked at it for a long moment, then recognized what it was for. He put it in the front door lock, twisted it, and the door drifted open.

Cathy stepped in, turned, and said, "Come on. It's the first day."

Ben smiled as he followed.

Stapleton's Dog

The sullen wasteland spread away from them until it met and blended with the overcast horizon.

They stared at it with approval. Around them, a cold wind carried with it a colder mist, and the mournful cry of a bird they did not recognize echoed through the desolation. October, that most melancholy of months, seemed highly concentrated in the 280 square miles of dead bracken, rotting vegetation, slimy moss, standing water, and quicksand.

"The greatest of the Dartmoor bogs!" exclaimed Tom Worthington, breathing in deeply. "Here we are."

"I wonder if it's as dangerous as the great Grimpen Mire." Stella, his wife of twenty-one years, rubbed her hands together to kill the chill. Even so, the flush in her cheeks wasn't just from the cold. She was excited, Tom noted. She was happy to be here. *Thrilled.*

"I'm sure it is," said Tom, scanning the distance. "I don't think Sir Arthur exaggerated his source."

Seventeen-year members of the Sherlock Holmes Society, they had been planning this visit for over a decade. Money was tight, but Tom's prompting had gradually won Stella over, and here they finally were. Both smiled as they took a few tentative steps closer to the bog's edge. Behind them the windows of the Gifford Bed & Breakfast glowed with light that promised warmth, food, and hot baths. Beneath their feet a fine, manicured lawn pushed away wildness with promises of croquet, picnics, and long walks on well-tended paths.

Neither of them paid any of that any mind. Their hearts were already caught in the mire.

"Doyle walked here," Stella said, nodding to herself. "On this very yard. On these very moors. In that very marsh."

"And now, so will we." Tom smiled.

"So many years of saving, and here we are, where *he* was," Stella went on. "And where he was is where Dr. Mortimer, Stapleton, Mr. and Mrs. Barrymore, Sir Henry, and dear old Watson and Mr. Sherlock Holmes himself *still* roam."

She reached into a coat pocket and withdrew a battered paperback. On the front cover a snarling, demonic hound glared out with fearsome red eyes.

"Yes, dear," said Tom. "You're absolutely right."

"I've always dreamed of standing in this spot with this book in my hand…with you."

"For a while, it looked like that would never happen."

Stella glanced at Tom sharply. "I know. But that's over now. It's forgotten…ancient history! I hardly remember his face." She grasped his warm hands tightly. He noted that hers were very cold.

"That's good to know," Tom said evenly.

Stella stared at him a moment longer, then took a deep breath. In the time it took her to exhale, she had cheered again.

"Well, what say we explore a little?"

"Certainly," said Tom. "Where shall we go first?"

"The mire, of course!"

She took six steps forward along what looked like a solid, mossy path. For a moment it held. Then the earth sucked, shifted, and gave way. Mud lapped at her heels, encircling them in a tight, clammy grip. She fell sideways. A heartbeat later she was knee-deep in stinking brown muck.

"Help me, Tom!"

A curse, a wallowing splash, a desperate heave, and soon Stella lay safe on the lawn, breathing hard. Tom, also drenched, drew in a ragged breath and laughed.

"What's so funny?" Stella snapped, still gasping.

"I was just imagining the pony that Stapleton and Watson watched…the one that sank, screaming, to its death."

"I don't think that's very funny at all. It was a horrible scene. Doyle used it to provoke a sense of foreboding and foreshadowing in the reader, and he succeeded."

"And what did Stapleton say about the great Grimpen Mire when describing it to Watson?"

Stella sighed, delved into her pocket for the paperback, flipped a few pages, and quoted, "'Even in dry seasons it is a danger to cross it, but after these autumn rains it is an awful place.' Fine, fine. I see your point. I should have known better."

Tom grinned. "And *then* what does Stapleton say?"

More thin pages flipping. "Um…'And yet I can find my way to the very heart of it and return alive.'"

"Yes!"

"I get it, Tom. All very clever."

"No, no. Don't be angry. Here."

He reached down and hoisted Stella to her feet. He dusted her off, removed a strand of slime from her hair, and grinned. "Now for the surprise."

"What surprise?"

"Did the water slop into your boots?"

"No. Good thing I wore the high tops."

"Excellent. Allow me."

Tom took Stella's hand and led her forward. For a moment he thought she would resist, but she followed him, even after her near miss. Whistling, he stepped, without hesitation, twenty feet into the mire without so much as a squelch…Stella right behind.

"Tom! How?"

"Nothing at all!" He bowed.

"But—"

"Oh, I did my homework. Corresponded with some of the locals and took notes. Got a map. Studied it. And here we are. And here we go!"

He led the way again, slowly but steadily, and when they stopped a second time the green grass of the lawn was very far away.

Stella could barely control her excitement. "I never imagined! It's…It's *wonderful*. Just like I thought it would be. How completely desolate! How horribly oppressive! Oh, Tom," she said, kissing him briefly on the cheek, "how can I ever *thank* you?"

"Oh, I'll think of something," Tom said. "But it's my pleasure. My way of saying, 'I want to start over.'"

Stella hugged him tight. "But how much farther are we going? It's getting dark."

"A ways yet," Tom said. "See that low hill?"

"What, way out there?"

"It's really more of an island. We'll walk out, take a look around, then head back for dinner."

They moved on, Tom picking his way carefully, Stella following in his footsteps. At last, with the bleached sun sinking into the heart of the mire, they reached the hill.

"It really *is* more of an island," Stella said.

"Yes," said Tom, climbing up the low rise to where two long stones jutted up like fangs. "See?"

Stella nodded.

"And you know something?" Tom asked.

"What's that?"

"This is the very spot that inspired Doyle's description."

Stella shook her head. "Description of what? The marsh?"

"No. The place where the demon hound tore out Sir Hugo Baskerville's throat."

"Really?" Stella shuddered. She reached out and took Tom's hand.

Despite the chill, his palm was very warm…so warm that she let go of it very quickly.

"Really," Tom said, then paused. "It *is* all very impressive, isn't it? Just the way we pictured it?"

"Yes," said Stella, but now her tone was low, somewhat distracted. The wind had grown very strong and very cold. Dead rushes moaned and sighed. She shivered.

"Bow-wow," said Tom.

She blinked, uttering a startled giggle. "What?"

And then he pounced.

Goodbye, Friend

The call came at five o' clock, barely an hour after Adam Mitchell's last class of the day. He was still cold from the long walk across campus, and Dr. Robinson's voice, booming out thoughts on Roman philosophy, remained a close memory.

He sat down on his dorm cot and answered the phone.

"Adam?"

"Hi, Dad."

"Tank is bad."

"How bad?"

"You should come home. Mom says the vet can see him within the hour."

Adam took a deep breath. "I'll be there in twenty minutes," he said.

*****

Tank lay in his kennel, breathing hard and staring straight ahead with cataract-stricken eyes that, even with limited vision, looked out at nothing anyone else could see. His lungs rasped and his chest heaved, over and over, and all the concentration he could muster was focused inward, oblivious to anything outside of his stricken body.

Adam knelt beside Tank and touched the long mane of hair on his neck.

"You remember what the vet said," Adam's father murmured.

"Yes, I remember."

"Will you do it?"

Adam paused. "I…I don't know. I'll see what the vet says this time."

His father sighed. "Tank has arthritis and cataracts, seizures and incontinence, all on top of his lung problems."

"I know."

"You need to do what's right."

Adam eased Tank out of his kennel and lifted him into his arms. "Right now, all I need is some help getting Tank out to the car," he said.

*****

The late-November day turned cold as the sun went down, the afternoon rain to ice, and the headlights of passing cars dazzled off the foggy windshield and cast halos into Adam's eyes.

He kept one hand on the steering wheel, one hand on Tank's chest. The dog lay beside him on the passenger seat, wheezing softly.

"Easy now," Adam said. "Easy."

The vet's office was twelve long miles away, at the end of a complicated gauntlet of back roads and congested highway. Adam already felt frustration toward it. Every time the brake grated down, Tank grunted. Every time he took a turn too tight, Tank whined.

"Easy now," Adam said again.

Norle Street flashed by on his right, a brief glimpse of sign and dark road in the relentless, driving sleet. As a child he had lived there, second house on the left. The memories of that time were all sunlight, sieved through age and years so only a vague feeling of childhood wonder remained—wonder at how the world worked, and especially how anything could ever change.

He looked down at the passenger seat and the memory of a long-gone Sunday morning came unbidden and unexpected. In that now-dark house, when he was five, he had looked at Tank and thought, "When I am twenty, he will be fifteen. When I am twenty-five, he will be dead." The idea had appalled him—that this young bundle, a reflection of himself, would die of old age long, long before he even knew full maturity—and he had taken comfort in the fact that such a time was so far in the future it might as well not exist.

But now it was close, and that other day, long ago in bright summer sunlight, felt faint and distant instead.

"Easy now," he said, patting Tank's neck. "Easy."

*****

The turn came swiftly and caught him unaware. Tank fell sideways off the seat. Adam's open backpack vomited books onto the floor. Tires squealed and gravel crunched. The car lurched to a halt.

Adam took a deep breath, reached down, and lifted Tank back onto the seat. Tank whined softly.

"I'm sorry," he said, stroking his fur, but Tank did not look at him. For a week he had not looked at anyone.

"We'll get you fixed up and take you back home," he continued. "You'd like that, wouldn't you? To go home?"

Once Tank had calmed, Adam reached into the back seat and picked up all the books. Absently, he glanced at a highlighted line from his Philosophy 121 textbook:

Never injure a friend, even in jest.
--Cicero

He paused, eyes frozen on seven words written by a man two thousand years silent who had found his voice again here, now, in a car at the side of a sleet-slicked road on a cold November evening.

He dropped the book and turned back to Tank. Tank, who had waited on the front porch every afternoon for him to return from school; who had kept vigil by his bed at night when he was sick; who had always, always put Adam first—unconditionally and without exception.

Never injure a friend, even in jest.

He started the car and pulled back onto the road, tears welling in his eyes. The whole time he kept his right hand on Tank, feeling the ebb and flow of the dog's belabored breath. He knew what he had to do.

Tank wouldn't be coming home.

Minutes passed slowly but inexorably. Twilight turned to night. Sleet turned to snow.

"You always put me first," Adam murmured.

As the lights of the veterinary clinic dotted the dark surrounding woods, Tank raised his head and licked Adam's hand.

Adam pulled into a parking space and turned off the car.

He looked down. Something had changed.

Never injure a friend...

He placed a trembling hand on Tank's cooling head, then on his still, silent chest. He closed Tank's eyes, then his own.

Without Power

Night came, and Rachel Phillips looked toward the ceiling. Darkness met her gaze and she saw nothing beyond it. The nothing scared her.

Her small hands clasped the corners of the quilt until her pudgy fingers went white in the knuckles. Far away, in the cold outside, a dog barked. She counted the barks until they numbered thirteen. Then the barks stopped abruptly, with a yelp.

Downstairs, no reassuring sounds came from the kitchen, the living room, the study or porch. In the other bedrooms no one spoke, snored, rustled blankets or fluffed pillows. She couldn't see the sliver of light that usually filtered under her door from the open bathroom. The back porch light didn't shine through the window.

The house was old. Once she'd asked Grandpa how old, and he'd said, "Older than you and me and your parents put together." That, she knew, was pretty old. In the past it was always warm and bright. Before two days ago. Before the sudden, cold-sweat drive through the snow and the quiet talk of hospitals from the front seat.

In the past it hadn't bothered her; the age hadn't been an issue and neither had the creaks and groans, the thumps and bumps, the far off murmurs and nearby squeaks.

Now they bothered her.

Now they kept her up, shivering, although February was stuck outside and the room was warm. Now they made her think of the dark fields beyond the edge of the back yard, past the picnic table and the maple tree; and of the forest; and of the church and grave-yard past the fairgrounds. And of the carpets still stained with mud from the paramedics' shoes.

And it was now, with everything dark and everyone gone, that she realized something—something very *close*—was wrong.

"It's just the dark," Mommy would have told her. "We'll keep the bathroom light on."

But Mommy was out, and Daddy was out, and Grandma and Uncle John were out, and Grandpa—

Under the bed something rustled.

A mouse, Grandpa would have said. And she would have believed him because it would have been true.

Now, though.

Now.

The rustling continued, and Rachel moved to the center of the bed, arms and legs tucked up tight around her. Her lower lip began to quiver.

Whatever it was, it was more than a mouse. Bigger. The wooden floor creaked beneath its weight as it shifted, scuttling across the cool beams then back again.

She wanted to scream. She wanted to holler, reach out a hand, slap on a light switch. But no one was home and the power was out.

"Stay in bed," Daddy had told her. "We'll be back before eleven, and I want you asleep by then."

"But I want to come too."

"Tomorrow. You'll see him tomorrow."

No way to tell what time it was now. It had been 9:30 the last time she checked, before everything went dark. She would have to wait for the tolling of the church bell.

The bed lurched, bumped from below. A shriek escaped her lips. She clapped a hand to her mouth, eyes wide and staring.

Instead of counting seconds, she counted the pounding beat of her heart. She soon lost track, distracted by the smell and texture of the quilt against her nose and face. She held it there, over her, knees pulled up to her chest. The quilt would protect her. It always had.

But it's just a quilt, a small voice whispered.

"No," she whispered back.

Yet she knew it was true. If whatever lurked under her bed chose, it could slide out, rise up, and grab her, quilt and all. She would be spider's prey already wrapped in silk, ready to be consumed.

Now her imagination, already heated from overwork, kicked into overdrive. Images flashed across her mental vision, captivating her the way a gruesome accident captivates those who drive by it— unharmed, but cognizant of the fact that the blood on the road isn't syrup dyed red, that the teddy bear in the dirt isn't a prop, that the broken bodies aren't dummies.

A rabid dog with glowing green eyes lay in wait, drooling white foam.

Her first cousin, killed in a barn fire four years back, had come home again, pallid eyes gleaming from a charcoal-black face, clothes smelling of cinders.

A giant rat had raced up through the sewer, through the heating ducts, and was clawing at the grate in the wall, yellow teeth grown long and crooked, red gums dotted gray with disease.

The huge salamander she'd hooked with Grandpa when she was six had somehow survived. She remembered its gasping, toothless mouth, how it had lunged up at her when she reeled it in, its slimy body squirming and wriggling until, with a moan, it gurgled and stilled. And now it was back.

Or—

Or...

No.

She sniffed the air.

No. None of those.

She forced herself calm.

None of them.

Breathe in, out. Deep, slow breaths. In. Out.

Nothing.

Up, down. Rise, fall. In, out.

Incredibly, her pulse slowed. Amazingly, she relaxed.

Mommy and Daddy will be home soon now, she thought.

Beneath her bed, nothing moved. Nothing breathed. Nothing clawed at the bedposts or tore at the edge of the quilt. Nothing smelled rotten. Nothing whispered in the dust.

She started to hum. At first it came out dry; she had no spit in her throat and her voice box didn't work. Then she swallowed twice and tried again.

The sound entered the room and everything was fine. The shadows receded. They lost depth and texture, fell back, faded out to make way for moonlight. The closeness of the room rose up above her head and dissipated. She extended her hands and feet again, feeling the edges of the mattress.

Rachel put words to the tune.

"Hush little baby, don't say a word. Mama's gonna buy you a mockingbird."

The high sweetness of her voice coursed warmth through her blood.

"And if that mockingbird don't sing—"

She stopped. Her breath caught in her throat.

"Mama's gonna buy you a diamond ring," the croaking voice beneath her bed finished.

In Rachel's nightmares, the worst moment always came when she reacted with a scream to whatever horrible thing happened, but no sound came out.

She tried to scream now, but no sound came out. Over and over. Again and again, until she tasted bile in the back of her throat. She didn't move. She didn't get out of bed. She didn't go rushing from the room. She was frozen. She was frozen, and something under her bed was perfectly willing to lie there and sing with her, sing her to death, scare her heart to splinters.

She was caught.

If Grandpa were here he'd take care of it, she thought desperately. *He always does. All he'd have to do is stare it down, and it'd go away.*

The thing under the bed growled softly.

He'd take care of it, Rachel thought, and despair shook her. Everything dark—above, below, inside, out.

The gloom was strong again. Something black, a shadow within a shadow, moved up the edge of the wooden bed frame with a rasping of claws.

Rachel saw it, heard it. She lay rooted, the pale skin of her ankle just inches from its scrabbling want. She felt her heart palpitate. The weight of the room's walls pressed down. With a whisper of breath she closed her eyes...

And then in a brilliant, shining instant, shifting light burned bright through the window blinds. Outside an engine purred, then stopped. Car doors opened and slammed shut. Boots crunched on snow. Daddy spoke quiet words. Mommy and Grandma responded.

The front door opened, and Rachel was free.

With a shriek she tore off her blankets and jumped out of bed. She sprinted across the bedroom and down the hall—straight into Daddy's arms.

"Whoa, now! What's this?" He hugged her tight, a flashlight in one hand.

She threw her arms around his neck, sobbing.

"Hey, hold on." Daddy held her at arm's length, smiling faintly. "What's the matter? It's just a power outage."

"There's a monster under my bed!"

"Oh yeah? Let's go take a look together, huh? See how he holds up under my flashlight."

"*No,* Daddy, it's—"

"Come on, now."

They went back to the bedroom. They looked under the bed with the flashlight.

Nothing was there but dust and dirty socks.

Ten minutes later Rachel finally felt tired for the first time in hours. Tucked in tight, Daddy sitting on the edge of the bed reading *Mike Mulligan and His Steam Shovel* out loud, the flashlight's beam reassuring as it spilled off the pages of the book and onto the blankets, her eyes grew heavy.

Daddy looked tired, too. She could see it in his face. Everyone would sleep well. She didn't need light. All she needed was to know they were sleeping nearby, in the rooms around her.

"Mommy," she murmured. "Grandma. Can they come say goodnight?"

Daddy stopped reading and looked at her. "Mommy's… Mommy and Grandma are real tired, Honey," he said.

"But it'll only take a minute."

"They're real sad now, Rachel. It—"

He stopped.

Rachel sat up so fast she knocked the flashlight from Daddy's hand by mistake. It flipped backward and fell to the floor. The light went out. The sound of batteries rolling across the polished planks seemed to die before it could properly be heard.

"Why are they sad?" Rachel demanded.

In the dark, Daddy fumbled for the batteries. She could hear him. There, he had one…there now, the other.

"Honey, in the morning. We'll talk more in the morning."

"Is Grandpa OK?" she asked, her voice very small.

Daddy said nothing. In the dark, all Rachel could hear was the sound of his hands fumbling with the pieces of flashlight and the batteries that made it work.

Then she heard something else.

"Daddy, turn the light on," Rachel breathed.

"Just give me a minute here," said Daddy, but his voice sounded odd, strange. It sounded upset in a way she'd never heard before.

"*Please*, Daddy. Hurry!"

"Hold your horses, now, I'm getting there."

"*Daddy!*"

Something black and hulking, a shadow within a shadow, stepped out from the corner of the room behind Daddy. It turned toward her. Two great tendrils of gloom reached forward.

"Almost got it, Honey. Almost."
"Too late," whispered Rachel, and shut her eyes tight.

Two Calls

O f course it was never as fine as his dreams, but still it was fine. The waves rolled on toward the shore. The world tilted on the edge of sight far out to sea. The sun slipped past its zenith and raced to fall, a comet across the water. Warm, bronzed people lay on the white sand, some already packing up, leaving for gritty showers at home, bare feet kicking up powder. A few, final Venice Beach street merchants plied their trades in the fading light—incense sticks, charcoal portraits, power crystals and sea-shell animals. Half a block down, a guitarist, case open for change, played a sad song about something lost forever.

Jacob stood, dusted off his swim trunks, and turned to his best friend.

"Dinner?"

"Sure," said Richard. "I should call Julie first. See how she's feeling."

"No problem. Call away."

Richard did. Frowning at his phone, he punched in the number to his home in Baltimore. His eyes took on a far-away look, glazed and sightless, and Jacob knew he could no longer see the great halo of light that glowed like a path from the shore to the rolling Pacific horizon. He saw other things instead.

Then Richard began talking, phone to one ear, a finger in the other, tuning out the far-away guitar and the hum of the waves, the sea gulls and the street vendors.

What, Jacob thought, are they saying to one another? He imagined a laundry list of things that needed to be done upon Richard's return: messages from work, small crises and tiny triumphs. The latest doctor report. Did the baby kick? Has it turned? Can Julie *feel* it?

Jacob walked toward the shore and sat down just above the tide line. He remembered his first vacation here, ten years before. He'd stopped the Venice Beach Hotel manager with a gentle tug of his sleeve and asked, "Do you ever get tired of this?"

"Of what?" the harried old man had replied.

"The beach. The people. Venice." He'd made a sweeping gesture with his arm.

And suddenly the old man's tired face had brightened. "Never," he said. "Look around."

Walking away, the manager had turned back. "Never!" he'd repeated.

Richard walked close and flopped down beside him. Jacob started to say something, then noticed he was still on the phone.

"If we go on Tuesday, that will give me two hours' extra time at work. Four days should be enough to find a decent rental. Yeah, OK. Fly out Tuesday, come back Saturday. Go ahead and book it for the end of the month. And don't let her get to you, Julie. You don't need the stress."

Jacob said nothing. He sat like a statue on the sand. Finally Richard tapped a button on his phone, folded it up, and put it in his pocket.

"Sorry about that," he said.

"No problem."

"There's lots going on at home right now, what with Julie's job and the baby coming soon. Insurance issues."

"That's fine. It's the same for me back in Pittsburgh...Hey, maybe we could wait on dinner for a bit. Let's walk over to those rocks. To the tidal pools. We could find a few more shells to bring home to the women-folk."

Richard snorted. "Already got eight jars full. Julie says she can't find anyplace else to put them! I'll give you whatever I've got back at the hotel and you can give them to Susan."

Jacob paused, blinked, then said, "Let's just walk awhile, then."

"Been walking all day."

"Just to the rocks."

"Fine, but my feet hurt."

They walked over to the rocks where the waves broke and climbed up on one, sheltered above the spray. Hermit crabs, starfish, mussels and minnows weaved in the ebb and flow of the pools beneath them. Three twelve-year-olds clambered up beside them, headed for a taller boulder. Years had passed since Jacob had climbed up that far: too much risk of a fall, of breaking something, and what was the point, anyway?

"Hell," he said, and followed the kids. At the top he stood next to them for a long moment, looking out to sea. A moment later he picked his way down again.

"Dinner?" he asked.

"About time," said Richard.

*****

They sat down at an outdoor table at the Sidewalk Café. For ten years it had been a mutual favorite—ever since they started taking their annual "buddy trip" following high school graduation. Through a long decade the restaurant had never looked any different from one year to the next.

"Remember," said Jacob, "when you tripped over that dead seal on the beach in the dark one morning? Your foot sank right in!"

"Look, man, I'm about to eat, OK?"

Jacob tried again. "Or the second time we came here, right off the plane, and I had five glasses of Merlot, I was so happy to be away from college? Right at that table over there."

Richard smiled. "Me and Patrick and Kevin had to carry you back to the hotel."

Jacob nodded. "But only after three hours wandering around Santa Monica. The Third Street Promenade. Hey, you remember that Costa Rican girl, how she gyrated those hips? I spent fifteen bucks on that band's album, just so I could give her the money and see her smile at me."

"Did she smile?"

"Nope!" Jacob chuckled.

"She *was* gorgeous," Richard agreed.

"Hey, why didn't we go there this time? To the Promenade?"

"Jesus, I guess I forgot all about it."

"Me too."

"We've seen it all anyway."

A one-armed waiter took their order. Jacob looked toward the ocean. The sun was falling into it so fast he could see it moving.

"Good view from here," he said.

"View of what?" said Richard. He was flipping through his wallet and looking at receipts. "Some of these dinners are tax-deductible," he murmured.

"Never mind," said Jacob.

"Hey, what time does our flight leave tomorrow?"

"Noon."

"Too bad. I'll miss sleeping in."

"One more chance to walk Venice Pier and go to the Cow's End for breakfast if we get up early enough."

"I doubt that'll happen. Long flight, long drive after that. I need my sleep."

Dinner arrived, they ate, and the plates were taken away. Dessert and decaf coffee followed.

Richard looked at Jacob for a long moment. "It was a good vacation," he said, voice suddenly bright.

"Yes," said Jacob. "I hate to leave."

"It'll all still be here. It's not going anywhere."

"That's true," said Jacob. "You're right."

The last sliver of sun slipped beneath the distant waves. Red and gold light disappeared in an instant, leaving the terrace in blue darkness. The waiter with one arm came around to each table with lit candles.

"Hey," said Richard, that artificial brightness still in his voice, "I think you're right. We should eat at the Cow's End tomorrow morning."

"I'd like that."

"And what about the Promenade tonight?"

"I think—"

Richard's phone rang. "It's Julie again," he said. "I'll be right back." He got up and left the restaurant.

Jacob paid the bill. Then he, too, got up and left. He walked past the candlelit tables, past Richard's voice talking distantly to a distant place, and into the darkness of the now-empty beach. He took a deep breath. Sea air filled his lungs. He listened carefully. Seagulls cried over the crash of waves. Behind him, all over Venice Beach, streetlights blinked on. Further down the boardwalk a group of teenagers laughed, a cloud of cigarette smoke billowing back in their wake.

He pulled out his cell phone. He dialed a number.

After three rings, someone picked up on the other end two thousand miles away.

"Hello, Susan?" he said. "Yes. Oh, I miss you too. Like you wouldn't believe. No, not since we talked this morning. Me too. Sure. We get in at eight. How's the baby?"

The Hunt

Biting wind whipped among the trunks of black trees, and branches, snow-laden, cracked to fall about the two young men as they pulled on hand-rolled cigarettes, loaded rifles under their arms. The slivers of sky they could see above the brittle canopy were deep gray. Moonlight reflected off clouds and spread bleak, shifting illumination across the land. Snow—incessant, pervasive—collected on the brims of their hats and in the cuffs of their trousers.

"Whittaker's field is only an easy half-mile off," said Samuel Holt, flicking the stub of his cigarette away. They watched as it tumbled through the air and came to rest, hissing, in the ice-crisped pine needles. The orange glow of the tip burned low, then out.

"Easy? Damned if that'll be an easy walk," said Arthur Hughes.

Samuel struck a match, and for a brief moment they stared at one another's pale, wide-eyed faces in the spluttering, abused light. A violent spat of wind plucked the match from his fingertips and blew out the flame in midair.

"Arthur, I swear you've seen a haunt. If you could see yourself like I see you, I doubt you'd argue the point."

"I don't need a ghost to scare me more. I guess this about caps it."

The woods ran up a gentle hill over Still Creek, then on, wilderness, for over thirty miles. People got lost and died in such woods. Arthur knew they were still within three miles of town, but in the dark and the cold and the snow, he wished they were out in Whittaker's field now, not a half-mile slog from it.

"Your father going to meet us by the oak?" Samuel asked, raising his voice above the crying wind.

"Said he would. Listen to that howl. It's getting bad again."

Samuel, always the better ear for such things, socked his arm. "Wait."

They listened.

"The wind…"

"No, not the wind," Samuel muttered. "Not the wind."

Arthur cursed and fumbled for the mining lamp at his side, touched the butt of his smoke to the wick, and shut the trap. A dull, faint glow took hold of the tallow and pushed back the night around them. In the distance, gunshots, then screams, superseded the howls that were not wind.

"They're flushing our way!" Samuel hissed.

"Should we make for Whittaker's field? I don't know if Pop'll still be there if—"

"That'd be moving away from them. We don't want to move away from them."

Arthur tugged the glove off his right hand with his teeth and stuffed it into a woolen coat pocket. The cold, naked flesh of his hand and fingers found fast reassurance around the colder wood of his rifle, and he grasped it until his knuckles went bloodless.

The cacophony grew clearer. Soon Arthur could make out faint lights coming down the hill. "They veering off?" he asked, pointing.

Samuel nodded. "*Now* we make for Whittaker's. They're driving them out into the open."

They ran until Arthur thought his lungs would bleed. He was a fine runner and he knew it, but the cold, the snow, the hill, the trees, the bushes and rocks all fought to take his air, fight his legs, slow him down, trip him up, and by the time the pale field opened up before them, the baying and the howling and the shouts and lanterns now very close and growing closer, he was just about spent.

Yet there was more to do.

Samuel gasped. "Jesus wept."

Arthur raised his eyes in time to see the first wolf, dark against the plane of snow, dart in for Mr. Rowling's hound, flip it over, and rip its throat out in a single, fluid motion. Rowling cursed and fired, and the wolf fell, even as the hound let out half a wet yelp and went still. Now, all around the field the lights of lanterns stood out like candles, illuminating Whittaker's land in a spluttering, shifting glow.

The wolf pack, half-starved, driven to desperation by the worst winter in a century, turned to take its stand.

Ten hours before, in the kitchen back home, Arthur's father had said, "Only once in a blue moon. All other times they keep to themselves, give or take a sheep. God willing, you won't see this a second time, even if you live to be an old, old man. The days of wolves killing men will be over after tonight."

Yet here, now, was that first and only time, the night not yet over, and Arthur felt the pulse of fear beat hard in his temples and wrists.

"Spread out, boys! Don't want no crossfire. Aim low!" Old Victor Eugene, who had somehow trawled his way through the hunt with his bad leg and weak heart, bellowed, demanded attention, and got it. The pinpricks moved apart.

Arthur couldn't count the flitting shadows. The hounds put up a frantic clamor, taut bodies pulling tight against their tethers, squirming and raging, jumping up in front of the lanterns. The men shivered, bodies moved by wind, adrenaline, and other, darker things. The wolves moved on the periphery of his vision, pacing out of the night and back again. The hip lanterns were erratic, disorienting sources of light. He felt caught in a nightmare; nothing seemed real.

"A baker's dozen," Samuel muttered.

"How can you tell?" Arthur had time to ask, and then the wolves came on.

Later, no one argued that the hunting party was surprised by the sheer vivacity of the wolves during the final attack. The hunt was nine hours old, and for seven the hunters had closely pursued the starving pack with dog and gun. The wolves were exhausted, beleaguered, and dying.

Yet when they charged, some of the men hardly had time to loose their hounds and raise their rifles. Suddenly the darting forms were no longer on the edge of Arthur's sight, but far too close, far too clear.

They fell upon the hounds first. For a moment the party could only watch. The animals grunted as they slammed against one other, and for a half-breath of time the wolves fell at bay.

But the hounds were outnumbered, and some of the wolves, used to fighting and desperate, struggled with a vigor that left dogs dead in their paths, regained their bearings, and continued the charge.

"Get 'em up! Aim! Fire!" someone shouted, and then the pinpricks of light disappeared as rifles exploded like canons across the field. Arthur blinked, eyes dazzled, and raised one hand from his rifle to his right temple.

"Look out! Arthur!"

Opening his eyes, Arthur saw the muzzle of Samuel's rifle flash. The percussion stunned his ears. A wolf, just spitting distance off, whined and began to limp away, then turned, disoriented, and plodded slowly toward Samuel again. It didn't growl, but its teeth shone bright in a wide, uneven grin, even as Samuel took careful aim and fired a second time.

Only then did Arthur hear a faster padding on the snow, and smell, through the fumes of powder sulfur and lantern oil, a deep, wild musk.

He turned. Fear clenched his bowels like a vise.

And then he was screaming and screaming, and suddenly the screams were no longer of fear but of fury, and everything, dream-like before, became very real. His teeth clacked together in a tight grimace. His hands grasped the rifle in a clenched lock, and when the emaciated wolf leapt at him, hackles raised, black eyes reflecting deep pools in the spluttering glow of his lantern, Arthur shot from the hip. One of the wolf's great eyes went darker but lost its depth. A gout of blood exploded out the side of its head and painted the snow. Its body somersaulted backward, legs and neck already rag-doll limp, and came to rest, curled in an untrodden patch of field.

Still screaming, he saw four-legged motion in the distance, ran forward, and fired again. And again. And once more.

When, finally, he heard only the clicks of the empty chambers, he flipped the rifle around and caught it by the barrels, ready to club whatever came on. Panting, rasping like a saw in the bitter air, Arthur looked about him wide-eyed, teeth reflecting moonlight.

Nothing else came on. For a moment Arthur was all alone, more alone than he had ever been.

Samuel started whistling behind him.

Arthur turned. On first sight Samuel seemed calm, but there was a shake to the tune that came from more than cold, and when he walked forward his gait was jerky, stilted and unnatural.

"Got a cigarette?"

"Here." Arthur dropped the rifle and fished in a coat pocket.

Samuel cupped his hand across the match Arthur offered him, pulled smoke deep into his lungs, and exhaled a fine, blue cloud from his mouth and nose.

A deep silence fell across Whittaker's field. To Arthur, the figures moving across it seemed somehow diminished. The field itself seemed somehow smaller. The night seemed less dark. The moon seemed less bright.

Without talking, men moved among the dark, still swellings on the ground, kicking or poking each one. Several of the forms whimpered. Rifle muzzles belched flame. The smell of scorched fur mingled with sulfur on the wind.

When Arthur and Samuel found Arthur's father, he was sitting on a rock underneath the big oak tree Whittaker never had the heart to cut down.

"You boys sound?" he asked.

"Fine, Mr. Hughes," said Samuel.

He looked to Arthur. "You?"

"Fine," said Arthur.

Mr. Hughes pulled out a plug of tobacco and bit off a piece. He chewed thoughtfully for a moment, then said, "You boys did good. I saw you."

He stood up and drew them toward him, put his hands on their shoulders, and shook them with gentle but firm earnestness. Arthur could never describe the expression he saw on his father's face at that moment, but he never forgot it.

Mr. Hughes then stepped back and sat down heavily on the rock again.

"They got old Eugene."

"What?"

Mr. Hughes turned and spit at the tree. "Victor Eugene's dead. Took a bad bite on the shoulder, but Moss Freeman saw the whole thing and thinks it was one part that, two parts heart attack."

"He shouldnt've been there," said Samuel. "Someone should've made sure he stayed home. He was too old."

Mr. Hughes laughed, face grim. "You ever get old Eugene to do anything he didn't wanna do? If so, you'd make a damn fine lawyer, but I have my doubts you did."

"Where's Dip? Where's the dog?" Arthur asked.

"Had to shoot him…I should've let him stay with you. Foolish of me. You needed him more."

"No," said Arthur, voice very soft, "No, I didn't."

Mr. Hughes looked up quickly. He nodded.

Arthur took a last, long pull at the stub of his cigarette, then turned and spit it from his mouth. He ached with exhaustion.

"Can we go on home? My feet are near frozen through."

"Yeah. Yeah, go on home. But don't mention Eugene. No one else need know about that until we've a chance to talk with his wife first, let her know what happened."

As they trudged away, Arthur could feel his father's eyes on his back. When he turned, his father was already walking back across the field to where a group of very quiet men stood in a half-circle around a still form covered by a coat already dusted with snow.

Samuel kept beside Arthur and neither of them spoke for a long time. Arthur's lungs felt like half-frozen balloons. His right shoulder ached from the kickback of the rifle. The balls of his knees throbbed and the joints cracked every time he took a step.

They found the trail at the edge of the forest and soon smelled the wood smoke of chimney fires just as the stench of sulfur began to fade. As the trees thinned, Arthur saw distant lights coming from the windows of homes that promised hot soup and warm beds.

"This will never happen again," he said to Samuel.

"That's what your father said."

"You don't believe him?"

They stopped at the edge of the forest atop a hill overlooking the back yards of the houses on Main Street. The yards and the houses looked small to Arthur. Still Creek seemed far removed even though it was close. He didn't feel well.

"I do, but somehow I find it hard," said Samuel. "It's the damndest thing."

"This will never happen again," Arthur repeated. "They're all dead. In the spring they'll make sure, take the dogs and root out any breeding dens left. Any dens at all."

Some of the pain went out of Arthur's lungs as they stood still.

"I'm gonna sleep well tonight," Samuel said. "Glad tomorrow's Sunday and no work. Come over for lunch at noon. Mother's making mincemeat pie."

They parted ways as they came down the hill.

Arthur let himself into the house and went to his mother's warm embrace, hot cider, potato soup, and bread by the fire. He answered questions as shortly as possible. He kept thinking about what Samuel had said—about finding it hard to believe it was all over. He knew it was. He was very tired and wanted to sleep, so he ate quickly then went to his room. The room seemed smaller.

Later, lying in bed and looking up at the slanted roof beams that met over his head, Arthur heard the back door close and his father's voice and footsteps. His parents spoke in hushed tones for a long while. For a time he heard his mother crying, but eventually those noises ceased. Finally, like always, the whole house fell silent.

I'm so tired, he thought all the rest of the long night.

Lorna Gould's Roses

Glenda Hall offered me another cup of tea, but I politely declined. Its aftertaste, mingled with the aftertaste of her muffins, was faintly appalling.

"It's good of you to visit, Henry," she said, setting down the pot. "Your grandmother always spoke so highly of you. You eat up and I'll give you the photographs you're after."

"That would be great, Mrs. Hall," I said, leaving the remaining muffins alone and checking my watch. "I *am* a bit pressed for time."

The old lady clucked her tongue. "The young are always in a hurry, but there's something to be said for taking the time to stop and smell the roses."

My eyes traveled to a glass vase standing next to the plate of muffins on the coffee table. It was full of red tea roses, freshly cut.

"You like them?" she asked.

"Very nice. From your own garden?"

"Oh, heavens no. I could never grow roses like that. Those are from next *door*. You saw the burnt house?"

"Yes. I meant to ask you about that."

"A shame, that is. Terrible. But the garden is still as good as when Lorna Gould planted it fifty-seven years ago. She had quite the green thumb." A far-away look came into her eyes. Macular degeneration had left them half-blind, but from the outside looking in, they seemed quite clear.

"What happened?" I asked.

"Hmm? To Lorna Gould? She died four years ago, age of ninety-two. I got her beat." Mrs. Hall winked.

"No, I meant what happened to the house?"

"Oh, that! *There's* a story for you. Got five minutes?"

I hesitated, then nodded.

"Well," she said, leaning in and setting a bony, confidential hand on my leg, "Lorna always kept her house nice. Took pride in it. You used to visit me with your grandmother when you were little, so you might remember."

I nodded, trying not to betray my distaste. Glenda Hall had never liked children, and I hadn't exactly changed her mind about them all those years ago, if memory served. But she and Grandma had belonged to the same bridge club, and Grandma had enjoyed showing me off to her friends.

"Nicest house on the block," Mrs. Hall continued. "Always a pleasure to have Lorna as a neighbor. Her husband was the last mine foreman in Still Creek, you know. It takes a special kind of woman to marry a man like that. Had to have an iron will to match his, and she did. But even strong wills bend with age, and when she died, she hardly knew her own name. According to some, her death, under such circumstances, was passing sad but long overdue. I visited her just before she went, and for what it's worth, I tend to agree."

I nodded, forcing myself to bite into another muffin. Echoes of bad childhood memories came flooding back with the stale taste.

"Well, once that house went up on the market, I knew there'd be trouble. And of course there was. It wasn't two weeks before the Danforths moved in, and right away things started going downhill."

"How's that?"

Mrs. Hall whistled. "First off, they had five cats. *Five cats!* You ever hear of such a thing? And a tall, mangy mutt to boot. Big and lanky, like a German Shepherd but not pure. Kept it chained up in the back yard beside an old wooden house made of particleboard. I thought it would wear a hole into the ground from all that pacing. And the barking! Night and day. Day and night. It was enough to send an old lady's nerves over the edge, let me tell you!"

"I can imagine."

"Well, the wife was fat and wore dirty shirts that said filthy things. And the husband swore enough to turn the grass black. And their *children*? Little urchins! Always screaming and crying and rolling in the dirt. The lawn was the first to go. Lorna's lovely lawn. And those children *rolled* in the remains!"

"Imagine that."

"Yes! Imagine that! And then Mr. Danforth, he started parking his old rusted pickup on the *front lawn*, and he dragged a davenport out on the *front porch*, and that was the middle of the end. Five months. *Five months*, and that was all it took to undo Lorna's lifetime of work on that nice old house."

"Hard to believe."

"Yes! Hard to believe! Here, eat that muffin, now."

My stomach churned. "Oh no—two filled me up fine."

"Nonsense!"

"No, really, I'm fine, Mrs. Hall."

For a moment I thought Mrs. Hall would say something more, but she didn't press any further.

"Well, anyway, pretty soon Mr. Danforth got to hitting Mrs. Danforth, and she always had dark glasses on to hide her black eyes, and then *she* starting hitting the *children*, and after that some of the cats even began to limp a bit. During Parade Day Mr. Danforth got in a great big fight right in the middle of the street with some other fellow, and that was ugly for everyone. Oh, and one time Mrs. Danforth threw a vase through the bedroom window. Things like that give Still Creek a bad name, you know."

I nodded.

"And the ladies up at the Bridge Lodge started talking about it, because really it was all getting to be a bit much. And then, one day, I heard Mrs. Danforth yelling at Mr. Danforth to—" she gulped, "to *dig up those goddamn roses*, pardon my language. Can you imagine the *nerve*? And I knew that just wouldn't do. Really, it wouldn't."

I shook my head in mock regret, glancing down at my watch.

"But things have a way of taking care of themselves," she continued, placing that confidential hand on my leg again. "At least, that's what my Samuel always used to say before he passed away, God rest him. And sure enough, late that very same night, when the Danforths were out at some drag racing contest by the fairgrounds, the house caught fire and burned right down to the basement foundation. Let me tell you, it lit up the night like the Fourth of July! A bunch of cats and that dog of theirs died, and all their junk burned up, too. Even that old davenport on the front porch!"

Her hand had closed on my leg like a talon. I winced but pretended not to notice. "Did...did they ever find out what caused it?" I asked.

"Oh, arson they think."

"Any arrests?"

"Nope! The police talked to lots of people, of course. But they didn't arrest anyone. Anyone at all."

I glanced up. Mrs. Hall was smiling, and that far-away look was back in her half-blind eyes. Again, to me they looked surprisingly clear, and when she caught my gaze she gave me a wink.

"I...I'm sure Mrs. Gould would have been pleased," I said lamely.

"Oh, Lorna hated her roses being bothered. She never gave a single one away through all her years. Not ever. Not a single one to anyone…and finally I knew that just wouldn't do. Really, it wouldn't."

Suddenly she snapped to. "You *sure* you won't have another muffin? I have to say, in my experience most people only eat like a bird when they don't like the food! I baked them myself, you know. And I *hate* to see a grown man go hungry."

No, I thought quickly. *That just wouldn't do.*

Without a word, I picked up a muffin and took a big bite. Then another. I smiled, chewed, and swallowed. Again and again.

"More tea?"

I nodded.

"There, now, *that's* better!" Mrs. Hall said, pouring another cup and giving me a sunny smile. "I'll go find those photographs."

She bustled out of the room. I looked down at the plate of muffins next to the vase of red tea roses, freshly cut, from Mrs. Gould's garden. There were four muffins left on the plate. Lifting my teacup to my lips, I vowed to eat them all.

Birthday

He could trace his motivation back to a single memory. All the years of work and toil; of diligent research and public ridicule; of failure, despair, more failure, and, finally, after half a *century*—

Success.

Seventy-six years old to the day, hair white, skin pale, eyes rheumy, David Halburn sat back in his swivel chair and looked at what stood before him.

A time machine.

"Thomas Wolfe, eat your heart out," he murmured through dry lips. "I'm going home again."

*****

"Mommy, what's that man looking at?"

David's sixth birthday party breathed magic. Outside, the world grew green and smelled of warm earth, flowers, and bees. Sunshine fell through white curtains, heating the yellow carpet, illuminating chubby faces of kindergarten friends. His house, huge in mystery and secure in comfort, blazed with banners, streamers, balloons and confetti. In the center of the living room, a great birthday cake with "E.T." carefully drawn on the top in icing awaited inevitable destruction. Chocolate ice cream sat cooling in the freezer. Wrapped presents, bulky in ways that promised Transformers and GI Joes, Star Wars figures and He-Men, rose up on the coffee table like an offering, a celebration, a reward for being born.

In the hallway, children played "Pin The Tail on the Donkey." In the den, an ATARI 2600 blipped to the soundtracks of "Pitfall" and "Tron." In the living room, his father, quick to laugh and easy with life, detached his thumb with causal aplomb, then wiggled it to applause before reattaching it. And sitting on a chair while his mother tied his shoe, David stared through the open bay window and wondered aloud about the strange man in the street.

His mother, still girlish in early womanhood, looked where he was pointing and smiled. "It's just an old man," she said. "He's probably thinking about all the fun we're having in here."

The old man stood in the street, staring at the house, an odd expression on his face. David looked again. Their eyes met.

"He looks sad," he said.

"Maybe he's remembering what it was like to be young like you," his mother said, turning back to the offending shoelace. "Maybe he doesn't have anybody, and seeing your party makes him think back on happier times."

"Will I ever be old like that?" David asked.

His mother leaned forward and kissed his cheek.

"Not for a very, very long time," she said. But that wasn't the same as "never," and David knew it.

Then the call came to light the candles on the cake, and for a long, long time—many years—his discomfort with time was forgotten.

*****

But time, whatever else one may say about it, is dependably punctual. Years passed as surely as clockwork, taking with them seasons, family, friends, and any feelings of security he once possessed. True, it gave as well as took; wisdom, perspective, knowledge, maturity, and love all found their way into his life when he wasn't looking, and all were welcomed. Yet loss, that feeling of watching sand run through your fingers all the faster as you try to stop it, became first a dim background distraction, then an annoyance...and then, finally, an obsession.

Favorite places changed. Favorite people grew old and passed away. Summer faded against a background of work in windowless rooms. Winter, no longer a wonderland, became a battleground for deep-freeze wars with cracked carburetors and icy roads.

And then...

Then...

David's father called his apartment, voice quavering, heavy with the news that his mother was riddled with cancer.

"This isn't supposed to happen," David told her as she lay in her hospital bed and tried to smile. "You're not supposed to die."

"Funny, I thought the same thing!" she said softly. Her laughter became a long series of wracking coughs before trailing off.

"Grandma Rose and Grandpa Ted, Aunt Emily and Uncle James. My rabbit, Flopsy. My dog. A dozen other pets and half a

66

dozen friends. All of them gone, each loss a chip with a chisel, a tap with a hammer. I'm being worn down by death, Mom. And you—"

"Me," she repeated.

"A great sledgehammer blow that will shatter me to pieces." Tears rolled freely down his cheeks.

"David."

He shook his head.

"David, look at me."

He raised his red eyes, and only then did he remember that long-ago birthday party so deeply buried by the past.

"This is the way of the world," said his mother, her voice drifting up into the room from a far-away place. "It's natural. A mother isn't supposed to outlive her son. Time rolls around and the great game continues, but with other players, each possessing a part of those who came before. You live in me, I live in you."

"It's damned unfair, Mom," he said. "Everyone says it's the way of things. I don't care. It doesn't make the loss any easier."

"You don't have a choice," she murmured, strength fading away. "*That* makes it easier."

We'll see, he thought, even as he nodded and tried to smile. *We'll see.*

*****

The time machine wasn't, of course, a constant project. He tinkered with it now and then, here and there, but always it was in the back of his mind, a comfort, tantalizing, a bright spot to stave off despair. He married, had children of his own, watched them grow. He didn't worry as his hair turned gray, didn't pine away as his little girl married, didn't flinch in the face of clocks.

Once it's done, I can see it all again whenever I want. The thought sustained him through long years and short, bad years and good.

Unlike Jay Gatsby, he had no illusions about repeating the past. Childhood was gone. The years behind were more numerous than the years ahead. But to be able to chat with his grandfather, pet his old dog, see his children young again, watch his mother laugh—*that* was the great desire, the burning hope. He was fervently convinced that loss was responsible for old age, more than anything else. To skip back and forth, skimming the surface of time like a rock across a still, clear pool—it would be a retirement gift fit for the gods, a chance at peace such as he had not known in a long, long time.

Now, a palsied hand caressed the cool metal skin of the device, finally finished. Gently, two brittle legs stepped into the machine's small chamber.

David closed his eyes, smelling the oiled gears, taking stock of a million choices.

After long moments, silent save for the tick of his watch, he brushed his hands across a series of buttons, pulled a lever, twisted a dial, and, eyes still closed, held on tight.

*****

1994, he thought, looking out. *A good year.*

More than anything, he wanted to see his mother. She wouldn't recognize him, of course, and he wouldn't say anything to even remotely suggest who he was.

On his sixteenth birthday, the teenaged David had been in Florida visiting friends over Spring Break. His father would be at work. His mother?

Home.

He stepped out of the machine, which had materialized in an empty lot at the top of his old street.

A man with car trouble, that's who he was. Could he use the phone? And she would say yes, and he would be inside his childhood home again—once more part of the world he had left behind, if only for a moment. During that moment he would breathe in the ambiance of living memories, feel the near-silent hum of youth reborn.

He whistled as he walked down the street, past the old, familiar houses that would eventually be demolished to make way for a new bypass, past the trees that smelled, for one glorious week a year, of apple blossoms that carpeted the street and paved the sidewalk with delicate white petals.

I remember when they were cut up by the construction men and uprooted by the bulldozers, he thought.

He breathed in, smiled, exhaled, and continued on.

His house, when it came into view, shocked him. It was far, far smaller than he remembered. Yet it felt familiar, like an old pair of shoes not worn in years that still retained the contours of his feet. It felt familiar, and that meant comfort. It was *right*.

But what *wasn't* right were the cars in the driveway. And the E.T. balloons tied to the mailbox. And the children who laughed and played beyond the open front door.

No one is supposed to be here but Mom, he thought. *Not in 1994.*

He stopped, lost in thought.

Which means...which means...

This isn't *1994.*

One inadvertent jerk of a finger, one wrong number. He should have paid closer attention.

Twenty feet away, his sixth birthday party was in full swing.

Just a quick glimpse, he thought, still planning on making that phone call. *Yes, a broken-down car, that'll do.*

His eyes, slightly glazed, focused again.

His mother sat framed in the great bay window, tying the shoe of a small boy he almost recognized.

"Mom!" he screamed, heart pounding. All thoughts of concealing his identity were instantly forgotten. There she was, young and healthy and smiling and full of life. "Mom, it's me!" he called out.

But no, all that issued up from his throat was a whisper.

I want my mother, he thought, and took a heavy step forward.

The child he almost recognized turned and caught sight of him.

"Mommy, what's that man looking at?"

His breath caught in his throat.

No, he thought numbly.

"He looks sad," the little boy said.

"Maybe he's remembering what it was like to be young like you," David's mother responded. "Maybe he doesn't have anybody, and seeing your party makes him think back on happier times."

"Will I ever be old like that?" little David asked.

His mother leaned forward and kissed his cheek.

"Not for a very, very long time," she said.

The offending shoelace now firmly tied and double-knotted, David and his mother rejoined the party. In the background, a dim shadow, his father placed candles on the cake, whistling cheerfully.

Outside, in a sunlight that didn't seem as warm or as bright as he had once remembered, David turned, smiling faintly, and walked slowly back up the street toward a time that was his own.

He missed it very much.

The Piano

A solid, cherry-stained Chickering, it has stood in Grandma's living room for seventy-two years. Her parents gave it to her in 1935, an early wedding present. Each key, starting with the first on the left, bears a tuner's date, and those run up until 1971. After that, nothing. Thirty-six years without a tune, and the river of people who touch the keys has slowed to a trickle, then run dry over slow but inexorable decades.

Apparently many played it back in the day, although I find that hard to believe. Ever since I can remember it has stood like any other piece of furniture: a silent prop—the bench a place for piles of newspapers and magazines, the flat top above the tuning wires a table for doilies, framed photos, and trinkets from Spain and France. I now sit by it, bumping a pile of *Newsweek*s that slide to the floor in a cascade.

"My fingers used to fly across the keys," Grandma tells me, rocking in her blue easy chair across the room. Only fifteen feet away, the piano is beyond her field of vision. "It's still a good piano, but it needs tuning, and I can't play it anymore."

"Did Mom used to play it?" I ask, stacking up the magazines.

"She sure did. She was very talented. All through high school she practiced on that piano. I don't know why she gave it up."

I nod, glancing around with mute contentment. The whole living room is a time capsule; a steady, warm element in a life full of change. I am almost thirty, and all the other places from my childhood have gone away—or I have gone away from them.

Then I turn to Grandma again, and my contentment fades. She is ninety-four, and the last three years have not been kind.

"I have no idea who's going to take it," she says abruptly.

"Hmm? What's that?"

"Who's going to take it once I'm gone." She's looking toward the wooden cover over the keys.

"Oh, don't worry about that."

"No one I know would want it. Your uncle doesn't have room and your mother no longer plays. I don't think you'd want it, either. It's a shame."

"Oh, Grandma, I'd love to have it, but there isn't much room in my house."

"That's all right. I understand."

"I'm sure Mom would be thrilled with it. Besides, there's no reason to think about that right now. You're not going anywhere anytime soon."

But she doesn't look convinced. I think of her losses, which are too numerous to list. She knows better. I wonder, fleetingly, if there is *anything* left from her youth that hasn't yet gone away.

A little while later she goes out to the kitchen and makes supper for us—chicken and biscuits. The chicken is too salty and the biscuits are burnt, but it's a good meal. I eat it all.

After we wash the dishes I say goodbye. She presses a check into my hand. Without looking, I know it's for fifty dollars. Without looking, I can picture her shaky script perfectly. I try to refuse it but she insists. Then I step out into the cool October afternoon and unlock the car.

When I was little, my grandparents always waved at me from the door as the family drove away. Now, as I drive off alone, it's just Grandma who sees me off. She watches until I'm down the road and long out of her sight. Through the rearview mirror I see her front door finally close.

Three blocks away, I realize I've forgotten a pot of russet mums she gave me for my front yard. It's still sitting on the walk beside the driveway. She'll be hurt if I don't go back for it. I turn the car around.

She doesn't hear my tires crunch the driveway stones. I pick up the flowers and pop the trunk.

And it's only then, holding the flowers in my hands, leaning over the car, that I hear it: faint but clear, the sound of the piano.

Through the closed front door I listen to my grandmother playing a song that is eighty-one years old. I know it because of a ninth grade history project I once completed on the "Roaring '20s." She knows it because it was a song of her youth.

She doesn't sing, but I know the words:

Blackbird, blackbird,
Singing the blues all day
Right outside of my door.
Blackbird, blackbird,
Why do you sit and say,
"There's no sunshine in store."
All through the winter you hung around.

Now I begin to feel homeward bound.
Blackbird, blackbird,
Gotta be on my way.
Where there's sunshine galore...

The piano hasn't been tuned in thirty-six years. Grandma has arthritis in her wrists and hands. She can hardly see, and misses keys.

I walk away before the song ends. It ushers me off, a living warmth from a long-gone time, an old thing that somehow hasn't aged.

That evening I call Grandma and tell her not to worry about the fate of the piano—when the time comes, I'll *make* room. And I'll be sure to play it.

"Well!" she says, surprised but pleased. "What made you change your mind?"

I make up an excuse. How can I possibly tell her that I heard her play—and that to me, every note sounded perfect?

Arachno

The night shift dragged on, and the two Rose Asylum attendants watched the camera feed from Cell 142 with all the interest they could hope to rouse. Most of the patients were asleep or restrained, either zonked out on hypodermic Quaaludes or strapped down to their beds. But the patient in Cell 142, Ms. Burgett, was wide-awake. That meant amusement for Pete Younker and Mike Cavell.

Tonight, Cavell noted that Younker had again taken up one of his favorite entertainments. The knapsack he carried bulged in a familiar way, and when Dr. Peterson finally checked out for the night shortly after eleven, leaving them alone, Younker slipped out the jar.

"Not a bad catch," he told Younker, eyeing the fat, sluggish flies.

"Two weeks of night duty in a row, I figured we deserved a bit of fun," Younker replied. "Let's go."

They left the front office and unlocked the gate, passed through, then locked it tight again. They walked in the middle of the corridor so none of the patients in the barred cells could get in a good grab. Some of them knew how to gum out their meds and play 'possum at night, waiting for the right time to lash out a fumbling hand or tripping leg. And that, Cavell knew, was sometimes all it took. Walking the patient halls always made him nervous. He was a thin man, tall but not strong. Younker, on the other hand, was a massive slab of rough muscle, which came in handy at Rose Asylum. Cavell always appreciated his presence.

They stopped at Ms. Burgett's cell. It was secured by bulletproof glass, not bars. Cavell turned up the lights, and the cell went from dark to dim. Ms. Burgett hated light; anything stronger than a forty-watt bulb sent her into a frenzy. She was also allergic to most sedatives, so following Dr. Peterson's orders they did their best to accommodate her in small ways.

The room's contents—a bed, toilet, rounded plastic desk, and several badly mangled sketchbooks—gained definition.

"Where's her latest creation?" Cavell asked. "It was getting big."

"Dr. Peterson had Delaney take it out earlier this afternoon. Said it was getting too difficult to move around in there with all that yarn."

Cavell was always impressed by Ms. Burgett's sheer, inexhaustible creative drive when it came to yarn. Dr. Peterson only allowed yarn that would come apart easily—in case Ms. Burgett ever got an urge to hang herself. If she acted up, Dr. Peterson removed the yarn immediately, but good behavior resulted in several bolts, all gray like she liked. Ms. Burgett would then immediately set to it with her fingers and teeth, prodding, pulling, licking, winding, separating each strand and stretching it from bed spring to desk, toilet to shelf. The more yarn she was given, the more docile she became. Sometimes she spent whole days sitting in the middle of her creation, weaving more, until Dr. Peterson decided it had grown too big, too unhygienic, and had it cleaned out. Then Ms. Burgett, after the inevitable violent fit, would begin again when given another bolt.

"Can't see her," Younker grunted. "Under the bed again, I guess."

Cavell knew Ms. Burgett got cranky as hell when her cell was bare. She often took to hiding under her bed with the sulks. There was one sure-fire way to get her out, though, and Cavell knew what it was. He scratched lightly on the glass with a fingernail, and Younker held the jar of flies up to the tray slot.

Ms. Burgett moved like lightning. Still pressed flat to the floor, she scuttled out from under the bed, completely naked, and covered the ten feet to the flies in an instant, still on all fours. Then, with a sudden lunge, she slammed herself against the glass, clawing at it with three-inch fingernails, licking at it with her bright red tongue, biting at it with filed-sharp teeth. Clicking noises came from the back of her throat. They hardly sounded human.

Cavell recoiled. He would never grow used to Ms. Burgett's appearance, and certainly not to her mannerisms. He shuddered to think the woman had once been free.

"Down," said Younker.

Ms. Burgett immediately fell back in a splayed crouch. She scuttled sideways a few feet, never taking her wide eyes off the jar.

Satisfied, Younker unscrewed the lid and held the open mouth to the tray slot. The flies quickly filled the cell, and Ms. Burgett went to work. The clicking rose in pitch and frequency as she scampered around the chamber, still on all fours, ropes of drool running down her chin as she gnashed her teeth and, methodically, efficiently, caught her prey and dined.

Younker chuckled. "By God, our Black Widow's a little Renfield, isn't she?"

Cavell, stopwatch in hand, couldn't help but shiver as he smiled.

*****

Like so many cases of criminal insanity, it was the smell that cost Ms. Burgett her freedom.

Cavell had seen her case file only once, and briefly at that, but had heard rumors in far greater detail: How the police had entered her apartment after neighbors reported the stench of rotting flesh emanating from beneath the door. How they had found three dogs, five cats, a dozen rabbits, and a seventy-five-year-old man wrapped up in fishing line, all hanging from the ceiling and quite dead. How Ms. Burgett had descended from a dense web of fishing line on a rope cord tied around her waist and attacked the officers with her sharpened teeth and nails. How her apartment was filled with a vast, moving carpet of tiny spiders, filling the cabinets, the washing machine, the toilets, the closets, and running rampant across the floors, walls and ceilings…

"Psychotic Monomania resulting in Schizophrenic Arachnophilia," was how Dr. Peterson offhandedly summarized Ms. Burgett's condition.

"The Black Widow," was what the attendants called her.

After finishing their rounds and settling back into the office, Younker shook his head and whistled. "I finally got a good look at the Black Widow's fingers."

Cavell had pulled out a report sheet and was starting to fill it out. A patient had vomited twice earlier that night, and Dr. Peterson and the morning nurses needed to be aware of it. "Hmm? What about them?"

"No prints," he replied. "I heard about that, but wanted to see for myself. They're smooth. Same with her feet and toes. Doctors think she sanded them off at some point, before she got caught."

"Jesus! Why?"

Younker shrugged and swung his feet up onto the desk, which creaked beneath the weight. "Why not? The chick's a loony. Anyway, that's why she's never been positively ID'd."

"I didn't know that."

"Sure. Peterson thinks she did it cause it was a way of 'further distancing herself from her human identity,' or something like that."

Cavell knew 'Ms. Burgett' wasn't the Black Widow's real name. She'd used it while in residence at the apartment building where she'd been caught, but beyond that the name had no apparent significance. The identification card the police recovered was false, and there were no credit cards, Blockbuster memberships, or telephone calls to provide further clues or leads. An intensive and extensive national records search had turned up nothing. If, like Dr. Peterson suggested, she had wanted to remove herself from the workings of human civilization, in that respect, if in no other, she had succeeded.

"Next time," Younker mused, "I think I'm gonna make her jump through a loop for those flies."

"She won't listen," Cavell said, turning back to his report. "She doesn't play games for anyone."

"Even spiders can be trained." Younker yawned, flicked on the desk radio, and settled down for a quick nap.

*****

"Hey, how long's it been since we last fed the Widow from the jar?"

For Cavell, time passed strangely in Rose Asylum. The redundancy and tedium of routine was largely to blame, but not entirely. The strangeness of the asylum's occupants: that played a part, too. News had no meaning on the inside. When he and Younker spoke of current events while on shift, the subjects seemed vague and distant. It was hard to talk of hockey games and presidential policy when people down the hall were screaming about bugs under their skin or how they intended to consume their parents. A day sometimes felt like a week, a week a month, a month a day.

"I don't know," Cavell replied. "Two weeks? Maybe less? I'm not sure."

Younker yawned. It was just after three in the morning. "Well, I thought we might have another go. I'm getting bored."

"Flies again?"

Younker smiled. "Nope. Check this out." He reached into his backpack and pulled out the familiar jar. But inside…

Cavell blinked. "*Fire*flies?"

"Easier to get this time of year."

Cavell wasn't sure how much fun fireflies would be. "It'll be over pretty quick," he said. "They'll probably just walk along the walls."

"Come on, let's go," Younker growled. "It's better than nothing."

This time, Ms. Burgett wasn't under her bed. Dr. Peterson had recently given her three bolts of yarn for good behavior, so she was now sitting secure in the middle of a great, connected mesh of damp fabric.

"Looky here, Black Widow," Younker said, waving the jar.

Ms. Burgett flexed, still in a crouch, then pounced against the window with a hiss.

Younker put the jar behind his back. He glanced at Cavell. "Let's see if we can make her dance a little."

Cavell looked at Younker uncertainly. "We shouldn't rile her up. You know she doesn't listen to anything but 'down.'"

"Oh, c'mon, it'll be fun." Younker returned his attention to Ms. Burgett. "Here now, spin a little for me." He twirled his finger in front of her face. "Spin round, little spider, spin round."

Ms. Burgett sneered at Younker, but kept an eye on the jar. She clicked and hissed and raked the glass with her nails, but Younker kept twirling his finger.

Cavell doubted she would listen even if she could understand…but then Ms. Burgett surprised him. Scowling, she suddenly crawled in a quick circle and hunkered down by the window, submissive but still clicking rapidly. Her eyes now never left Younker.

"There, you see? She learns fast." Younker flashed a grin at Ms. Burgett and unscrewed the lid of the jar. Carefully, he knocked the fireflies into the tray slot and stepped back to watch.

Ms. Burgett pounced. She took two immediately, one in each hand, slammed them into her mouth, and scurried back to the center of her nest. She chewed with gusto, grinning in a way that made Cavell want to lock himself back in the office, safe until the morning crew arrived.

"Look at that smile," said Younker. "She couldn't be happier."

Yes she could, Cavell thought. *From all accounts she seemed pretty damned happy in her old apartment, when the prey was bigger.*

And then, abruptly, Ms. Burgett stopped chewing. Her eyes became white saucers. Her lips, glowing dully with stains of fading luminescence, drew together in a tight, bloodless line.

"Younker?" Cavell stepped back.

Ms. Burgett took a long, deep breath.

Younker frowned. "Hey, what's her problem?"

The ensuing shriek was so loud Cavell and Younker called out and clapped their hands to their ears. Immediately the other patients, ripped from slumber, began to moan and cry.

"Now you've done it," Cavell said. "Come on."

But Younker was still staring at Ms. Burgett, entranced. Shrieking and hissing, she flailed at the glass, scrabbling at it in a mad fury. She fell back, ripping at her tangled black hair. Blood spilled from her mouth; she had bitten into her tongue and lips with her filed teeth.

"Get the jar and let's go," Cavell said. "We have to let her calm down, and she won't with us here."

"Fine," said Younker. "Jesus, look at her."

"I already did. Let's go."

The shrieking ceased.

Cavell and Younker stepped carefully toward the cell, peering into the dim depths.

Gray yarn swayed in the aftermath of Ms. Burgett's frenzy. Through it they could see her crouched against the far wall. She was staring at them and smiling.

Cavell tapped Younker's sleeve with a shaking finger. "All right, she's calm now. Let's go."

"Yes, let's go."

Their footsteps echoed loud and rapid down the long corridor.

*****

Cavell slammed a book down on the table.

"I figured out what went wrong yesterday," he said. "Fireflies. Listen here: 'Firefly bioluminescence is caused by a chemical reaction in the light organs. Predators avoid eating fireflies because these chemicals give off a bitter, musky taste, and can be toxic to amphibians, reptiles, arachnids, and other insects.' There you go. She thought you were trying to poison her...or at the very least didn't like the taste."

Younker picked up the book and looked at the spine. "*A Field Guide to North American Insects*. You just happen to have that lying around your house?"

"I like to read."

Younker chuckled. "Whatever. Good job, detective." He handed the book to Cavell and nodded toward a slip of blue paper pinned to the bulletin board. "I guess we'll find out tonight whether she bears a grudge. You see what's at the top of our duties?"

"I haven't even taken off my coat yet."

"Check it out."

Cavell squinted at Dr. Peterson's nearly indecipherable handwriting.

"Wait a minute."

Younker slapped Cavell on the back. "The Widow's nest has gotten too large again! And who gets to clean it out? Me and thee."

Cavell sighed. "I'd just as soon clean the latrines."

Younker grinned. "That's on the list too."

Ms. Burgett's web had grown impressively dense during the last few days. The floor, walls, and ceiling were covered with yarn. The bed and table could hardly be seen.

"The yarn...it looks almost *sticky*."

"It is," said Younker. "She licks every strand."

"I hate spiders," Cavell said, shivering slightly. "I don't mind them behind glass or on TV, but...anytime I see one I kill it if I can."

"Yeah? Try stepping on this one."

"Oh, shut up."

"We'll need to secure her arms," Younker said. "That's how the day shift usually does it."

Cavell turned up the light in the cell to forty watts. "I can't see her."

"Keep your stick handy, and your Taser, too." Younker held up a pair of scissors. "I'll cut away a few of the bigger sections close to the door, you hang tight next to me, and then we'll see about getting her secure and finishing the rest of the cleanup. Ready?"

"No."

"Good enough for me." Younker typed in the lock code and the glass door slid quietly aside.

"It's humid in here. One of us should talk to Peterson about having the ventilation checked." Younker started snipping away. The skein of yarn began to slough off in great clumps he then kicked out into the passage.

"Do you see the Widow?"

"No. Ouch! Jesus!"

"What? *What?*" Cavell raised his stick.

"Put that damn thing down. Oh, man." Younker sucked on his thumb. "A goddamn spider bit me."

"Come again?"

"A spider! A spider, Cavell."

"Come here."

"Eh?"

Cavell stepped forward and pulled Younker into the light of the hallway. "There's two more on your shirt." He pointed to the tiny brown spiders but made no move to brush them away.

"The Widow's got her own little fan club in there, don't she?" Younker batted the spiders off with his stick. They drifted to the floor on gossamer threads, hit ground, and scurried back toward the cell. Younker was too quick. He brought his boot down hard. They sounded like bitten grapes as their abdomens burst.

Ms. Burgett moved quickly. Before Younker could turn she was on his back, shrieking as she slashed at his face with her claws.

Blast it, Younker, first the fireflies, now you kill her friends, Cavell thought, then brought the night stick down on Ms. Burgett's arm. There was a *crack*, louder than Younker's screams, and Ms. Burgett fell off his back. Cavell raised his stick again. Ms. Burgett lunged forward and caught it with her good hand. Younker, still screaming, fumbled for his Taser, flicked it on, and jammed it into Ms. Burgett's neck. Blue lightning sizzled across her face, leapt across her filed teeth, and arced down her chest.

Younker pulled away.

Ms. Burgett fell.

Breathing hard, Younker and Cavell leaned heavily against the glass. Younker sobbed in distress, his face a criss-crossed pattern of welts and scratches. Cavell had his hand on his heart. It was pounding furiously.

"It...it shouldn't have done that," panted Younker. "The taser. She was damp. The current hit her too hard. She...check her pulse, Cavell."

Cavell inched forward as Younker slid down the glass and slumped to the floor, patting his bloody face with his shirtsleeve and moaning.

Ms. Burgett lay on her face. Her limbs looked wrong, somehow. Cavell reasoned the taser juice must have tightened them up. He grasped her unbroken arm to turn her over, but recoiled as he touched the skin. The arm felt funny, like the bones were in the wrong places. Not broken, just...

Cavell turned to Younker. "I don't think I can—"

"Come on, Cavell, get a pulse on the bitch. Hurry up! I—"

Younker stopped in mid-sentence. His eyes left Cavell's face and looked up, up, far over and behind Cavell's head, as Cavell sensed, but did not see, something rising tall, too tall, behind him.

"Younker?"

Younker breathed in. Breathed out. Breathed in again, then opened his mouth for a bellowing scream that came out silent, like air in a great, hollow tunnel.

Cavell turned.

The bloated, dark shape swung down and bit him quickly on the neck, twice, before running back up its silk line, scuttling across the ceiling, and falling on Younker like a leaden weight. Immediately Cavell felt ice in his veins as the poison pulsed into his body. His face and shoulders already numb, he could hear Ms. Burgett working behind him, but could not turn. All he could see was the mass of tiny, brown spiders seething across the webs of yarn and over a wet, deflated mess that had disguised Ms. Burgett well for a long time.

A touch of something thin and sharp behind him, and he found himself turned about to face her again.

Your children, Cavell mouthed silently as she spun her webbing tightly around him with hairy spinnerets. No more yarn, now.

"Adaptable!" Younker shrieked beside him. "I'll give you that! All these years. Good for you! You had me fooled. You had..."

Younker's face went slack. He spoke no more.

Ms. Burgett, Cavell mouthed. *Ms. Burgett, please.*

"*Mrs.* Burgett," she snarled, looming over the stricken man. The voice from the wide, slavering mouth was like night wind hissing through dead grass. She dipped her fangs toward him again, hairy pedipalpi caressing his face, the red hourglass on her raised black abdomen shining wetly in the dim fluorescent light, and added, "*I'm a widow.*"

The Day After

Christmas Day was sixteen hours over. Presents lay open and scattered across three cluttered rooms. The house was full of people sitting in scarred furniture, smoking cigarettes, drinking beer, eating cold ham and warm chicken salad. Cats snaked around the legs of children. Children ran into adults, bumped their heads, cried. On the floor of the kitchen, in front of the dishwasher, a black poodle puppy with a red bow around its neck slept soundly, oblivious to the nearby trampings and voices.

One of the men at the kitchen table, fifty-two years old, had just arrived. The engine of his white Toyota Camry still ticked with heat by the ice-slicked curb. His wife, prim in a tan turtleneck and red wool sweater, sat beside him, making small talk with his sister. Outside, on the front porch, his son smoked a cigarette next to strange relatives and stared at the ground.

The man had been in the house a month ago for Thanksgiving and four months before that for an unexpected visit. Beyond that, he seldom saw the place. He lived far away.

Although eight people sat crammed around the table and half a dozen children crawled and toddled across the linoleum floor, the man was only concerned with one person: the old woman sitting across from him.

She had no teeth because she refused to wear her dentures and her hair was long, straight, and white. Although almost blind, she didn't wear glasses. That was something else she refused to do.

The man reached over an ashtray filled with cigarette butts and beer tabs. He took the old woman's palsied, wrinkled hand in his own. She clutched it with surprising strength.

"I went to Spain last week, Mum," the man said at last. "Did I tell you that?"

"I don't think so."

"It was beautiful," he said.

"Oh yes?"

"Yes."

Both of them fell silent, but neither let go of the other's hand. Kaitlyn, the eight-year-old granddaughter of the man's brother, ran into the kitchen and demanded someone play *Hungry Hungry Hippos* with her. She threw the game up on the table until someone did. The

85

marbles made loud rattling noises until the man's wife lost to her. Then she dragged it off the table and ran out of the room.

"Jeff's doing well in school," the man said to the old woman.

"What?"

"Jeff's doing well in school."

"He must be in high school now."

"Actually he's in college, Mum. Remember?"

"Oh, yes. Yes, of course."

"He's a junior. He even has an apartment downtown. He can walk to all his classes. He's doing really well."

"That's good. That's very nice."

Out of the outdoor cats, a white shorthair the size of a Shetland Sheepdog, had found its way inside and into the kitchen. The man's sister-in-law screamed at it, then screamed at one of her daughters to throw it outside. The daughter told her seven-year-old daughter to do it for her. The seven-year-old grabbed it and carried it out of the room by its armpits. She returned a moment later with a four-inch scratch on her arm, bawling her head off.

Together, mother and daughter went off to the bathroom. The man's sister-in-law shouted medical instructions from across the house.

The man tried again.

"I remember when John and I were kids," he said. "Remember how we used to make Christmas ornaments out of papier-mâché?"

"Um."

"We used to make two dozen at a time, all shaped like stars, then sell them door-to-door. Remember that? We used to sprinkle them with glitter."

"Oh. Oh, yes. Sure."

The old woman fiddled with her empty teacup. She picked it up off the saucer, looked inside, and set it down. Then she picked it up again and started clinking it against the saucer. She clinked it so rapidly the man couldn't keep track of it. Then she stopped and placed it gently on the table beside the saucer, running a yellowed thumbnail along its cracked rim.

"Janet and I both have next week off," the man said. "It feels good to have some time away from work. We've both been so worn out."

"Oh, yes."

The man nodded.

The old woman's gaze rested on her teacup again. She picked it up and started clinking it against her saucer a second time. Then she stopped abruptly and looked him in the eye. "I have to find my keys. It's late and I'd better be getting home now."

"Mum, you are home," the man said gently.

"This isn't my house."

"You've lived here for three years. Remember? You live with John now."

The old woman shook her head violently. "No I don't. I live on the farm. They must be getting tired of me. I've been here all day."

"Mum, it's okay. Don't worry. It's okay."

A pause lengthened between them. Everyone else kept talking, but they did not.

"I'm sorry," the old woman said at last. "I get confused by things."

"It's not your fault," the man said. "Don't worry. It's just how things are."

The old woman looked at the man and smiled. The man squeezed her hand and she squeezed back.

"You remind me of my son," she said.

In the other room, one of the little boys knocked over a glass of Pepsi. Everyone in the kitchen knew it was Pepsi because three other children came in and started yelling about it.

Come Spring

They tramped up the back yard, through the woods, to the clearing at the top of the hill. It was very steep and the dew-wet grass made each step tricky, so Jake grabbed his grandfather's hand and held it tight.

"You tired?" his grandfather asked.

"Course not, Grandpa. You?"

"No siree." Sweat ran down the wrinkles of the old man's face and into his white beard.

"I never been this high up above town before," said Jake.

"It's a special place," said his grandfather, stopping to catch his breath. "Whenever a forest ends somewhere up high, you know you're in for a sight. And beyond the hill, far down below, there's a stream where I used to fish when I was a boy. Caught trout the size of my forearm!"

Jake stared at his grandfather's forearm, trying to picture it.

"Can *we* go fishing there someday?" he asked.

His grandfather didn't answer, just stared up the grassy slope. After a moment he reached into his jacket pocket and pulled out his pipe.

"Don't tell Grandma," he said, and struck a hidden match off his thumb.

Jake, impressed by this profound and casual trick, forgot all about fishing for the time being.

They continued climbing. "Can you do that again?" he asked.

"Sure can," his grandfather said, then leaned over and snapped fire off the brim of Jake's cap.

"There used to be butterflies here in the summer," his grandfather said. "Huge. Some yellow and black, some bright blue, hard as all get-out to catch."

"Did you ever?"

"Sometimes. Had a big case full of bugs when I was your age. Maybe I can help you start your own. We can make a case out of some pine scraps I got in the shed."

"Yeah?"

"Well sure, why not?"

They tramped on. The sun, bright and warm despite the early November morning, blazed down, and the wild grass began to dry.

Suddenly Jake remembered something he didn't want to remember. Without thinking, he stopped cold.

"What's the holdup?" his grandfather asked, turning back.

"Nothing," said Jake.

"Then let's go! Grandma will murder us both if we let breakfast get cold. We best keep moving."

But Jake just stood there, grass up to his knees, looking up at his grandfather with different eyes.

"You feeling better now, Grandpa?" he asked quietly.

His grandfather puffed out a circle of silver smoke and smiled. "That what's bothering you?"

Jake nodded.

His grandfather nodded back. "Well," he said, spitting expertly out the side of his mouth, "That's a funny thing. Funny odd, I mean."

He looked around for a place to sit down. Off to his left, the old stump of a once-enormous tree lay like a flat, smooth rock in the grass. He eased himself down slowly, motioning Jake to sit beside him.

"This heart," he said, poking his chest casually with his pipe, "is what all the trouble's over."

"That's why you had to go to the hospital over Christmas?"

"That's why."

"And did the doctors fix it? Is it OK now?"

His grandfather stared at him evenly for what felt like a long time.

"You having a good morning so far?" he asked.

"Sure am," said Jake, "but it'd be better if I knew you were doing OK."

"You don't like liars, do you?"

Jake thought about it. "No sir," he said. "You told me I shouldn't have no truck with liars."

"Well, I guess I had a point there." Chewing on the end of his pipe, the old man seemed to balance two things in his mind.

"No," he said at last.

"'No' what, Grandpa?" asked Jake.

"No, the docs couldn't fix it," he said.

Jake, shocked, felt tears well up.

His grandfather smiled and let out a dry laugh. "Well goodness gracious, Jake, that's all right."

90

Jake shook his head. "No! No, that's not right at all! How can you *say* that, Grandpa?"

"Well, I'm here now, ain't I?"

Jake said nothing.

"*Ain't* I?" his grandfather demanded.

"Yeah, Grandpa. You're here now. But you—"

"Won't be soon?" The old man tamped out his pipe on the stump and put it back in his pocket. He ground out a last bit of smoldering tobacco with a calloused thumb. "That what you mean to say?"

"Yeah," said Jake.

"We'll see," said his grandfather, squinting up the hill into the bright sun. "Come on, now. I was honest with you, you've got the truth, but for now we've got a good day ahead of us. That's what's important. No matter what, we can't let it go to waste. I do so hate a ruined day."

The old man slowly eased himself up off the stump and started climbing the hill again. Jake stood behind him, staring at the familiar figure but not moving.

"Come on, Jake! Don't you want to see the view?"

A fast decision made, he ran to catch up. A moment later he met his grandfather on top of the hill and gazed out at a wilderness of golds and greens and browns and reds, all glistening and brilliant in the early morning sun.

Far below, in the valley, a silver thread of stream wound its way from someplace out of sight to someplace out of sight.

"Is that where you used to fish?" Jake asked, pointing.

His grandfather took a moment to answer; he was gasping for breath.

"That's where I used to fish," he said in a hoarse voice.

"Can we fish there together sometime?" Jake asked for the second time that day, taking his grandfather's hand again.

"Why…why sure we can. Sometime we can fish there together. Come Spring. When the fish come out of hiding."

"Promise?"

His grandfather looked down at him and smiled. "What did I say about truck with liars?"

Jake smiled back, squeezing his grandfather's hand tighter. Then he blinked. For a brief moment his mind had wandered.

He looked down at the child holding his hand.

"Grandpa Jake?" the child asked.

"What's up, Doc?"

"You feeling better now, Grandpa?" his grandson asked in a small voice.

Jake nodded, trying not to cough. When he started it was hard to stop.

His grandson tugged his hand. "Is that where you used to fish?"

Jake looked down at the stream far below, a ribbon of silver winding its way from someplace out of sight to someplace out of sight. "No," he said. "But I always wanted to."

"You wanna go fishing there sometime with *me*?" his grandson asked.

"Yes," he said, without hesitation.

"When?"

Jake smiled. "There's a good day ahead of us. We'll come back this afternoon. Pack a picnic lunch. I'll drive down to Stockton's and buy us some gear first."

"Really?" the boy exclaimed. "*Promise?*"

"I don't have no truck with liars," Jake said, then closed his eyes and breathed in the smell of spring.

Wolf Stone

B rewster was melancholy—a vague adjective that can mean anything from mildly glum to virtually suicidal. His case fell somewhere in between.

"Melancholy" usually conjures up mental images of an ennui-stricken consumptive from the nineteenth century. Brewster was luckier—a twenty-first century college graduate, physically fit, education paid for and completed, and more than a little spoiled by doting, upper-class parents. But his degree in eighteenth-century European theater was worse than useless; it was pointless. Everyone had told him so from the start, but after five years spent working as an assistant manager at Blockbuster Video with no brighter job prospects in sight, no lasting relationship, and no greater understanding of the world around him, he'd finally come around to admitting it to himself.

So in a listless, self-pitying state of mind Brewster sold his apartment in Killington, moved back in with his parents, and wondered what to do next. Not finding any ready answers, he started losing weight, stopped shaving, didn't bother washing his clothes, and seldom left the house. He made a nest for himself in the basement, complete with television, couch, computer, and mini-fridge...and there he hid.

Three weeks after the return, his father came downstairs.

"You should go back to the doctor. He helped you before."

"No."

"Then you're going to Aunt Margaret's."

"Aunt Margaret's dead," said Brewster.

"Very observant. But the house is still there, and you're going to spearhead a restoration operation. That's lakefront property, prime real estate. You're going to have the place inspected, hire contractors, live there while the work is underway, make sure nothing gets stolen."

"I don't want—"

"And get your shit together while you're at it." He patted Brewster on the shoulder and clumped back upstairs.

*****

There wasn't much to do in Bethany. All the wonder from Brewster's childhood visits to his aunt's had died with her. Lake Erie still held some appeal, but autumn pushed him away from dark water and the darker thoughts that came with it. While the contractors worked, he walked. Too much noise to watch TV. Too much sawdust and commotion to sleep.

One of his only mildly satisfying discoveries was the Bethany Historical Society, an old, three-story clapboard built in the 1880s. Except for Stockton's Grocery and Drug, the post office, Paige's Pizzeria, and a VFW hall, it was about the only building in town open to the public.

He signed in at the front desk, much to the delight of the blue-haired woman behind the counter, and declined a guided tour for two dollars—much to the woman's obvious dismay. After falling back into sullen silence, she returned to her faded paperback and ignored him completely. This left him free to explore in a bored, haphazard way.

It was on the third floor, under the slanted attic eaves, that he found the portrait. Stacked among photos of the Bethany Flood, he almost overlooked it, but a hint of color—of *skin*—caught his attention among all the black and white.

The frame, too, was different from the rest: ornate gilt and arabesque patterns instead of unpolished oak. He turned it over. A date on the back, in flowing quill pen: *1792*.

A sharp breath of air cleared away the heavy cover of dust. Brewster stared at the young woman and she stared back. Her eyes, a faded green similar to his own, gazed at him with playful vitality. A pile of red hair, held in place with jeweled combs, accentuated the pristine, almost translucent ivory of her skin. *She can't be more than twenty*, he thought, *and she knows what that means…all those years stretching ahead. So much time. So many possibilities. Look at that poise, that confidence…*

Embarrassed, surprised, he found tears verging in the corners of his eyes. Worse, he heard footsteps on the stairs. Clearing his throat, he looked at the portrait with close interest, trying to regain his composure. Doing so, he was surprised to notice that the girl didn't have any teeth. She was smiling—grinning, actually—but the artist had chosen to leave a swath of pink acrylic gum lines where her teeth should have been.

The woman with the blue hair waddled up behind him. "Closing in ten minutes!"

"Oh, sure…I'll be going."

She peered over Brewster's shoulder.

"That's not supposed to be out for public viewing," she said in an accusatory tone.

"Sorry. I didn't know."

"Not your fault. Bernice, the other guide…she's always moving stuff around. Should be back in the basement. No one wants to see *that*."

"It's a good painting. Was she one of Bethany's first citizens?"

"Who, Roberta Kirkpatrick?" She snorted.

"Is that her name?"

"Sure is. Was. No, the town's far older than her. If you'd taken the *guided* tour, you'd know that."

"Oh. Yes."

"No, she was just a girl who died young. Lots of those back then. Nothing special."

"What happened to her teeth?"

The woman leaned in close. "Don't know," she said, recoiling quickly.

"How'd she die?"

The woman looked at her watch. "Closing time!"

*****

Brewster couldn't get the portrait out of his mind. Or the name. "Roberta Kirkpatrick," he whispered that night in the dark, as the wind clattered tree branches above the house and pushed waves against the shore of the lake. She fascinated him—close to his age, but separated by over two hundred years.

In the morning he walked up Bethany Hill to the end of the paved road. A half-mile up the steep dirt path beyond, he came to the old cemetery. Forty-five minutes later he was kneeling in the dead grass by Roberta Kirkpatrick's grave. The chiseled letters on the headstone were almost worn away, but the massive slab of granite that lay across the length of the grave bore a deeper inscription, along with two dates: 1773-1794.

"She was twenty-one," Brewster murmured.

"Twenty," said a voice behind him.

He whirled, heart slamming.

An old man stood behind him, smiling apologetically.

"Didn't mean to startle you," said the stranger. "I keep a home over the crest of the hill. Watch over the graves. Stupid kids come up once in a while, especially round this month when it's close to Halloween. Do all kinds of mischief if you let 'em."

"I just came to look for her," said Brewster, nodding at the grave.

The old man clucked his tongue. "Name's Dwight Farnum. You from around here?"

"My Aunt was Margaret Peron."

"Oh, hell, I knew her! Fine lady. Nobody never said a bad word about her. You selling the property?"

"Yes."

"Damn shame. You know, I used to—"

"Do you know anything about *her*?" Brewster interrupted, pointing to the stone.

Farnum paused, rubbing the back of his sunburned neck. "Well…not much," he said slowly.

"I saw a portrait. How come she didn't have any teeth?"

Farnum's face drained of color so fast Brewster thought he'd have to save him from a fall.

"There was a good reason," Farnum said thinly, steadying himself, "but I can't rightly remember what it was."

"You don't look so good. Here, sit down on the slab a minute."

"I won't sit on no wolf stone," said Farnum quickly. "And I'm fine, thank you very much. I'd best get on. You keep away from here, now."

And Brewster, too surprised to speak, could only shake his head while the old man walked away.

*****

That afternoon, Brewster looked up "wolf stone" on Google.

"A slab of concrete or stone placed on a grave to keep wild animals from disturbing the remains of the recently interred," he murmured. "Popular through the mid-nineteenth century."

The rest of the evening Brewster felt increasingly anxious. He hadn't had a monomaniacal impulse since high school, but he recognized the signs that he was now in the grip of a developing obsession. He struggled against it for hours, but couldn't shake the thought of Roberta Kirkpatrick's body beneath that massive slab; of her decay; of her skeleton surrounded by stained, disintegrating burial cloth. Alone, far from anyone he knew, she felt like a friend, and he grieved for her passing.

He missed her.

He thought of her wolf stone. What a terrible necessity—a monstrous reminder of a long-gone culture's fear. Images of corrupt, defiled graves coursed through his mind. And wolves, of course. They skirted his thoughts like dark figures on the edge of firelight.

Later, in tormented sleep, Brewster tossed and turned, haunted by dreams of Roberta's face. The eyes, the hair, the smooth marble skin...even the toothless mouth didn't detract from her striking beauty. That face promised great things—friendship, love...*other* things; fulfillment in all its great and many forms...

He woke up bathed in sweat, loins throbbing, eyes wet, and knew his father had been right to send him here. And he continued to know this as he threw on his clothes, went out to the shed in the back yard, grabbed a crowbar and shovel, and trotted silently up Bethany Hill.

"There are no wolves now," he said, digging around the base of the slab as quietly as he could. "No wild animals." He giggled. "All dead. All dead."

He pressed down on the crowbar with all his weight, heaved at it until a blood vessel burst in his left eye, and laughed wildly as the wolf stone moved an inch, then two.

"You called to me the only way you knew how," he whispered two hours later, three feet down in the grave, "and here I come."

Soon the coffin, surprisingly intact, began to take form beneath the dirt. His shovel struck old sheet metal.

"Roberta," he said, and dug at the box with his nails. Earth fell away in wormy clods. The rotting casket lay fully revealed. He pulled a flashlight from his back pocket, turned it on, and clamped it between his teeth. He reached up for the crowbar, eyes wide, smiling with expectant glee.

"My purpose," he whispered, and forced open the coffin.

*****

The heart attack that killed Dwight Farnum came two weeks after he found the young man's body, but nobody doubted that the shock of the discovery contributed heavily to his demise.

Just days before his death, Farnum drove down to Tap's Bar outside of town, a rare enough event, and when some of his cronies started asking questions he waved them quiet.

"I didn't come to talk, I came to drink," he said. "But all I'll say is that I never seen a body like that before." He downed a big gulp of lager. "Throat ripped out an' all."

"Police say it was like claws did it," someone said.

"My last words on the subject," Farnum muttered, setting down his empty mug and reaching for his hat, "are that Mr. Brewster learned three things. First, he learned why they took out that Kirkpatrick girl's teeth all them years ago. Second, he learned they probably should've taken out a few other things, too. And last of all, I guess he learned what a wolf stone's *really* for."

He tipped his hat and left the bar, which had gone very quiet.

And shortly thereafter, he died.

All, Always

Paul Burton sprouted up in a small town called Plumville, and in Plumville the Christmas season officially began on "Light-Up Night" down at the courthouse, where a few dozen strands of colored lights sparked off a speech by Mayor Davidson, two competing choirs, the train display down in the station shooting range, and an earnest bake sale by the formidable ladies of the Plumville Historical Society.

But for Paul, Christmas *truly* began when his father and mother piled him and his sister into the old Ford truck and headed out to the McCullough farm to choose the family Christmas tree.

Choosing was a laborious process. His mother always wanted a *thin* tree, his father always wanted a *fat* tree, Janey always wanted a *little* tree, and he always wanted the biggest one they could fit in the house. Beyond that, the pros and cons of ten-dozen Frasier Furs, Douglas Furs, Blue Spruces, and White Pines had to be weighed, debated, and argued over.

Ultimately, the final decision was based on compromise—and a "thinnish chubby tree, not too tall," was invariably purchased, tied to the back of the truck, and driven home. Once the roots were bundled up in sacking and the tree balanced up, they decorated it with home-made stars, cranberry garlands, silver tinsel, bubble lights and winking lights, white lights and colored lights. Then Mom heated up cinnamon cider and cooked sweet and sour beef-log, and Christmas was officially under way.

So it had gone when Paul was two, six, twelve, twenty-four, thirty-two, and all the in-between years that, once past, weave together into a glowing sheen of memory. But his mother's passing, shortly before his thirty-third Christmas, had marked the beginning of the end— a time of downward-spiraling change that destroyed ritual and froze warmth. Crisis followed crisis, and now, six days before his forty-fifth Christmas, there *was* no tree—only a hospital room.

"Dad," he said, gently shaking his father's shoulder. The skin felt warm and dry through the thin paper gown.

"Mmmm." The old man opened jaundiced eyes and peered out at the small world of pastel walls and mildly alarming plastic machines that counted down his life.

"Dad, I have to go now. I wanted to say goodbye. I'll be back first thing tomorrow morning."

For a long moment Paul's father didn't seem to comprehend what he was saying, or even realize he had spoken. It was hard for Paul to tell. Paul cleared his throat, opened his mouth to repeat himself, then stopped as his father raised a hand.

"Janey," a broken-reed voice said.

Paul sighed. "Sorry, Pop. I tried every number I had. I called Information, old friends… I even contacted Bob."

"Bob's a son-of-a-bitch." The disused voice gained confidence. "If I'd known what he was really like, I never would have let Janey marry him. And if she hadn't divorced him, I would've killed him myself."

"I know. And he hung up on me, so that didn't help."

Paul's father grinned. "Almost Christmas and our holiday sucks. Ho ho ho!"

He smiled back. He couldn't help it.

The old man chuckled. "Not much fun, is it? Your mother gone, me on the way out, your sister MIA, you divorced. Shit. What are you going to do? Who are you going to spend Christmas with?" He held out his hand. Paul took it. The skin was like tissue paper. The grip was palsied but oddly, desperately strong.

"It doesn't matter, Pop." The words were listless and hollow, dark emptiness behind false nonchalance.

Paul's father snorted. "Sure it does. I'm stuck in this bed, but *you're* not. I don't want you moping around, even if there *is* plenty to mope about. I got you a present. I think you'll like it. If you do, then I know you just as well now as I did when you was a little kiddo. You always loved Christmas."

"That's right. It used to be my favorite holiday."

"Mine, too. And it still is. So listen up. In my bathrobe—"

A nurse bustled in, humming, and administered a shot. The old man gave her a dirty look, began to extend his middle finger, then sank abruptly into a deep sleep. The hand that held Paul's relaxed its grip slowly, a worn bundle of bones and sinew.

Paul placed it gently on the coverlet over his father's chest, then quietly left the room.

*****

He threw his keys down on the coffee table and collapsed into an easy chair. The apartment didn't feel like home. Outside, Pittsburgh hummed with late-evening life. Inside, sterile walls, much like those of the hospital he had just left, stared blankly back at him and did not comfort.

Paul liked to talk, but since his divorce and his father's illness had forced the move from his house and town, there hadn't been many people to talk to. So he talked to himself.

"This isn't Christmas," he told the dark television screen.

He got up and made himself a cup of instant coffee, took one sip, and splashed the rest in the sink. He took a shower, shaved so he wouldn't have to do it in the morning, wiped the foam off his face, and stared at the medicine cabinet mirror.

"I can't remember what Christmas was like," he said softly, looking into his own hollow eyes. "I know it was good, I have the memories, but the feelings are gone." He dropped his head, and when he raised it again the face that stared back at him was very pale. "It's like all those Christmases happened to someone else. Or like they never happened at all."

The telephone rang in the other room. After staring at himself for a moment longer he went and answered it, and learned that his father had died in his sleep.

*****

"In my bathrobe."

The words haunted him as he drove back to the hospital in the freezing rain. They haunted him as he stepped through the hospital's sliding doors. They haunted him in the elevator, in the hallway, in the room with the empty bed.

They haunted him as he reached into his father's bathrobe, still hung up on the hook in the tiny closet, and slid a hand into the pocket.

They haunted him as he pulled out a piece of paper and unfolded it.

He read the letter in his father's shaky print, re-read it, put it in his pocket, then went to take care of all the details that suddenly rear up to confront the grieving when someone dies.

*****

On December 25, Paul drove the three hours to Plumville. He rented a room with Mrs. Diller, his old piano teacher who now owned a bed & breakfast, and let her make him a nice lunch. He sat down and ate it in the deserted common room. Then, as dusk began to fall and a few stray wisps of snow took flight on the cold, gentle wind, he donned his hat, buttoned up his coat, and stepped out onto the sidewalks of his old hometown—a tiny Western Pennsylvania hamlet slowly fading away as the abandoned coal mines lost definition and caved in upon themselves, dotting the landscape with sinkholes.

After two blocks he stopped walking. In the light of one of the town's telephone pole Christmas stars, he unfolded his father's letter and read it for the tenth time:

Paul,

> *Go to Plumville. Rent a room with Mrs. Diller, let her make you a nice lunch, then, when night begins to fall, walk over to the old house, up the back yard path, and into the woods. Remember when we used to walk in the woods after Christmas dinner? Once you hit the old train tracks, turn left and keep going till you reach the station house. I bought it years ago. It's yours, but that's not the present. Your present is inside. And outside.*

> *Pop*

Paul folded the letter again and walked up the driveway of a small, abandoned house, empty ever since his father had moved into the nursing home in Pittsburgh four years before. The windows were broken, black and vacant like empty eye sockets. Inside, the rooms that had hosted his youth lay in deep shadow, wallpaper peeling, floors warping without the century-long treads that once kept them flat.

He walked up the river stone path his father had built by hand fifty years before. Shivering, he stepped under the first of the trees that flanked the end of his old back yard. Deep, deep in on the old trails, then to the rusted tracks and left, on and on, the cold creeping into his blood, the darkness almost alive, the woods immense and silent, everything brooding above the small, warm town below. And then the station house, faded green shingles and wooden slats framing a door that opened like a dark mouth into gloom.

"Why," Paul murmured, "did he bring me all the way out here?"

He snapped on a flashlight, unlocked the door, and stepped inside.

Dust lay thick on a creaking, empty slat floor. In one corner a small desk stood next to a stuffed outdoor rocking chair. On the wall, above the desk, was a red fuse box. A sign attached to it with masking tape read, "OPEN ME." Paul did. Inside was a single switch. Paul's breath smoked hotly on the freezing air and hitched hard in his throat. He flicked the switch up.

The world blazed with light.

It took him a moment to figure out where it was coming from. Then he did.

Paul stepped back outside into a forest of evergreens, each one decorated with thousands of lights, strand upon strand, color upon color, a glowing wonderland in the middle of cold, darkened wilderness. Some of the trees were stately, tall, and full-bodied. Others were younger—smaller, shorter, and more recently pruned.

In the thin winter breeze that moved and shifted the lights in a kaleidoscope of branches, Paul stumbled forward. He leaned down by the base of a particularly large pine and shone his torch on a small brass plaque nailed to a stand.

Christmas 1971, it read.

Paul shook his head. He moved on to one of the smaller trees. It, too, was marked.

Christmas 2000, read the plaque.

He didn't understand. Blinking rapidly, he returned to the station house to look for a clue. He found it on the table below the fuse box—a thin slip of paper with his name on it, covered in dust.

Written in his father's hand, but in stronger script, before he became ill, the message was short and simple:

Paul,

> *These trees grew for me. Now they grow for you. They are all here, always.*

Pop

And suddenly a gear clicked into place in Paul's head and it all made sense. He ran back outside in a fever, cold and warm, jaw slack and tight, slack and tight.

"All our Christmas trees. Every single one. From every year."

He stared out at the illuminated forest and said nothing else. His father had always brought their Christmas trees home alive, roots and all. No one ever questioned why or what he did with them after Christmas, when the chore of taking down decorations distracted them with melancholy. "Just another late December afternoon," Paul had thought on such days, "and Christmas so far away again."

But it hadn't been. No, not at all.

A gentle snow began to fall. A great deal gathered on Paul's hat and shoulders before he turned off the power in the station house and hiked back to town.

*****

Mrs. Diller found him in the living room, feet to the crackling fireplace, a mug of hot cinnamon cider steaming gently by the arm of the overstuffed rocking chair.

"Mr. Burton!" she exclaimed. "Oh, I hope you haven't been alone long. I was over at my niece's for Christmas Dinner, and time slipped by so *fast*."

Paul grinned. "Don't think anything of it. I made myself nice and comfy."

Mrs. Diller paused, opened her mouth, shut it, then pursed her lips. Clearly, she wanted to say something. Finally she said it.

"Paul, it's none of my business, but you didn't spend Christmas all *alone*, did you?" Apparently she decided she had gone too far. "No, forgive me, don't answer that. It's none of my business. It's just...family makes all the difference sometimes. Even a quick visit or a phone call. Don't you think?"

"I couldn't agree more."

"Well, I hope you got to see or talk with your family today. Here, I'll go get us some Santa cookies." She bustled out of the room.

Paul, staring into the fire, nodded distractedly. "Yes," he responded once she was gone. The warm room embraced his voice. "I saw them, talked with them. It was quite a day."

He smiled, raising his mug. "What a gift."

Steel

In the early dawn light, Jacob Fields felt a hand on his shoulder and rolled over in bed to see what it wanted.

"Five o'clock," said his father. "Get up."

"I don't want to go."

"You're going," he said firmly. "Meet me outside in ten minutes."

Jacob took his time. He clumped downstairs eight minutes late, eyes sullen and fixed on the floor.

"Too late for breakfast," his father said from the kitchen. "Gear's in the back of the truck. Let's go."

Outside, Jacob changed into his camouflage jumper and orange vest in silence. His father looked on appraisingly. They climbed into the truck and his father gunned the engine to rattling, spluttering life.

Jacob's father had built his house on the edge of a long tract of forest in Western Pennsylvania, three miles from the nearest village and its silent, crumbling coal works. He drove them deeper into the trees, into true, rarified backcountry. The paved road soon turned to gravel, then dirt.

After a long silence, he jabbed Jacob in the side with a stubby index finger. "You like nature, kiddo. You'll like this. I got a blind nailed up in an old oak tree so hard to find nobody knows where it is except me. Real natural. You'll see."

"I'll sit there but I won't shoot," Jacob said softly. "You can't make me."

His father slapped him hard across the back of the head. "I want a dead deer, and I ain't doing no shooting today. Understand? We been through this before. No books this weekend. No goddamn flower walks. Jesus, thirteen years old and you've never even skinned a knee."

Jacob rubbed the back of his head and said nothing.

"Too bad there ain't a war with a draft on right now," his father continued. "World War II made men of a whole generation. So did 'Nam. On and on back, up to now. If I had any money, I'd truck you off to military school. Get your head of out the clouds. But this'll do just fine, I guess. Nothing quite like a good hunt. You wait an' see. It'll open up a whole new world for you."

Jacob opened his mouth to say something, closed it again, then said, "I never meant to make anyone ashamed."

His father grunted.

"I do real well in school. Mom taught me every day when I didn't understand something. I never get in trouble. Last year I won an art contest. They showed my painting at the mall."

His father sighed. "I don't mean to talk badly of the departed, kiddo. Your mother was a fine type, even though she treated me so shabby."

"She did *not*—"

"You did good by her," his father cut in, "but all those years without a man in your life—it ain't natural. Gives you no sense of yourself. You're getting your ass kicked at your new school twice a week, and we can't have that, can we?"

"It'll pass. They'll get tired of it soon."

"You need a little steel in your heart, kiddo. Something that won't bend to everyone else. This'll help give it to you. It'll be a start, at any rate."

Jacob opened his mouth to say more, but noticed that same steel in his father's face, in his gray eyes and hard mouth. Now, at least for the time being, he chose to keep his silence.

*****

The blind was nothing more than a handful of boards tucked away in the upper branches of an old, lightning-struck oak. Covered with dead branches and camouflage canvas, it smelled of mold, decaying leaves, gun oil, and dried whiskey.

"Now what?" Jacob asked, breathless from the climb up the half-rotten ladder.

"Now we have our quality time," said his father. "We wait for a deer and catch up on the last ten years."

But neither volunteered much, and so it had always been, ever since the funeral. Their lives, so different, refused to gel, even when forced to touch. Silence descended like a curtain between them, until the only sound was the ebb and flow of the forest—the minute resonance of flora and fauna that, combined, hum their routines out to the world.

Jacob's father pulled out a battered pack of cigarettes and flicked open a Zippo. Soon the acrid smell of tobacco smoke cut an unnatural swath across the other scents of the wild. To Jacob, it was sickening; his mother had always hated it. Suddenly he missed her terribly, more than he had in the four months since her death, and he started to cry. He tried not to, but he couldn't help it. Everything was different. Everything was strange.

"Stop that." His father said it quietly.

He didn't.

"Stop that," his father said again. "You'll scare the deer."

An open hand cracked across his face. An angry red welt rose to throb tight and hot on his cheek.

Jacob stopped crying.

"That's what I mean," his father said, still in that soft, wooden voice Jacob could neither fathom nor penetrate. "Steel in your heart, kiddo. You need more than a little, but you ain't got none at all. Hey…"

He leaned over the blind, eyes squinted, peering out through the canopy.

"There." He pointed, then grabbed Jacob's shoulder and pulled him forward. In a slight clearing of fallen trees, a small doe ate calmly, quietly grazing among the ferns.

"Two-year-old if a day," his father muttered, reaching for his rifle. "You'll love the taste, Jacob. Meat tastes different when you kill it yourself. You *earn* it, then. It always tastes better when you earn it."

He proffered the rifle to Jacob, who shook his head.

"This ain't an option, Jacob."

"I'll miss on purpose."

His father's eyes were like slate.

"No you won't," he said. He turned, took careful aim at the deer, and fired. A jet of flame shot from the end of the rifle. The forest shook, the very air traumatized by heat and noise. Beyond it all, Jacob could hear intense silence, and as the echoes of the shot faded away, that silence took over, alive in the vacuum of life holding its breath.

Then, very faintly, leaves crinkled, ferns bent, as a small body fell among them and upon them.

Jacob stared out at the fallen deer. He bit his tongue until he tasted copper.

The deer wasn't dead. His father had shot it in the back flank, and it had fallen, too stunned to rise. It pawed the air feebly.

"It's suffering, Jacob," his father told him. "Let's go."

Jacob followed his father down the ladder and across the forest floor. In the clearing, the deer lay in a bed of blood-soaked fern, moaning softly.

Jacob's father handed him the rifle. He took it with numb fingers.

"You can't miss now," his father said. "Finish it."

Jacob shook his head.

"Finish it."

"No." A whisper.

"Finish it, Goddamn it! Finish it!"

Jacob aimed the rifle the way his father had taught him. A sob choked in his throat. He felt faint. *Steel*, he thought, and the image of his mother appeared behind his closed eyelids.

He fired.

Thunder rumbled across the land. The deer stopped moving.

"You did it!" his father exclaimed. "You did it, Ja—"

Jacob fired a second time. Then again. He riddled the deer's carcass. He squeezed the trigger, released, and squeezed until the last thunder died away and all the damage he could do was done.

Sounds of life returned slowly to the forest. His father stared at him. "You ruined it," he said softly. "Buckshot all through it. No one can eat the damn thing now. Goddamn it, Jacob!" He pulled his fist back to strike, then paused, breathing heavily. After a long moment the hand uncurled and fell to his side.

Jacob opened his eyes. He felt different. No tears welled up to fall. Slowly he bent down and picked a small cluster of yellow wild flowers from the forest loam. Not looking at his father, he placed them by the head of the still, silent deer, then reached out to stroke its cooling head and close its brown, staring eyes.

He stood up and handed his father the rifle. Wordlessly, his father took it.

Without looking back, Jacob walked quickly out of the clearing, back to the path that led to the truck. He murmured something in parting.

"What's that?" his father asked sharply. "What you say, kiddo?"

"Steel," Jacob said a second time, louder than the first, and continued walking.

An Unknown Shore

It was a passion, and passions can never be fully explained. Why the Civil War? people asked. A hundred and forty years old and not getting any younger. Sure, a visit to Gettysburg is an eye-opener. Antietam Bridge is provocative. Harper's Ferry? A good way to spend a Saturday if it's not too hot. But why the full Union uniform? Why live in a tent ten weekends a year? Why the collection of bullets and bayonets, the library stocked with Shelby Foote and Walt Whitman, Sherman's memoirs and Lincoln's speeches?

There were many things Tyler Adams could have told them, but if they had to ask, there was no way they could ever fully understand.

But eventually, against all odds, he found a woman who *didn't* ask, who didn't mind pretending to be Clara Barton at reenactments and whose idea of a fun holiday was a weekend in old Richmond followed by a three-week voyage starting at Sumter and ending at Appomattox. Eight months later, Tyler married Paige Sayer and his life was finally full.

The Civil War. It had brought them together: Tyler a born-and-bred Bostonian, Paige a die-hard Savannah belle.

Yet now, ten years into a happy marriage, two weeks into a twenty-day battlefield tour, something happened that had never happened before.

"I think," Paige said, looking out at yet another of the endless strip malls between Antietam and Fredericksburg, "that I've had enough of the Civil War for awhile."

Tyler almost choked on his granola bar. "*What?*"

Paige turned and looked at him sadly. "Not forever, mind you. But for a little while. Perhaps a long while. We should spend the rest of our vacation elsewhere—someplace the Civil War never touched. Hawaii, maybe. Or Alaska."

"Secession!" he exclaimed.

Paige smiled. "Not quite as bad as that. It's just…" She broke off, face crumpling.

"Oh now," Tyler said, putting his hand on her arm. He pulled the car over and turned off the ignition.

"I feel…*too* close," Paige explained.

"To me?"

"No! Gracious, no. To *it*. To those four bloody years when the House was divided."

Tyler was silent. The car ticked in the hot day.

"It was Gettysburg that did it," she continued softly. "Time always seems *thin* there, have you noticed?"

He nodded.

"Like time is a veil, and all you need do is push it back..."

"Yes. Yes, I've felt it too. Many times. So much happened there, so much death and emotion, it's like a physical weight on the present. But Paige, we've been there *dozens* of times! Why now?"

"Because two days ago, when we packed our bags and said 'goodbye' to the Farnsworth House, that feeling *didn't go away*. Something followed us. Something that should be dead and buried and safely filed away in the history books. I wouldn't be scared, but...but..."

"But *what?*"

"But it's *inside* of me."

"What? What's inside?"

Paige took a deep breath. "Ever since Gettysburg I've felt things I've never felt before. Seen things I've never seen before. When I opened my eyes just now, I didn't see a paved highway...I saw a *dirt road*. And yesterday, when I woke up at the motel in Antietam, I could have *sworn* it was a farmhouse, and that two horses stood waiting outside where our car should have been."

"Nonsense! You're just imagining things."

"*Am* I? I've never had a very vivid imagination, Tyler, but when we stopped for gas in York an hour back, I didn't see a service station, I saw a clapboard inn, and in front of that inn stood two dozen dusty Union Blues, dismounted, watering their horses. Three were wounded, bandages soaked with blood. And I could *smell* the horses, that sweet musky smell of hay and manure. I tell you, *it wasn't my imagination*."

Paige got out of the car. Tyler followed.

"And it's more than that," she continued, beginning to pace. "I'm not only seeing with someone else's eyes, I'm *feeling* someone else's *feelings*. Oh, the sorrow, Tyler. The *heartache*. We can never know what it was like to be a soldier then. Never. We *think* we can, and the feeling thrills us. But that's all. Never have I felt such despair as I have felt since leaving Gettysburg. And it is not my own."

She leaned against a rail fence a little way off the road and looked out on a field of golden wheat that stretched away into the distance.

"I don't know if I'm looking at a field now, in 2007, or a hundred and forty-five years ago," she murmured. "It's all too much. Can you understand that? Too much."

Tyler sighed. "I'm sorry," he said. "I brought this on."

"How can you say that? It's not your fault."=

"There's a fine line between passion and obsession. We must have crossed that line somewhere along the way, and this is the result. All those reenactments. Those were my idea."

Paige shook her head. "You didn't force me to do anything. I've always loved this stuff." She paused. "You *do* believe me, don't you?"

"I believe you *think* you're seeing these things," Tyler said gently. "But they're not really there."

"But what about what I *feel?*" she demanded, voice rising.

"That's real enough, but it's *not* a ghost inside your head—"

"No," she interrupted, "It's a person from *another time*."

"—It's *you*," he continued, "overwhelmed by the magnitude of the tragedy."

She shook her head. "You don't understand."

Tyler raised his eyebrows. "Well, maybe not. But I think your idea is a good one. Let's use the rest of our vacation and go somewhere different. How about a cruise? Hawaii was a great idea."

*****

Five days later, on the deck of a great ship plowing across the Pacific, Paige reclined in a chair and sipped a Cosmopolitan. The sun beat warm on her face. The breeze of the ocean cooled the warmth until everything felt just right.

"Three days until we reach Hawaii," Tyler said beside her. "This was a good idea. This was a very good idea. For us, for now, the war is over."

Paige nodded. The visions had almost ceased. Whoever it was that had traveled with her in her mind had all but packed his bags and left—headed, she hoped, back from where he had come.

Even so, something gnawed at her. Some other angle she hadn't considered. It didn't panic her like before, but nonetheless a small, distant worry remained.

"I wonder," she said softly. But Tyler, not hearing, left to find a magazine.

"I wonder," she continued to herself, "if what came with me from Gettysburg could look out of my eyes the way I could look through his? Time is thin there. And war divides some, yet brings others together. That's what history teaches. What visions did *I* give to *him*—whoever he is?

"And what, oh what, would he think of what he saw?"

She made no effort to answer her own questions. Putting on her sunglasses, she forced her mind silent, and focused instead on the incessant gold and white rhythm of the sunlit waves as they met with the distant horizon.

*****

The man awoke suddenly in the pale sunlit room. Distracted, bemused, he dressed, washed, and descended the stairs to assume the duties of the day.

The Executive Cabinet awaited him in the morning room, seated around a long table of polished oak.

"You look tired, Mr. President," said Secretary of War Edwin Stanton.

The man rubbed his brow. "Gentlemen, several times in the last four years, always before some important event or disaster, I have had the same dream. I had it before Antietam, Fredericksburg, Gettysburg, and, lately, the surrender of Lee. I had this dream again last night."

He took a seat at the table. His deep-set eyes looked careworn and haunted.

"In my dream," he said slowly, "I stand upon the deck of a ship that is rushing on some vast and indistinct expanse...toward an unknown shore." He looked up with a tired smile. "I take it as a good omen, that perhaps reconstruction will commence quickly, and all animosity be buried in the efforts to come."

"Let us hope, sir," someone said, breaking the silence in the suddenly quiet room.

"Yes," said the man. "But the dream does leave me tired. Well, tonight will bury that fatigue. Mrs. Lincoln and I will attend a performance at Ford's Theatre. General and Mrs. Grant may be joining us."

The cabinet then shifted to other matters, but all the rest of that day Abraham Lincoln appeared thoughtful, and sometimes raised his head—exactly, some reflected in the chaotic days that followed, as if looking toward a horizon he alone could see.

A Sense of Duty

The four men worked hard with handkerchiefs tied around their faces. The September floods had been very bad, the worst in a hundred years, and the graveyard by the woods outside town had paid the price. Now someone needed to clean up the mess.

"Ain't no work for a man," said one, shoveling clear a load of muck from the top of a disintegrating pine box.

"We volunteered, Hugh," said another. "It don't do no good to complain."

"We didn't volunteer for *this*, Carl," Hugh insisted.

"Stop your whining and shovel," Carl said, lifting the handles of a broke-down wheelbarrow full of bad earth and turning away with it. "Whining ain't fitting a man, neither."

"Carl's right," said the third. "Volunteer firemen are in for it, no matter the calamity. You signed up as a volunteer fireman, you volunteered for this. So here you are. It's for the good of the town... 'Course, it sure is nasty," he added, peering into the dank hole before him...mostly empty, but not quite.

"I guess, but it strikes me this here's a bit above and beyond the call of duty, or what have you," said Hugh. "You'll change your tune if you fall in there, Ted."

The fourth man, the groundskeeper, returned from his trip to the storage shed, pulling an empty cart behind him. "That was Mr. Wilbur Collins I just unloaded. Wiped off the name plate," he said. "The newer boxes all have 'em."

"Never did like Old Man Collins," said Hugh. "Shot me with rock salt once for cutting across his north pasture."

"How many we got in there now, Mike?" Carl asked.

Mike let go of the cart and wiped his brow with a gloved hand. "So far there's eleven, and some spare...odds and ends. Phew! For late September it sure is hot." He looked sick and pale.

"Eleven," said Ted, turning away from the open grave only to face another. Carefully, he picked his way back to clear ground. "That means," he continued once safe, "there's a good...well..."

"The chart says ninety-two," Mike said, rummaging in his overalls for a battered sheaf of papers. "Yep, ninety-two. But to be honest, this one hain't been updated in some time. The new chart, I'm afraid it was warshed away. Can't say as I can recollect all the names, seeing as I just took the post six months ago, but there's probably a few dozen more than what we see here."

"Jesus wept," groaned Ted.

"With all the stones strewn about, we got our work cut out for us," Mike agreed.

Hugh thumped Mike on the back, grinning. "Ain't you glad you got the job when you did?"

"Pineville's a small town, thank God for that," said Carl. "It could've been worse."

*****

Around three they rested on a log at the far end of the cemetery, carefully checking before they sat to make sure there weren't any surprises lying nearby.

"Looking at it from this vantage point, I think I'm gonna cry," said Ted. "I don't wanna go back there."

From where they sat it became apparent just how little their day's work had achieved. One corner of the yard was mostly clear, tombstones neatly stacked against the low stone wall, nothing else in sight but a long hole every now and again or a bulge in the matted grass signifying a risen coffin the waters hadn't entirely freed.

The rest of the yard, sixteen square acres, was a charnel garden. Tombstones law strewn about, some face down, some face up, some cracked, some broken, some sticking in the earth by a corner after being tossed end over end by the current. Only a few of the heavier, expensive granite stones remained mounted and upright. In almost all cases the remains they memorialized were no longer where they belonged.

It was an old cemetery, some coffins planted so long ago there was nothing *left* to float, but Pineville had also been gifted with several generations of skilled casket makers who knew how to prolong disintegration and fit boards tight together; thus, many had risen when the waters called, only breaking open when those same waters currented them into trees, tombstones, rocks and each other. Scores of broken wood caskets littered the yard, along with their long-hidden contents that turned the stomach and watered the eyes...some still under lids, others strewn across the muck. Friends, family, and progenitors society had long ago accepted as lost had now returned, but they were not wanted.

"If only everything wasn't so *damp*," said Ted. "A little sun, a little heat—"

"Heat would only make it worse." Carl sniffed.

"But at least it would make everything less…less *dead*. I hate autumn. Cold mists, colder rains, and never enough sun. It's the sun I need more than anything. Besides, we won't be able to rebury any of these folk until the ground dries. We should pray for sun."

"Prayer is good, I won't argue none with that, but we should pray for strength more than sun," Mike said, "and hurry up and get on with our job before what strength we got left gives out." He stood, stretched, and trudged slowly back to his cart.

The others, equally slowly, followed.

"What we *should* pray for is a miracle," muttered Hugh, bringing up the rear. "Something involving me never having to see anything like this ever again."

*****

By sundown the shed, formerly used for storing shovels, spades, hoes, rakes, bags of peat and wheelbarrows, housed three dozen occupied coffins and the remains of a dozen and a half Pineville citizens without, the latter securely tied up in burlap sacks. Outside, four stacks of tombstones lay in front of the shed, to be sorted through and restored to their proper places later.

"Another two days should do it for the gathering," Carl said. "Then we can help Mike here with the sorting and put everybody back proper who can *be* put back."

The night was clear but moonless, the wind gentle but cool. They slept in Mike's cottage on the hill next to the shed, setting up two-hour shifts to guard the cemetery from animals that might worry the exposed remains. Mike lent out his rifle for the purpose, along with an oil lamp so no one would take any bad steps in the dark.

Carl picked the short straw and kept watch first. He walked the grounds carefully, handkerchief tied tight around his face, trying not to think. For two hours his only excitement was chasing a red fox away from what was left of Abigail Wilson. At two he gave Ted a kick in the leg and turned in.

Ted didn't go through the graveyard, just circled around it. He didn't want to stumble into any gaping holes in the dark, didn't even want to *risk* it, so he kept to the perimeter, scaring off rats and raccoons, before stumbling into, not a hole, but a wooden coffin that gave way as his boot pressed down.

Forty-five minutes later, still wiping his heel on the grass, he shambled, muttering, back to the house and woke Hugh.

Hugh chose sitting rather than walking, and parked himself on Mike's porch swing for guard duty. It was in pretty poor shape, the weather-worn wooden seat hanging from rusted chains which looked ready to break, but it felt good to sit, and everything held. In fact, it felt so good that after a while, probably not more than a couple of minutes, he drifted off into uneasy sleep.

He dreamt fitfully of mildewed linen, dank holes, and the sighing of fretting winds through dark tree boughs. The sound conjured images of waving doors that shouldn't be open; clattering attic shutters in abandoned mansions; cold, wet-ashed chimney flues…and after a time it grew louder, more distinct and insistent, until with a start and a cry he awoke.

But the sound did not cease.

"What's that?" he hissed, then clapped a hand over his mouth. "What *is* that?" he hissed again through white fingers. He looked back toward the front door and the black inside space beyond. Silence there, save for snores.

"Christ Almighty, that ain't *them*," he said, and fumbled for the dark lantern. "Gonna see," he said. "Gonna see what that goddamned sound *is*."

But he couldn't bring himself to strike a match.

The sound was like a tide, cries washing over voices, voices demanding answers. The sound was faint but resonated with the power of a multitude. Over the voices came the tread of feet on grass and leaves, the knocking of knuckles against wood, the ripping of fabric with fingernails.

"Lord a' mercy." The words could have been Hugh's but were not. They came from *behind* him. He spun like a top, arms raised to fend off or strike.

Carl grabbed him. "Now, now, it's just us." Mike and Ted stood beside him in the dark, holding their breath.

Together they stood on the porch and listened.

"It's coming from the bone yard," Mike whispered.

"Some of the kids from town come back to cause trouble?" Ted whispered.

"Hell no," Carl said. "No one would cause trouble with *that*." His shadow nodded toward the cratered lawn.

Mike took a deep breath and said, "Come on now, let's not get panicked. It's my job to see this property's residents are kept safe. I'm turning on a lamp." He fumbled with a match. Yellow flame sprang up, touched an oiled twist of hemp. The lantern glowed.

Hugh gasped. Ted shut his eyes tight. Carl grabbed the rifle from Hugh's hand.

Mike raised the lantern.

As though of the wind itself, the noise rose for a moment, then, protesting, faded quickly and completely away.

Nothing moved in the cemetery but rats and leaves.

Even so, no one caught a wink all the rest of that long night.

*****

"Well, I'd say something looks different."

Everyone looked at Mike, who was surveying the cemetery, hands on hips and nodding slowly. "It don't look as messy today."

"That's cause we worked our behinds off yesterday," said Hugh. "Now my first order of business is to get that damned pine tree to give up her goods. It just don't look *right*, that thing all the way up in a tree." Shouldering a coil of rope, he walked over to the Spruce planted in the middle of the lot and looked up into its cover, where the glint of a brass handle betrayed the presence of a coffin lodged between two branches some eight feet off the ground.

"I'd better help him," said Carl, following. "If the damn thing drops sudden it'll probably land on his head."

"Bag duty for me," said Ted, holding up a pile of burlap sacks with a grimace. "Gonna go in the woods and search for strays. Feel free to trade whenever you're so inclined."

"Gonna try and start matching pieces together, one stone to one coffin, one coffin to one body," Mike said, and went off to the shed.

The sun was bright and warm, good for drying out the earth but bad for what needed to be re-interred beneath it. They found their cologne-soaked handkerchiefs, tied them in place, and the work went on. There was no talk about the previous night.

Not until noon did something happen to put everything else on hold for a time.

It was Ted, out in the woods, who picked up on it first, and when he did he came running from among the trees, waving his arms and wringing his hands. Everyone stopped and stared, and when he got close he called out, "There's a child in there! I can hear her crying!"

The search began immediately.

"No way anyone's in here," said Mike, turning to Ted as they weaved their way through the trunks and branches. "You sure it wasn't a barn owl? They sound kinda like tikes when they're riled."

"Hey now, I know what I heard," Ted grumbled.

"It don't make no sense. The nearest farm—"

He was cut off by a wail the likes of which none of them had ever heard. It came from farther in the forest, but not too far, and worked its way into their bones until their footsteps slowed and they all grew still. It started high and ended low, but not low enough for an adult, and there could be no doubt it was a person. Ted was right. It sounded like a child, hurt and terrified.

"My God, that was it, that was the sound," Ted whispered, grasping Carl's arm.

"Leggo," Carl hissed. "Someone needs help." But for a long moment all they could do was stand in place looking toward the thickening cluster of pines that stood before them, and Ted held on.

The silence was deathly.

Then the cry went up again, the desolate wail of someone utterly lost and alone. "Mama!" that someone called. "Mama!"

It was Hugh of all people who was stirred into action by the sound. He was a father and knew *that* call of duty when he heard it. "Come on now," he said, and trotted off toward the noise. As if waking from a dream, Carl tore free of Ted's grasp and followed Hugh. Mike and Ted kept pace behind him.

Hugh moved rapidly, trying to pinpoint the location of the sound before it died away again. He pushed through the dead lower branches of some pine trees just as the wail was fading away, and arrived at the source of the sound before the last echo died.

There could be no doubt who had made it. The sound had led them to her, and they had found her.

The little girl in the faded pink dress lay in a shallow mud puddle in the shade of the trees, but there was no need to help her up.

She had been dead for a long, long time. The skin of her face was stretched tightly over her skull, dehydrated and tanned by many dark years underground. Her long, blond hair rested in dusty, disintegrating braids across her chest. Her hands were clusters of brittle white twigs. Her hollow eye sockets stared vacantly.

Around her lay the shattered remains of a small, white coffin.

Hugh let loose a yell that sent blackbirds flying off in fright. Mike and Ted simultaneously turned and were sick. Carl leaned against a tree, swallowed his risen gorge, and shut his eyes. When he opened them again he looked up and said, "The waters took her all this way. Guess it would be a good turn to take her back. Guess that's what she wants."

Like a funeral procession they filed slowly through the woods and back to the sun-struck graveyard, a small bundle in burlap carried between Carl and Mike. After depositing the bundle in the shed they went quickly back to Mike's house, trudged inside, and worked no more that day.

Later that night before they fell asleep in front of a cheery, popping hearth fire, Hugh sneaked over to the door and latched it tight.

No one asked where he had gone when he came back.

****

By morning they had collected themselves enough to return to work, and for the next three days labored diligently, ignoring flitting shadows and sheltering themselves at night by laughing too hard at jokes and sticking cotton in their ears when they slept. Although they remained on the property out of a sense of duty, they didn't keep watch on the grounds after dusk anymore.

They made fine progress. Soon all the "litter" was gone from the grounds and Mike began making a great many identifications, due in part to his own detective work, but mainly to a somewhat disturbing discovery he made one bright morning: during the night, someone had used a sharp stone, branch, or (here Mike shuddered, thinking of it) fingernail to scratch names onto all the coffins, and mud to write names on all the burlap sacks. Despite the issues this raised, it helped a great deal, and the four men figured that no matter how it had come to happen, the act was a gift.

One afternoon, after the reburials had begun in earnest, Carl was touching up a hole when he saw Mike sitting off by himself on a rock at the edge of the yard.

"Everything dandy?" Carl asked, but was taken aback by Mike's appearance. He looked sicker than any man standing he had ever seen. There was sweat on his forehead and upper lip, but Carl could tell it wasn't the good sweat of work, but the kind that comes with brain fever. He looked so pale the light seemed almost to shine through him, and his breathing was labored and loud.

"Lord a' mercy," Carl said, and put his hand out to touch Mike's shoulder. Mike shied away, and Carl withdrew with a raised eyebrow and a frown.

"You look mighty sick, Mike. I don't know what to make of it, but I think you'd best get inside and lie down."

"I ain't *sick* sick," said Mike. "To be honest, right now I just want out of here for a bit. I want this over. I need time away."

"Well why don't you go, then?" Carl asked gently. "You've worked damn hard. No one can say different."

"Because if I leave now this job is history, and I need it bad. What with the Depression on and a score's score of people ready to take over if I up and run, I'd be a crazy to walk away."

"Depression?" Carl said. "I don't follow."

Mike gazed at him long and hard, then motioned for him to sit down beside him. This time he didn't shy away.

"I found something 'bout an hour ago," Mike said.

"Yeah?" said Carl.

"I found the updated chart of the cemetery."

"Oh yeah?" said Carl.

"Just sittin' there right as rain, a little stained but still readable, right on top of my desk like it had been there all along." He pulled out a folded sheaf of papers from the front pocket of his overalls. "Here it is."

"Well that's fine, Mike, just fine. Now we can know for certain if we're missing anybody. But I don't see—"

"It'd please me if you took a gander at it. 'Specially the bottom of the second page."

Carl took the list, flipped to the second page, scanned it, and stopped short.

He breathed in and out, long and deep.

"My oh my," he said.

Mike swayed beside him, mopping his wet brow.

"Oh my," Carl continued. "Oh my oh my."

*****

"What you need, Carl?" Ted asked. Several hours had passed. Carl had taken some time to collect himself, then gathered everyone together on Mike's front porch.

"Ted, Hugh, I got a question for the both of you. Before this job, what's the last thing you remember?"

Hugh snorted. "You drunk, Carl?"

"I just wanna know."

"Well...I..." He trailed off. "It's kind of hazy, now that you mention it."

"Ted?"

"Well hell, Carl, I guess my house and my wife and working in the mines. I got lotsa memories."

"I know you do, but what about *right* before? What do you remember about the flood? Who came and told you we needed to do this job?"

"Oh, now, Carl, that's easy...I mean...That is to say..."

Mike stepped in. "Hugh, what year is it?"

"1912," Hugh said immediately. "What the hell year you *think*?" He stood up. "You've all gone crazy, I —*ouch!*"

"Oh!" Ted grunted, grabbing his hand. "What'd you do that for?"

Carl held up a knitting needle.

"The year," Mike said flatly, "is 1934."

"Look at your fingers, fellas," Carl said.

The two men raised their fingers. Eyes, suddenly wide, suddenly terrified, examined them closely. A thick, clear liquid dribbled down both hands in slow rivulets.

"Embalming fluid," Mike said. "Unless I'm mistaken, I'm the only man here with a pulse."

*****

There was a great stir on Mike's porch, and after the screaming and the exclaiming and the accusing and the shaking heads and frantic cries had ceased, three men walked the dirt road to Pineville and sought out their homes.

A short time later they returned, glassy-eyed and resigned.

"Now do you believe me an' Carl?" Mike asked.

Hugh and Ted nodded their hanging heads. Their houses were abandoned, their families gone.

"What year you say this is again?" Ted asked quietly.

"1934," Mike said. "Pineville's been dead since the early twenties, when the coal gave out. I'm the only one here. All I do is tend the cemetery, see that no one bothers anything. Come from Pittsburgh, originally. Paid by the county."

They trudged back into the living room and slumped down in rocking chairs by the fire. Outside the wind blew cold, sending dried leaves scuttling across the porch boards and stressing the roof beams.

Mike said, "According to this chart, you all...er...passed away on the same date: May 23, 1912. You remember anything at all about it?"

They thought for a moment. "Come to think of it," Ted said, slowly, "I do remember something...something about water. But it's distant, like an old dream."

"The mines!" Carl exclaimed. "Culver Lake. The flood."

"The roar...the rocks," said Ted.

"By God," said Hugh, "the collapse."

"We all work—or worked—the same midnight shift," Carl explained. "Looks like we didn't make it out of that one with all our *faculties intact*, as the doctors say."

Mike moaned. "This'll teach me for not taking an interest in other people's lives. If I'd only asked what you all did and where you all lived when you first got here...I just assumed you lived in Still Creek over the hill and were sent down to help. I never thought...that is, I never...I should have known when you was talking about Wilbur Collins. He died in 1893, and you all look so young, I—"

"Enough," said Carl. "Don't worry yourself over it. What we need to worry on now is the best course of action. There's something going on here that ain't natural, we've all guessed that since Day One, but now it seems we're a pretty big part of it ourselves. Well, to be frank I've got to say I don't think we belong up here, walking and talking, anymore than the rest of the folk out there who seem to be a tad restless too."

"Agreed," said Ted and Hugh.

"And I think we'd also agree that this is a fair bit, well, *upsetting* for us, what with us being dead and our families all moved on and away...upsetting for our friend here too, who ain't done nothing to deserve this kind of stress," Carl continued, nodding to Mike. "So the sooner things get back to normal, the better. Now, we've laid out there quiet for twenty-two years and change. Why we up and walking again now?"

"The flood," Hugh said.

"That's how I see it," Carl agreed. "The flood warshed us all up, something needed done to fix it, so we came back to ourselves. Taking care of this kind of thing is our job as volunteer firemen, after all."

"Agreed."

"But what about the others?" asked Ted. "Why are they up and about too?"

Mike said, "It's like that saying my granddaddy was fond of, the morbid cuss: 'The dead take care of their own.'"

"Sounds about right, given what's happened," said Hugh.

"Everyone out there in that yard and in that shed is doing their part, and we're heading up the project," Carl said.

"So all we got to do..." Hugh began.

"...is finish what we started, and things'll fall back into line around here." Carl turned to Mike. "After all this, you mind if we stay on at the house a little while longer? That fire feels good, even if we ain't supposed to notice such things in our condition."

"Well hell, boys," Mike said, and they were glad to notice the color had returned to his face, "I'd say you deserve that at the very least."

*****

They had the cemetery back in good order at the end of two weeks. Some gravestones needed replacing including Carl's and Ted's (Hugh's was found in a rain gully a short distance from the grounds, a little chipped but otherwise fine), but Mike made a trip over to Still Creek and came back with a half dozen new stones. Finally, on October 27, they lined up in front of Mike's cabin and looked out upon the graveyard, grass neat, stones straight, and declared it finished.

All except one thing.

"Everything trim and tidy again, everyone tucked back in," Carl said. "Guess it's time you saw us off, Mike."

"Boys, it's been my pleasure." Mike shook hands all around. "You ready?"

They were. Three open graves lay side by side. Carl, Hugh, and Ted, dressed in smart, new tailor-made suits, climbed carefully down into the holes, minding the dirt, and lay down in the pine boxes they'd built for themselves the previous day.

"Feeling a bit tired, to be honest," Hugh said, reaching up to close his lid. "Miss my kids. Maybe if I go to sleep I'll see them again. So long, folks. Catch ya again sometime, I guess." He shut the lid, knocked twice, and Mike stepped down and latched it.

"I guess all this was fitting," Ted said, squirming slightly to get comfortable. "There ain't many people left to look after us…it would've been too big a job for you to do alone, Mike."

"You did great, Ted." The lid creaked shut. Mike latched it.

Carl shook Mike's hand again. "I want your honest opinion…you think this place looks good? Really good?"

"Even better than before."

"An untended grave is a shameful thing. It was quite a shock, this, but I'm glad we came back to do it." He reached up, grabbed the edge of his lid, and started to pull it closed over himself. "Oh, hey!" he added. "I almost forgot!"

"What's that, Carl?"

"We talked it over, and if you ever need any help keeping your house in good order—a paint job, new roof, whatever—don't hesitate, eh? We owe you."

The lid shut. Mike latched it.

Later, he found himself whistling as he shoveled on the dirt.

Welcome Home

The cat first appeared in the middle of winter. It came in the evening, after Scott Gardner finished shoveling the latest snowfall from the driveway so it wouldn't turn to ice. He wouldn't have noticed it if he hadn't heard the cries, but it was hungry, and cried to let him know.

"There's a cat under the car," he told his wife while taking off his boots. "Should we feed it?"

Emily's eyes brightened. "Do you really need to ask?" She went to the pantry, grabbed a can of cat food from a half-empty carton on the floor, and picked up a small blue bowl sitting next to it. She threw on a sweater.

Outside, shivering, she looked under the car, then all around in the falling dark. Nothing.

"I can't see under the car," she said. "Are you *sure* it's there?"

"Positive!" Scott called from the utility room. "It was *loud.*"

"But did you see it?"

"Nope! But I know a hungry cat when I hear it—after Hider, I'd better."

Just then, the cat cried again. It sounded like it was under the car, but Emily couldn't be sure. Kneeling down, she peered into the oily shadows beyond the tires and saw nothing—but the light *was* fading.

She set the food down on the pavement beneath the eaves. Shivering, she closed the door.

*****

Next morning the food was gone. Every bite.

"Should we put out more?" Scott knelt down and touched the light dusting of snow that had fallen during the night. "That's strange…no paw prints."

Emily shook her head. "No. We shouldn't have done it yesterday. I don't want to start that again."

"Start what?"

"You know."

"My allergies?"

She nodded.

Scott set the empty bowl back down. "Now that's not fair."

"No—it's just...with Hider, we fed him, we cared for him, but in the end we couldn't offer him a home. He cried to come in and we did nothing. And one February afternoon I found him on the road."

"Because we couldn't let him inside," Scott finished. "Because of my allergies."

"I don't want to get attached like that again. I know what will happen if I do."

She went back inside and closed the door—not angry, just resigned. And resolved.

Scott remained, staring at the slate-gray sky and bare, windswept trees. A gentle snow began to fall around him.

Great sadness descended upon him with the snow. Their twenty-year marriage had produced no children, and now, after a long season of growing unease, he recognized the missing element that had gnawed at them through all the seasons as their hairs slowly turned gray and their backs slowly bent: love between them was not enough. They needed something to love outside of themselves, something to care for that would care back gratefully and unconditionally, a give-and-take that left all for the better. A heart, however full, slowly goes bad without an outlet. Their hearts, however full, now needed release. But even something so humble as a cat was beyond their grasp—all thanks to his allergies: an inconvenience in his youth, a full and major setback now, as their capacity for love threatened to vanish with the last warmth of the dying year.

Without another thought, he went inside and returned a moment later with a can of cat food.

"There you are," he said, forking it into the bowl. "I can't see you, but at least I can feed you."

An hour later the bowl was empty again.

*****

It was only after two weeks of clandestine feeding that Scott realized just how *odd* the new cat was—no paw prints was one thing; cats could step like feathers when they wanted. But to *never* see it? Several times now he'd heard it crying, meowing, purring—but could never place it. He'd searched all the possible hiding places, and nothing doing. Once, he'd left food, returned five minutes later to take the trash to the curb, and the bowl was already half empty. A moment later, walking back to the house, it had looked from a distance as if the rest of it was *disappearing before his eyes.*

It *can't* be, he thought at the time.

Now, however, he was seriously beginning to consider the possibility that it was.

Later that evening Emily walked into the den with a dazed, dreamy look on her face and said, succinctly, "I think I'm going crazy."

"You always say that," he said, not lifting his eyes from his book. Then, thinking back, he reconsidered. "Why?"

"Just now a cat brushed against my leg."

"And?"

"And nothing was there."

He sat up. "Where did this happen?"

"Outside. I was raking leaves."

Scott was silent a long, still time.

"Think I'm crazy?" Emily asked.

"No. No, I don't. That cat we fed a few weeks ago—it's... it's...I think it's a..."

He couldn't bring himself to say the word.

"I've been feeding it," he said instead. "I didn't tell you because you were upset about it before. I've never seen it, even after two weeks. And I *should* have. But it was never there. Or it *was* there, but...oh hell, you get my drift."

Emily went to the window and stared hard into the cold evening.

"You mad at me?" Scott asked.

"Yes," she said immediately, then turned. "Be sure to put out more food tonight. But put it in the parlor."

"Inside the house?"

"Inside the house," she repeated.

*****

In the morning the food was gone.

The following evening something stepped up onto Emily's legs and into her lap so gently she wasn't even startled. For the next hour she sat with a rare smile on her face, watching television and petting the warm, invisible motor engine that rumbled contentedly on her legs.

"Why?" she asked later that night.

"I don't know," Scott said, although he was beginning to think he did. "The purring...does it sound familiar?"

"I don't know. It just sounds like a cat."

He looked at Emily for a long time. She sighed under his gaze.

"It sounds like Hider," she said finally.

Scott nodded. "He's come back to us."

"But why?" Emily's eyes welled, springs long dry replenished now, suddenly, in the eleventh hour.

"Because we cared for him when no one else would," said Jacob.

"But he cried and cried by the door, and we didn't let him in!"

"Yes...and we always went out to see him instead. It was enough. And now he's finally inside. That's all we really need to know. And I haven't sneezed once."

The room, suddenly warm, brought sleep quickly, and as it took them both they felt the mattress shift as something small and soft lay down between them. And they knew, as sleep gave way to dreams, that for all the winters that followed they would never feel the sting of ice or the oppression of gray skies again.

"Welcome," Scott murmured, rolling over.

"Welcome home," Emily said, and took his hand.

Armistice Day

He was 109 years old, and breathed like a brittle leaf harried by cold wind. Lungs rattled, moth-wing ears twitched, and hair like spider silk downed the crown of his head as dreams roved his mind like trenchant guards.

"Mr. Farnon is fading." A hospital attendant named Ainsworth looked at the doctor's chart by the foot of the old man's bed and clucked his tongue. His on-duty partner, Brian Holdman, crossed his arms in the doorway but did not approach. Behind Holdman the halls were shadowed and silenced by midnight, a distant life support machine the only sound that broke the Witching Hour's calm. Even so, Ainsworth felt uneasy, as if some terrible catastrophe was about to come crashing down on them like an irrepressible wave.

"Come away from there," Holdman said. "He's not to be bothered."

Slowly, looking back over his shoulder several times, Ainsworth did as Holdman said. He closed the door quietly behind them as they left.

In the attendant lounge, Ainsworth took a sip of his Coke and shook his head. "The reporters have been gathering like vultures. Just this morning he granted an interview, can you believe it? *Newsweek*, I think. But that took it out of him. Doc Jordan says no more, but I don't think he could give another anyway."

Holdman snorted through a bite of ham sandwich. "I don't see what the big deal is. He's old, and he's going to die, and that's the way of things. That happens to lots of people without all this fuss."

"But he's the *last*," said Ainsworth. "The final one. Fourteen *million* men fought in World War I, and they're all gone now. All except him."

"I know, I know, you keep saying that. It had to happen sometime."

Ainsworth shook his head. For a moment he seriously considered punching Holdman in the eye. That, he figured, would get through to him better than anything else he could do. But instead he said, very quietly, "I want you to imagine something. Can you do that, Holdman?"

Holdman muttered something unintelligible.

"Close your eyes," said Ainsworth, and closed his own without waiting to see if Holdman complied.

"I want you to picture," he continued, "Yankee Stadium on a packed fall day. Now imagine *two hundred* packed Yankee Stadiums. That's how many people fought in World War I."

Silence from Holdman.

"Now imagine the front lines of the trenches, like Wilfred Owen described in his poems."

"Who?" asked Holdman.

"Imagine 'No-Man's Land,' bodies rotting in the sun and rain, yellow pools of toxic sludge filling up around them, men watching the carrion birds from deep-dug trenches laced with barbed wire, and machine guns popping dull and thick without any rhythm, incessantly, all day and into the night. The charges. The disease. Biplanes scattering men like ants…Mr. Farnon saw it all. When he dies…"

Ainsworth opened his eyes. Holdman was gone.

He walked back down to Mr. Farnon's room and stood outside the closed door for a long time.

When he dies, Ainsworth continued silently, *fourteen million men die with him a second time. Every single one of them becomes a second-hand story…or, worse, nothing. Not even a name in a faded ledger. He keeps them alive, all of them, in that egg-shell fragile body. Even the ones he never saw or met. Because he breathed their air, drank their drinks, shared their world…*

When he dies, Ainsworth thought on, *a generation dies with him. When his eyes close for the last time, no one will ever again look into eyes that saw the first tanks trundle across the blasted fields of the Somme. When his mouth shuts for good, no one will ever again hear a voice that shouted up at the Red Baron as he flashed overhead, a dazzling streak of lethal elegance.*

He opened the door to Mr. Farnon's room quietly, carefully, and sat down gingerly on the edge of the old man's bed.

Ainsworth wanted to ask Mr. Farnon a question. Very badly, he wanted that. As far as he knew, no reporter had ever asked it before. Even if one had, Ainsworth didn't care. He wanted to hear it from the man himself.

The question he wanted to ask was, "What was it like at the eleventh minute of the eleventh hour of the eleventh day of the eleventh month? When you were nineteen years old and the guns went silent?"

But he hadn't the heart to wake Mr. Farnon. There are some lines that even the deepest desires shouldn't cross.

Without a word, Ainsworth stood up and left the room, silent as a moth.

*****

Just before dawn, Holdman popped his head in the door of the public bathroom where Ainsworth was washing his hands.

"Your friend just bought it," he said simply, and ducked out again.

Ainsworth turned off the water and waited for the last drop to fall from the faucet. Then he left the bathroom and walked over to Mr. Farnon's room a short way down the hall.

No one had arrived yet except for one doctor, who was now at the main desk making some hurried phone calls in a low voice.

Holdman stood beside Ainsworth and they both looked into the room, now completely shadowed, and at Mr. Farnon, now completely still.

Neither man said anything for a long time. Finally, Ainsworth spoke.

"Hear that?" he asked quietly.

Holdman stared at him like he was crazy. "No, man, I don't hear anything."

"Silence," Ainsworth said. Somewhere deep, a part of him had expected fourteen million voices to raise shouts against time, a thunderous barrage.

Holdman walked away, shaking his head.

"Complete and utter silence," Ainsworth added.

"I wonder…" he finished, "…if *that's* what it was like?"

GREGORY MILLER

146

Hollow's End

The forest stretched across long-abandoned fields and deep red-rust valleys. It hedged back roads leading to lonely white-washed houses and dipped through night streams that inhaled leaves and exhaled cold. As the sun fell and the day died, icy wind flowed down from the high October sky. Boughs creaked and clattered, a desolate cacophony that roused owls to flight and sent mice scurrying for shelter. And in a sunken field between two hills on the outskirts of a nestled country town, all darkness was doubled, all creatures red-eyed.

In one small house at the end of a thin dirt lane at the far end of that town, James Holt, ten years old, listened to the wind rattle skeletal bonewood trees and felt his blood run cold.

"James?" His father stepped into his bedroom and looked around. "Hey, champ, where are you?"

"Under the bed," a soft voice replied.

Mr. Holt sat down on the bed while James crawled out. "Mom's been calling you down to dinner for ten minutes. She's going hoarse! What's the problem?"

"Nothing." At that moment an especially strong gust of wind gibbered through distant tree trunks and slammed against the window-panes, insistent, clamoring. James gasped, jumped, and grabbed his father's arm.

Mr. Holt smiled. "It's the wind. That's all, champ. Nothing but the wind."

"No," James said urgently. "It's not the wind—It's the *hollow.*"

Gently, Mr. Holt removed his arm from his son's tight grip. "You still scared of the hollow?"

James nodded, wide-eyed and pale. "Even the wind is scared of it. The wind don't scream until it reaches the hollow."

"But you're home, safe and sound! Bright lights, warm blankets, good food. Speaking of that, come on down for dinner. Mom's pork chops are getting cold."

James sighed and followed him down the stairs.

"Oh, hey!" His father turned. "I'm taking off early tomorrow. Wanna pick pumpkins after school?"

"Yeah, sure! But…but the pumpkin patch is through the hollow, Dad. You know that."

"You went last year. And the year before. We do it *every* year."

Mr. Holt looked at his son's quavering lip and sighed.

"We'll go while the sun's still high in the sky." And under his breath: "*Also* like we do every year."

*****

Even by day, the hollow was a dark place. Trees grew thicker in its cool depths, down in the gully between the steep hills of Old Man Turner's far fields. Ancient trunks rose from loam made thick by a thousand years of fallen autumn leaves. Cobwebs laced across skeletal branches and strange things howled from the shadows of the inner forest where no one ever stepped. Rumor had it there were stone cottages lost among the shifting boughs, unseen since before the Civil War. In those woods, ghosts held court with murderers, and things that shouldn't walk crept and slithered on the far edge of sideway sight.

"C'mon, Dad, let's hurry."

The thin dirt path cut through the trees like a scar. James walked it like a tightrope.

His father followed behind, pulling a small wagon. "There's nothing to worry about, you know. I keep telling you but you don't listen."

James sighed. "You haven't heard the stories."

"Ha! I've heard 'em all! This place is older than Grandpa by five hundred years. It looked the same when I was young."

"OK then, you ever been deep in those trees?" A branch cracked in the distance and James shot a wide-eyed stare across the orange and red curtain of leaves.

His father shook his head. "Never. When I was your age we were scared, too. Then I grew up and never saw the point. Here we are."

They stepped into a small, wheat-sifted glade beside an ancient, towering oak. Left over from some long-dead settler's reclaimed fields, the pumpkin patch grew in coiled russet luxury beneath the lowest branches, its heavy orange burdens shockingly bright in the fading autumn sun.

Together, eager, they started the search.

But finding the *right* pumpkins took longer than expected. James wanted a thin, tall one and a fat, squat one—no rotten spots, no green streaks. By the time that was done, the sun, much to his surprised horror, had already begun to set.

"We'd better hurry," he told his father as he raced to load the pumpkins onto the cart.

"What could happen? If some ol' ghost comes after you, I'll knock it on its head."

James didn't look convinced as they started back. By day, the hollow was a dark place. By night, even by *twilight*, it was a living shadow, a force to ice his spine and darken his dreams. As long as he could remember, its proximity to his house had impressed him…that something so mysterious, so *dangerous*, could exist so close to his life.

"Nothing to worry about," his father added as they strode quickly through the encroaching gloom—James in front and impatient, he lingering behind, enjoying the evening.

It happened just moments later.

A freezing night wind rustled through dead leaves, bringing with it a cry to convulse stomachs and shudder spines. James stopped dead, heart rabbit-pounding, sitting prey to whatever might come.

"That sounded like a wolf," he whispered.

His father shook his head. "There aren't wolves around here. Not since Grandpa was a kid and they killed off the last of them. A dog. Old Man Turner's hound."

The howl rose and fell, buffeted by currents of air, distinctly close.

Then it faded, ceased, and silence settled…followed quickly by laughter, faint and distant. A child's voice, somewhere in the dark trees where children never ventured.

"It's the Crying Ghost!" James hissed, grabbing his father's hand tight.

"Nothing but a cat," Mr. Holt reassured him, but James knew better.

Why, he thought, *is my father so blind?*

*****

Every day after supper the children gathered in the park. Between kick-the-can and catch, they huddled around red picnic tables and rope-board swing sets. Every year, when the first skeleton cutouts appeared in windows and the first Halloween Trees bloomed in yards, their conversations turned to the same thing.

"Grandpa says that sometimes a boy wearing old-fashioned clothes can be seen tramping around among the trees. Always at dusk. If you try following him, he leads you deeper and deeper in, always a dozen steps ahead, until he reaches an old stone well. Then he turns, and you finally see his face, only he don't got no eyes. And he tries to grab you and drag you down into that ol' well. Cause that's where he died a hundred years ago."

Ed Graybill nodded his head, confident in the truth of his story. The other children murmured, entranced and wide-eyed. James felt cold sweat bead his brow.

Brian Lumley took up Ed's torch. "I heard there was a p'fessor who went hunting a rare spider back in there. Wanted it for a study. So he went lookin' deep in, where no one goes, an' found one of those old stone huts from back before the Revolution. It was as picture-perfect as the day it was left empty, only *everything* inside was full of spider webs. Floor to ceiling, corner to corner. An' in the fireplace was the spider he was lookin' for, only it was big as a dog, an' all gray and furry, an' in its webs was all kinds of things—birds an' rats an' rabbits an' squirrels. An' it made a start for him, so that p'fessor stumbled out, an' when he got home his eyes was all wide an' starey an' *he never spoke again.*"

Murmurs. Then Sarah Fuller said, "If he never spoke again, how we know *what* he saw?"

Brian rolled his eyes. "Cause he wrote it *down*, silly! An' that's why you don't see many animals down in that hollow, an' why so many's pets go missing."

"You ain't gonna have to worry about *that* much longer."

Everyone turned. One of the high school boys, Pete Gifford, stood beside the picnic table, hands in jeans, chewing a plug of tobacco.

"Whatta ya mean, Pete?" Brian asked.

He grinned, displaying stained teeth. "I mean that starting tomorrow, Heinz Construction is gonna bulldoze the hollow clear away. It's got a new owner, and he wants to plant on that land."

The children looked at one another in shocked amazement.

"They...they can't do *that*," Ed Graybill exclaimed.

Pete Gifford spit tobacco and straddled the picnic bench, forcing everyone else over. "They can do any damn thing they want ... and what's more, I'll be running one of the dozers! After all these years, we're gonna get to the root of all those dumb stories—then shovel over and bury every last trace of 'em."

He smirked, spat, got up, and loped away.

No one said anything for a long time. Then a few chimed up:

"I wanna be there to see *that!*"

"It'll never happen. The hollow won't *let* it happen."

"I wonder what they'll *find?*"

"Grownups ruin *everything.*"

But James kept silent, though his mind was a turbulent riot of joy and relief.

He smiled discreetly. And when it came time for dinner, he whistled past the entrance of the hollow without a second thought, stopping only long enough to notice the gleaming row of hulking chrome bulldozers lined up and ready to destroy.

"Your days," he murmured at the ancient trees, "are numbered."

*****

Gone, he thought that night, no longer *under* his bed but *in* it.

Not yet, but *soon.*

Gone soon, he thought again, and stared up at the ceiling in the moonlit dark. Soon was close enough.

After a long ten minutes he rolled over. *So quiet,* he thought. The wind blew, rattling the window, but it didn't scream or cry. Far off, a howl echoed faintly over the hills—quite likely Old Man Turner's hound, and certainly not a wolf.

James rolled over on his other side, twisting beneath his blankets, then kicked them off in frustration. The night felt dull. His mind chased itself in circles.

He slipped out of bed and walked over to the window, wide awake even as midnight tolled downstairs on the grandfather clock. He looked out over the milky fields and sighed.

He raised his eyes farther. Beyond the fields, past the cornhusks, a place loomed where no moonlight had ever dared fall.

Tonight, however, the hollow was bathed in faint silver light that softened its shadows and reflected the great steel shovels poised on the brink of its earthen skin. James stared at it for a long time, breath even and calm, face warm against the cool windowpane. Then, bored and confused, he returned to bed.

Two long hours later he sat up with a start, still wide awake, a recent voice now replaying in his mind as a surprising truth: *Grownups ruin everything...*

Shortly thereafter, had anyone been looking, they would have seen a small figure in red checkered pajamas running across the darkened fields.

*****

"Cut clean through, every one!"

Ed Graybill nodded his head, confident in the truth of his story. "All the gas lines, all the brake lines. All the tires slashed, too. And sugar in all the tanks! Pete Gifford is *pissed!*"

Excited murmurs rose and fell around the red picnic table.

Brian Lumley took up Ed's torch. "They say Heinz Construction's gonna walk. The job's off, at least 'til spring. The hollow's not going anywhere for now."

There was a long pause. No one spoke.

Then, hesitantly, someone piped in, "I heard there's a madman who lives in there, way back in a hidden cave. He escaped from an asylum back in the fifties, an'—"

Later that night a storm rolled through town and across the distant farms. The wind shrieked. Distant trees moaned. A wolf howled.

And under his bed, scared to death, James Holt shivered, smiling a jack o' lantern grin.

The Forest and the Trees

An abundance of forest borders Still Creek, but the small expanse of Still Creek Wood stands alone on the hill above my grandparents' house. When I was young, Grandpa and I walked it every time I visited, even the last Christmas before he died, when he knew his heart was almost kaput and that any kind of outdoor walking was full of risk.

Unlike other forests that fringe town, there is never any trash in those woods, and hunters shy away from them. So Grandpa, who spent his youth working underground in the coal mines and his middle age teaching in classrooms, liked it up there, beneath the rustle of leaves and the sigh of branches. I've almost forgotten what that feels like: to be at ease in a quiet place you know is safe.

But it wasn't always safe.

Four months after Grandpa died, in early May, right after my tenth birthday, Grandma sat me down with a piece of pumpkin pie and a glass of milk.

"Promise me you won't go in the forest behind the house anymore," she said. "Promise me you'll leave Still Creek Wood well enough alone."

I was surprised. "But I go in there all the time! And it's the easiest way to get to the top of Still Creek Hill and over to the fairgrounds."

Grandma stood firm. "That may be, Dennis, but it isn't safe without your Grandpa. When you're older, maybe I'll explain."

"Why not now? Why not for sure?"

"Just promise me. There are plenty of other places around here for a boy to explore."

Well, I promised, even though I didn't understand why. But I was ten, and I was told not to do something for my own good. What choice did I have? On the final day of the visit, hours before Mom and I started the three-hour drive home, she and Grandma went to Plumville to shop for crafts, and I stayed behind and did what I promised not to do.

I trotted up the back yard, past the flower garden under the maple tree, the flagstone walk, and the tool shed; past the burn pile, the three pine trees, and the old stone spring, until the long, wet grass of May became strewn with mildewed leaves and the forest loomed.

When I was very young, I thought there were man-made trails through Still Creek Wood, but as I got older I realized they were due to the natural placement of the trees. The trees grow tall and full without being smothered. Their branches intertwine but don't compete for sunlight or air. No one made the trails. The trees did.

I followed a familiar path. Grandpa and I used to walk to the point where the forest ends atop the hill, then over to the western edge bordering Mr. Collins' wheat field and back down to the yard. I went that way, since it made me think of Grandpa; only three months after his death, I had already come to realize the importance of routine as a method of remembering what has gone away.

For the most part the forest floor was dark, but sunlight broke through in places, and every so often I stopped to look up at the fractured rays that filtered down among the softly groaning boughs high above. I enjoyed the rustle of leaves and the noise of branches clacking gently together. Far off, I could hear the bells of the church on Pugh Street tolling the time: five o' clock.

The only evidence of human presence within the forest was (and still is, so far as I know) toward the bottom of the western edge, a couple dozen yards from Mr. Collins' field, where an old set of seven stone steps had been hauled out from an abandoned barn many years before. Whenever Grandpa and I walked in the woods, we'd always stopped by them. I don't know why they fascinated me. Maybe it was seeing stairs in a place where they didn't belong. Maybe it was seeing the stairs slowly, gradually begin to look more and more like they *did* belong, as moss, fallen leaves, and weather did their work. Regardless, they had been in the forest since before I was born, lying among the trees but not touching them, not *of* them, and I liked their strangeness.

But this time, as the angle of the falling sun sent long shadows reaching out behind all standing things, I realized something had changed.

I came to where the steps should have been…and couldn't find them. For a few unhappy moments I thought maybe someone had finally broken them up or taken them away again, but after circling the area carefully, eyes focused on the closely-patterned landscape, I suddenly realized, with a start, why I'd missed them.

The stairs now leaned against a full-grown oak tree, forty feet tall if an inch. Its straight trunk gave way to branches that arched over my head like open arms. Now the stairs rose, upright, to the lowest branch of the tree, supported by the rough, solid trunk.

I walked around the tree several times, trying to tell for sure whether I was in the right spot. Yes. A flat boulder Grandpa used to rest on still sat in its usual place amid a bed of fern just a spit away, rain-stained and covered with pale green lichen. A squat poplar still grew nearby as it always had.

My heart raced and I remember letting out a thin sigh, confronted for the first time in my life with something that didn't make sense and couldn't be explained.

Somehow, in the five months since Grandpa and I had taken our final walk together, an oak had grown from nothing to full, stately height, moving the steps with its growth until they climbed, with rediscovered purpose, to meet its boughs.

I crept over to the steps, ran my hand over the worn, moss-covered slab, and clambered up the old stone cuts. Reaching the top, I grabbed the oak's lowest branch, hoisted myself up, twisted around, and then, with a gasp and a grunt, plunked down on it.

Above and around me the leaves of the tree rustled softly. I looked about, impressed by the height and view, hardly realizing how comfortable the crook of the branch had become. And as I sat there, I gradually became aware of my own feelings: for the first time since bitter, cold February, I had allowed the preoccupations of worry and grief to fall away, lulled by the murmur of sap-blood and gently shifting leaves. The great, crushing wheel of loss had been halted, if only briefly. Security and comfort had taken its place.

A short time later the town bell tolled six. Mom and Grandma would be returning from Plumville soon. Jolted, I felt for the top of the stone with my feet, and, finding it, trotted back down the steps and broke into a jog. The back yard was close, only a hundred yards away. It would just take a minute, and I'd be home. Just one minute—

The feel of rough, hard fingers digging into my arms is one I would like very much to forget, but the memory will not fade. As I was lifted off the ground, shrieking and hollering, legs pumping the air, it flashed through my mind that Grandma had been *right* to warn me, that I should have listened, and that promises should never, ever be broken…

I remember the strong, heady smell of pine sap and the creak of the limbs that lifted me, high, high, oh, a good fifteen feet off the ground, and it wasn't long until I had thrashed my way around and finally saw what held me.

The pine tree was massive, dark, and ancient. I'd walked past it with Grandpa many times but never stopped to look close. It was one of those trees that always looks dirty, and not very good for climbing, and even kind of scary in an indefinable sort of way. But now I knew that the deepest, gloomiest part of the tree, high in the upper boughs, had never before revealed itself. I could sense it: a brooding night of death-preserving amber sap, tangles of brittle twigs, and the soft, warm egg sacs of spiders. It was a blackness palpable, a deep gulf—and, having sensed it, I knew that if I didn't free myself from those hard, creaking branches I would come to know it well, know it intimately, and that such knowledge would be enough to darken my world forever.

With a massive, desperate twist, I wrenched myself away, dropping to the ground with a *thud* that didn't break anything but left my shoulder purple, yellow and brown for weeks to come.

Freed, sobbing, I ran.

And I never explored Still Creek Wood again.

*****

But I did go back to Grandma's. I went back often. And it was just before the Spring Break of my senior year in college that my psychology professor gave us the assignment of conducting "20 Questions" with an older relative. "If done properly it will provide an illuminating picture of how the lives of older generations differ from the adolescents you will soon be teaching yourselves," she told us. "No 'yes' and 'no' questions in this game, though. Ask open-ended questions and encourage your subject to elaborate."

So that's what I did.

Grandma was eighty-four that year. Her eyesight was beginning to fade, but she was still sharp as ever and a willing subject. I asked about her courtship with Grandpa during the '20s, about her parents, about school conditions and grading and cars and long-dead relatives, about World War II and ration books and the Great Depression, about meeting FDR during a Gettysburg speech and attending, when she was a very little girl, the last public hanging in Pittsburgh.

After an hour, I'd exhausted my set of prepared questions and started to wrap things up, but she didn't make any motion to indicate we were through. Instead, she nodded at the paper and said, "There's only nineteen questions there. You still have one to go!"

I looked down at my paper in surprise, realized she was right, and sat back in my chair to think. I heard the steady breath of spring wind as it rattled the kitchen windowpanes. Listening harder, I noted the distant sigh of branches. "Tell me why Still Creek Wood is dangerous," I said abruptly. "Tell me why I shouldn't go there."

Grandma glanced up sharply. For a moment her fingers tightened their grip on the armrests of her chair, then slowly, slowly relaxed again.

"It isn't something people speak much about," she said.

"I understand," I said quickly, embarrassed. "We don't have to talk about it. I shouldn't have said—"

Grandma threw her arms up with a great sigh. "Oh, of course you should have. You're an inquisitive soul like your Grandpa and, if I do say so myself, like me. It's in the blood. And you have a right to know, as I see it, even if you don't live in town."

Something burned behind Grandma's rheumy eyes: a knowledge that had grown ripe for imparting.

"Have you ever noticed," she asked, "how those woods are never touched by loggers?"

"I guess I figured the trees were protected. You know, by the town board or something."

"But no trash? No vandalism, no hunters? State-protected wilderness isn't well guarded, kiddo. Not in places like this."

I thought about it for a moment, realized she was right, and said so.

"All these years, the town filled with trouble-seeking boys, vandal teens, and no-good adults, and Still Creek Wood never became a club house for any of them," Grandma continued.

"So why not?" I asked.

"Because the trees protect themselves," she said simply.

And I nodded, because I knew it was so.

*****

Like a wave held back since that long-ago day when Grandpa's loss was fresh, childhood still slipping away as the true nature of death sank in, I told Grandma everything I remembered, much of it feeling like an old half-recalled dream until my words made it real again.

And, finishing some time later, I looked up to see Grandma's cheeks were wet.

"Oh, child," she said. "You should have listened. You should have stayed away."

"Tell me why," I said. "Make me understand."

Grandma sipped gingerly at her iced tea, heeding the cold, and said, "A fair number of old folks like me know what I'm about to tell you, though we each came across the truth in different ways. In my case, and your grandpa's, it was our first next-door neighbor, Mr. Adams, who let the cat out of the bag. He was old when we were young, and had seen things in Europe during the First World War that drove him to drink. When he drank he often came over to talk with your grandpa. I didn't like it at first, but Mr. Adams was never violent or rude, just liked to talk, and one night I overheard him say, 'If you walk in Still Creek Wood enough times, you'll notice how none of the old trees were ever young, and none of the young trees ever grow old.'"

Grandma leaned forward. "He was right, you see. If you ever go up there again—though I'm not saying you should, even if you *are* older now—you'd see the same young saplings in the same places, same height, same branches, that were there when you were a child. There would be a few more, since Mrs. Forester had a still-born baby two years back and that sweet Schretengoss child died of leukemia, but besides them the saplings in the forest would be the same. And the older trees? The ones when I was young are the same as the day they appeared, but have since been joined by many, many others."

I shook my head. "What do you mean, 'appeared?'"

"Just like you saw all those years ago," Grandma said. "A tree that hadn't been there before, full-grown, pushed those old steps up so you could swing your legs from the lowest branch." She paused, allowing me to piece everything together so I could say it back to her, paraphrased and simplified, evidence of my understanding.

But I wasn't ready. Not yet.

"You mean…" I began.

"…that when someone in Still Creek has to leave, and that leave-taking involves a funeral home and last rites, Still Creek Wood gets a little larger," Grandma finished. "One tree larger, to be exact. Yes. You've got it."

I looked up the incline of the back yard, to where the tops of Still Creek Wood waved in a cool spring breeze.

"I believe it," I said at last, quietly.

Grandma took my hand. "Say it back to me."

"Whenever someone in Still Creek dies, Still Creek Wood gains a tree."

"Good."

Then we were silent, and it was the silence of deep thoughts.

Finally, "But why was I attacked? I did nothing wrong."

Grandma sighed. "Because some of those trees, like the people they used to be, are cantankerous. Some downright bad. Rotten. Your grandpa got along with most everyone in town, won the respect of all he knew. That's why he felt safe when he went walking in there, and why I didn't worry too much when you went along with him. But given half a chance, the bad will always work what mischief they can, and by yourself you weren't protected. Now maybe you can go back, if you have a mind. But if you do, promise me you'll be careful."

"But why would I want to go back?" I said.

"Oh heavens, did you forget the tree by the stone steps?"

"No, but…"

"Goodness, haven't you *guessed*?" Tears again came freely to my grandmother's eyes and spilled down her creased cheeks.

And I made the last, great connection.

Grandma must have seen the light in my face. "That's right," she said softly, and patted my hand. "That's right."

*****

And now, age thirty, married and on the cusp of another era in my life, I wonder if I should finally go back. I didn't that day. Perhaps I was still too incredulous. Or too frightened. But now I want to go, I really do. Loss, that crushing wheel, has turned again.

I got the call this morning. Sometime during the night, Grandma passed away.

I keep wondering… will it be there if I go?

I'll choose a sunny day in early spring, the season when life in *all* its forms is granted renewal. I will walk up through the yard of the empty house, past the flower garden under the maple tree, the flagstone walk, and the tool shed; past the burn pile, the three overgrown pines, and the spring. I will enter the woods and find my way, with great care, to the old stone steps.

And will it be there? The second oak beside the first? New but not, full-grown and splendid?

Will the two trees rustle their leaves in the warm, still air, just for me?

The Saver

Their car broke down thirty miles from Bedford, the nearest town with a gas station. Mabel and Tony Palmer sat for a moment in the softly ticking Oldsmobile Cutlass, the rapidly warming air thick with mutual disbelief.

"Shit," said Tony, simply.

"There go our plans with Adam and Kathy."

He sighed, she sighed, and they both got out, slamming the doors shut behind them. Immediately the strong, cliff-side wind whipped at their hair, their clothes, bringing with it the salty tang of the sea and making them blink rapidly. On the driver's side a guard-rail marked the edge of the road. Just beyond it the cliff descended, all sheer drop and red stone, for three hundred feet to meet the crashing waves.

"No reception," Tony muttered, sliding the useless phone back in his pocket. "This must be the last place in America that doesn't have it."

"There's a house up there," said Mabel, pointing to the top of the hill that rose steeply across the street. "We can ask for help."

"I hate asking help from strangers," said Tony.

"Then start pushing."

The seashell-paved driveway was winding and uneven. At the top, sweating and out of breath, they found themselves standing on a green, closely-manicured lawn. A small wooden windmill spun frantically in the wind. Glass and metal chimes clinked and rang from the porch of a small, neat cottage that seemed within inches of sliding down the hill, back end first, onto the road far below.

"It's quaint," said Mabel.

"In Big Sur, with a cliff-side view of the ocean, it's probably worth a million," said Tony.

"More than that," said a voice behind them.

Mabel let out a tiny yelp. They turned.

An old man of perhaps seventy was smiling at them beneath a frayed straw hat. The sleeves of his denim shirt were rolled up, his browned skin slick with sweat. He held a mud-encrusted shovel over one shoulder.

"Sorry," he added, and gave them a reassuring grin. "I was working yonder, in the field over the lip of the hill, and took the side path around when I saw you coming up."

The next thing he said was unexpected: "You need saved? They don't usually come up to the house if they need saved. Usually I got to go down to them."

Mabel and Tony cast a quick glance at each other and locked eyes. *A holy roller*, Tony thought. *Just great. Thick as flies everywhere.*

"Um, no, we don't need saved," Mabel said politely. "Our car broke down and we don't have cell phone reception. We need to call for a tow. That's all."

"Oh, hey, why didn't you say so?" The old man swung the shovel off his shoulder and impaled it with surprising force in the packed, shell-strewn drive. It stuck there, quivering, then stilled. "You can use my phone, and we can sit a bit on the back porch and have some lemonade while you wait for your tow. It'll take a little time. Name's Carl Budren. Pleased to meet you and come on in."

They followed him into the prim, tidy cottage. Dozens of sea-shells, stones, sea glass, and starfish, carefully glued into patterns, adorned the wood-stained walls in driftwood frames. The wicker furniture, worn but not dilapidated, was simple and inviting—a perfect fit. Mr. Budren dug a phonebook out of a drawer in his kitchenette, licked a calloused finger, found a page, found a number, and soon the local towing service was on its way.

Minutes later they found themselves sitting on the rickety, whitewashed porch overlooking a dizzying drop to the road, cliffs, and dark, crashing waves far below. Mr. Budren joined them, a cold, sweating glass of lemonade in each hand.

"An hour 'til the truck comes, huh? Well, it's nice to have some company, even if you don't need saved." He sat down in a spare chair, sighing as his knee joints popped.

"No, sir," said Mabel. "We aren't the religious type. I'm afraid converting us is a battle you just won't win, if you'll excuse me saying so."

The old man's eyebrows narrowed, then he smiled and chuckled. The sound was faint, like a distant motor. "No, no, ma'am, you misunderstand me." He nodded down toward the cliffside road, where their car sat like a squat, injured beetle. "You don't know this spot, I take it. Just a random place your vehicle happened to break down."

"That's right," said Tony, bemused.

The old man reached into his pocket and pulled out a battered pack of cigarettes. "You mind?"

"No," said Tony and Mabel in unison, though both did.

Mr. Budren lit up. "Across the highway by the cliff, and about twenty feet further down the road from your car, there's a little jut of rock. An outcropping, like. On the other side of the guardrails. See it?"

They looked. They saw.

"For about forty years now, that's been known as End Point. Don't know why, but there's been more suicides there over the years than anywhere along this coast for two hundred miles in either direction. Hell, you'd have to drive down to Frisco's bridge to find a hotter spot."

They both looked again, longer this time.

"How many have jumped?" Tony asked, chewing a piece of ice from his lemonade.

Mr. Budren stroked his chin.

"In the last twenty years or so, I'd put the number somewhere around forty, maybe a few more. There was more before that, but I don't have the exact numbers."

Both Mabel and Tony started. Tony's mouth worked a little, but he said nothing.

"No one knows why?" Mabel finally asked.

"Well, I guess it's a couple things." Mr. Budren took a drag off his cigarette. The smoke plumed out his nostrils like the exhalation of a geriatric dragon. "First, it's a good view. Of course, there's plenty of those, but I guess that's something. I reckon the dying like a good view before they go. Second, all it takes is one or two jumpers before word gets out about a place. Then others copy the first. I don't know why, except maybe the desperate like being part of something, too. Something they can share with like-minded souls."

"Like a club," murmured Tony.

Mr. Budren nodded. "That's right, Mr. Palmer. An *exclusive* club."

He took another drag off his cigarette, and a far-away look palled his face. "An exclusive club," he repeated, voice little more than a murmur.

"Mr. Budren? What does that have to do with saving?"

Mr. Budren turned to Mabel, and in that quick moment his eyes focused again. "Ah! Yes, oh yes. Well, my daddy owned this cliff-side property for going on half a century but never did nothing with it. When he died I was about retirement age. I'd heard of End Point, so since I got the rights I thought I'd build a little house up here. Figured I could save some people if I spotted anyone who came by and looked ready to jump."

Mabel leaned forward. "That's the reason you moved here and built this house? To keep people from killing themselves?"

Mr. Budren nodded. "Yes, ma'am."

Tony shifted, his wicker chair creaking. "So how does it work?"

"Hmm?"

"Saving people."

Mr. Budren smiled widely. "It's real simple, mostly. I keep an eye out, you see. When I spot a car parked near End Point, or a motorbike, or whatever else, I head on down the drive to the road and see what's what. Usually someone'll be sitting in the car, or on the bike, or even standing on the point, sometimes on one side of the guard rail, sometimes on t'other. If I get there in time, that is. And if I do, I go on down and have a talk with them."

"You don't call the police?"

"No time for that, son. Not if they're settling in to jump. No. I just go down and have a talk with them. It's what works. It's what the moment needs."

Mabel took a small sip of lemonade. The ice clinked against her teeth. "But what do you *say*? I couldn't imagine being put in a situation like that, with a life on the line and everything riding on what words you choose."

Mr. Budren grunted. "Well, miss, you do have a point. It's a mighty tight spot, sometimes. But I knew it would be when I moved here. And that stress is worth it, when you save someone. To know they're *safe*. That's the payoff.

"But as to what I say..." He paused, thinking. "It depends, but usually I ask them what their favorite thing to do is in all the world. I keep 'em talking, have them tell me all about it. Everyone has something they love to do. So if I'm lucky they start talking, and I listen, and prod, and ask more questions, and finally I get around to saying, 'Now don't you want to do that again? Because you sure as hell can't if you're fish food in the Pacific.' Or something to that effect."

Tony raised his eyebrows. "That's it?"

Mabel jabbed him in the ribs, scowling. But Mr. Budren just smiled again. "One time it took five hours. Another, I made dinner for a woman and brought it out to her because she got hungry after talking so long. It was just the two of us sitting there, on the edge of that cliff, with Death circling round and round us. But she ate, and she came to, and she was saved."

He stubbed out his cigarette in a stained seashell ashtray and sat back in his creaking wicker chair.

"That's really something," Tony admitted.

"It really is, Mr. Budren," added Mabel. "That's incredible."

"Well," said the old man, sighing, "it soothes me, to do something. But I can't save 'em all. When I come down some mornings and find an empty car by End Point, I know I failed because I can't be there all the time. Then I call the police and they call a tow, and sometimes a body washes up down the coast, carried far on the current. Most often it's never found."

He brightened. "But it's worth all that. And I'm very content. Now, unless I'm mistaken, that's your tow truck! So I won't keep you any longer."

They looked. It was.

As they reached the front door, Mabel turned back and gave the old man a quick hug. "You're an amazing man, Mr. Budren. I'm glad we met you."

"Well thank you, darling," he replied, flashing a final warm smile.

Tony held out his hand. "Yeah, those are lucky people, Mr. Budren. The ones you saved. Glad we could meet."

The couple walked quickly down the hillside drive, Mr. Budren watching from the top. Faintly, he could hear Tony hailing the tow truck driver. He watched them for another ten minutes until the car was latched to the truck, and both truck and car were nothing more than glints of reflected sun, far away and receding, on the winding, cliff-side road.

Then he turned, retrieved his shovel, and walked purposefully across the well-tended yard and over the crest of a small rise. Beyond, a long, sunken field of scrub grass stretched away into the distance, just out of sight of the house.

"Lucky people," he repeated.

He picked his way carefully down the other side of the rise and stopped beside a half-filled pit. Next to it was a small mound of dirt.

Whistling tunelessly, he smiled as he resumed shoveling—the young couple's interruption already all but forgotten.

A pale, thin hand stuck up from the pit like a wilted, diseased plant. Moments later, dirt covered it.

"Lucky people," he said a final time. He stopped to rest, wiping his brow and looking out at the dozens and dozens of faint, rectangular depressions in the earth that even the tall grass could not completely obscure.

"I sure did save them."

Shells

My cove is rimmed on all sides by high, steep outcroppings of sharp rock. Only one gravel road leads through them down to the beach. The beach is white sand and small pebbles. And shells, of course. Lots and lots of shells.

I've collected shells as long as I can remember, ever since I was a very little girl. I've always loved them. First, when we stayed at the cabin every summer, I collected everything I could find, but after my family moved here for good, I became more selective. Otherwise, where would I keep them all?

*****

There are some wonderful rare kinds in the cove. You can find the best ones in late spring, in tide pools by the black rocks that jut out from the sand. And after a storm. Even in winter there are good shells to be found after a storm.

I get lonely real easy, now that we're at the cove all year round. There aren't many children nearby. But one evening in late-November, I looked up from my shell hunt to see a boy walking toward me from the opposite end of the beach.

He was tall and lanky, about twelve. A little younger than me. And he kept his head down. I knew what that meant. He was hunting shells, too.

I met him down by the rocks near the tide pools. Boy, was he surprised! He looked me over, real shy, and said, "I didn't know anyone else lived here."

"Me neither," I said. "Isn't it a little late in the year for a vacation?"

He shook his head. "My grandpa had a house on the other side of the cliffs. He died last month and my folks and my uncles have to go through everything and decide who gets what." He paused. "They fight a lot, so I got out of there. I can't take it."

I felt bad for him and nodded in what I hoped was an understanding way. "What's your name?"

"Sam Gerts. What's yours?"

"Mattie. Hey, you like shells?"

Sam nodded. "Every beach I go to I look. But I don't see any good ones here."

"No, not this time of year. Not unless there's a storm, and then there's some great ones, really! But let's check over there."

I led him to a little tide pool basin separated from the dark ocean by just a foot or two of jagged stone.

"They collect here at high tide. Even in fall and winter you can come across nice ones if you're lucky."

We scanned the pool, its rocky bottom covered with shifting sand. Tiny, black fiddler crabs scuttled in dark corners. A hermit crab climbed among the mussels.

"There!" I said, as the current shifted the sand and revealed something white, pink, and sharp. "Grab it!"

Sam leaned forward and gave a yank. "It's heavy! I can hardly budge it!"

"Give it a *big* tug. A real hard pull."

He did, grunting, and the huge whelk sucked out of the sand.

"Hey! Hey, look at that!" he cried, beaming at the beautiful shell. It was a full foot long, its spiral perfect, the inside a smooth, polished pink.

He handed it to me. "You keep it. You saw it first."

"You grabbed it, it's yours."

"Thanks. That's really nice." He looked it over again. A big, goofy grin spread across his face. "It's the best one I ever got."

Then his watch beeped. "Oh, shoot. Dinner. I gotta get back." His face fell. "I don't want to, but I'll get in trouble if I don't. Mom's been real stressed through all this mess. Can't say as I blame her." He clambered down the rocks and back onto the sandy beach.

I felt real bad. I'd just made a new friend and now he had to go home.

"How long you staying at the cove?" I called out. He was already walking away.

Sam turned. "A week. Maybe a little longer. 'Til after Thanksgiving, at least. We just got in today. Hey," he took a few steps back, "you wanna meet again tomorrow? Same place?"

"Early in the morning or in the evening as the sun begins to set. That's when I come down."

"I'll be there."

My heart swelled.

*****

The next week was terrific. We met every day, usually in the morning and evening, and spent the time walking, skipping stones in the surf (trying to make them go through as many wave crests as possible), and poking around in the hills.

And collecting shells.

I asked Sam about where he lived and he said far inland, in Arizona, and that he didn't really like his school. And I told him all about my family and the town we used to live in before we moved here full-time. But he never invited me to meet his parents, and I never invited him to meet mine. We were both shy, and besides, for Sam our time was a chance to escape all the family problems and sadness he had to deal with.

The cove was a place where we both felt comfortable and easy. And we found some great shells, too! Over a few days we gathered up a couple dozen good cowries, some beautiful, purple-streaked scallops, and even a conch the size of my fist. Sam found some shark's teeth, which really thrilled him, and I snagged a handful of ray egg pods, which I took home to dry.

At one point during those long days, Sam turned to me and said, "I think fighting is the dumbest thing ever. People say and do things they regret and can't ever take back. Take my Uncle Brock. He used to be nice. But he wants some paintings that belonged to my grandfather because he wants to sell them. Mom and Uncle Alex want to keep them in the family. Uncle Brock said they were selfish and always ganged up on him, and then Dad said something, then Mom, then Uncle Alex, and all back and forth until they were screaming and stamping and threatening, and now they're not talking anymore. I don't think I'll ever see Uncle Brock again."

Sam had never told anyone that, except me. He trusted me. That meant so much, even though I'd only known him a little while. And I understood how he felt.

*****

The storm struck just two days before Sam had to leave. I should have been glad, but this one hit at a bad time. Sam and I were still out on the beach, skipping stones. The clouds got dark, but we just thought twilight was falling. Then, finally, Sam looked around and whistled. "We better get inside."

"Oh, we'll be fine," I replied.

And then the storm hit.

It was a real bruiser: a cold, hard shower with black, pressing clouds. The whole cove was covered in gloom and shifting light from blue, scattered lightning. Strong, gray waves lashed the shore. A bitter, spray-flecked wind drove us toward the water, but we fought our way back.

Sam shivered, raising his voice to be heard over the thunder. "Is your place close?"

No, I thought. *Don't tell. Not yet.*

"You go ahead home, Sam!" I yelled back. "I'll meet you tomorrow. I'll be fine!"

"No, I live too far away!" The rain had plastered his hair against his head and his chattering lips were pale. "Is your house nearby?"

I thought a moment. I was shy about my home. But I knew Sam trusted me. The things he'd told me all said so.

"Fine," I said after a long pause. "Follow me! We'll ride it out and you can head home later."

I led him along the beach, farther than I'd gone before with him, then up a thin path into the hills that ringed it. The rain was really hammering down now. Lightning flashed and thunder rolled across the sky.

"Almost there!" I called back to Sam.

We reached the cave: a small, black hole in the side of the hill—all by itself, hard to find, invisible from the shore.

"What's that?" Sam asked.

I shook my head and pulled him in after me.

It was very dark inside, but the falling day and the lightning provided some light. I shook out my hair and Sam ran a hand through his.

"Where are we, Mattie?" he asked, still breathing hard, water dripping off his nose. "This is a *cave*."

"It's OK," I said softly. "Come on."

I led him farther in. He followed slowly, hesitantly, and soon I heard his shoes crunch.

"Careful!"

"What is it?" he asked. "I can't see."

"Why, it's my shell collection, dummy! You're stepping on it!"

He stopped walking. I could barely see his face. "What is this place? Why are we here?"

"It's my home," I said. And before he could speak, I stepped forward and lit a candle. "Here, now you can see all my shells!"

I looked around the long, low space and smiled. It was cold but dry, and for ten feet back into the cave the floor was covered with shells. My shells. My whole collection. Every kind you could imagine. All shapes and sizes. Most of them perfect. They lay two feet deep in some places, piled almost to the ceiling in others.

"Your…your collection is *here*? Home? Mattie, I don't understand. I—"

He stopped.

"What's that smell?" he demanded in a hollow voice.

I winced. "Nothing. I mean…Sam, we're all here, you see. I would have told you before you left, but the storm kind of rushed things. Still, you trusted me. I know I can trust you, too."

"Mattie…" Sam's face was very pale. "In the corner, way back there… what *is* that?"

I followed his gaze. In the shifting candlelight, in the flashes of lightning, I could make out two dark shapes I knew very well.

"Give me the candle." Sam yanked it from my hand.

"Wait, Sam, I just—" I tried to hold him back but couldn't.

He thrashed through my shells, not bothering to be careful, until he stood over the slumped forms. He stared at them for a long, long time.

"Sam?" I said softly. "They're my parents, Sam. Or used to be. I was so worried what you'd think, I couldn't tell you…"

Suddenly, almost casually, he turned and threw up. He breathed hard, fast, and wiped his mouth. He stumbled away from the half-rotted bodies and moaned.

"It was my father, Sam," I told him quietly. "He had a bad time. He'd lost his job. One night he and Mom got to fighting. You know how it is. Anyway, he wasn't thinking straight. He took us up here, and that's when I saw the gun. He shot her, Sam. Then he shot himself."

"No," he wheezed, eyes wide. He stepped back from me slowly, like a sleepwalker, and tripped over something else.

Sam fell.

Don't look down, I thought.

He did.

"Dad shot me, too. Right after Mom."

And then Sam bolted upright, screaming and screaming, his face a white mask of shock. He stumbled around me, crunching shells as he passed. He sobbed, pulled in a harsh breath, screamed again, and ran.

"No!" I said, starting to cry. "Come back! That's not me, Sam! Not any more! It's just a shell! Just an empty shell!"

But he was already gone, his shrieks lost in the howl of the wind, and once again I was alone with my collection.

Wood Smoke

"My grandfather tilled this farm," Benjamin Collins told Blake Riggs, his grandson. "It ain't proper and it ain't right."

"You should buy one of those townhouses they want to build on it. You could, with the amount they're offering." Blake was 26, ambitious, with a master's degree in business management from Penn State. He lived in Pittsburgh, fifty miles away.

Collins looked at him with bemused impatience.

"Offering? *Demanding*, you mean. And to share all this with a hundred townies, talking into earphones like crazy people, power-walking, with manicured lawns and little, red foreign cars and rat-terrier dogs? No. I won't do it. *Can't* do it."

"*Have* to, Grandpa."

Collins sighed. "Come outside, kid."

With a hidden smirk, Blake followed him through the kitchen to the back porch. The view of the property was almost complete from this vantage—fallow ground, long untilled, and a great expanse of woodland. Maples, oaks, birches, and spruce pines sighed in a mid-summer breeze.

"See, Grandpa?" said Blake. "What do you need all this for, anyway? It hasn't been an active, productive farm in twenty-five years, and even then it didn't bring in much money."

"Money," Collins echoed.

"Right. And besides, look at all those trees! You're the proud owner of a half-assed scrub forest. To sell is the best option. But, hey, it isn't even an option now, is it? Not the way the town council raised your taxes."

"When I was a boy," Collins said quietly, not looking at his grandson, "my daddy used to thin the forest. Lots of trees die in a year, and of course saplings start to grow in the fields. Every autumn, close to Halloween, he and my uncles and my older brothers and me would cut them down and stack them all in great piles and set them on fire. Always around apple-harvest time. The *smell...*" He closed his eyes. "You know the smell of wood smoke, Blake?"

"I guess," Blake replied absently. "I don't know."

"There's nothing like it. If you did, you'd not forget. My daddy, he used to smoke cherry tobacco from his corncob pipe while he worked. Always did when he was outside, and farmers are *always* outside. And on those days when they lit the fires and Mother made hot apple cider and baked pumpkin pies, and all the neighbors came over, I remember sitting here on the back porch, smelling his tobacco and the wood smoke mixing together, and it felt like everything would always be all right and nothing would ever change."

"That's sweet, Grandpa, but things *do* change."

The faraway look in Collins' eyes faded. "Anyway, I'll sell, but they're letting me keep the old house; that's the condition if I stop fighting. Isn't that nice? A stand-up thing to do. Change... yeah, things change. Some things. So it goes." He passed a hand across his brow, wiping off a sheen of perspiration. "And I'm getting tired, so I think I'll head upstairs and let you head home. Thanks for coming out and visiting your old ancestor."

He led Blake to the front door.

*****

An hour later and three blocks away, the steamed windows of Maggie's Eat n' Smile Diner hid the two men in the front booth from the view of anyone walking down Main Street.

"Does he know?"

Blake snorted. "How can he? Anyway, he's keeping the house, so we'll have to work around that, but I don't think he'll be any more trouble. Not like before, when he went up against the council with that damned petition. He'll sell. He told me. He can't afford the tax increase. That's got him."

Max Nelson, President of the Still Creek Town Council, beamed. "That works out for all of us, then."

"He got quite a piece of change from the deal. I'd rather inherit that when the time comes than a useless bit of wilderness."

"Well, hell, kid, you're overlooking the best part!"

"What? That my company's doing the developing?"

They both laughed.

"Here's to a mean, ornery son-of-a-bitch."

"Which one? Him or me?"

Glasses clinked. Steaming dinners arrived.

*****

"I haven't seen you for upwards of a year." Collins, a little older, a little slower, appraised his grandson with shrewd but tired eyes.

"Sorry, Grandpa. I've been snowed under, that's all. Lots of work."

"I figured. Busy man. Plenty to keep up with out there in the city. Thanks for coming."

Blake nodded. "It was nice you invited me. How's the view from the back porch now?"

"Come see."

They stepped through the kitchen door into the crisp autumn air that filtered through the screens.

"There's your view," Collins murmured dryly.

The old fields and forest were gone, cut down, bulldozed over. All that remained was a muddy, flat expanse from which the wooden shells of four-dozen townhouses rose like matchstick models in perfect rows.

"Wow, they're really making progress!" Blake exclaimed, absently rubbing his hands together. "Amazing."

"Yes, ain't it though?"

"See? Everything changes, Grandpa. Just like I said. Everything changes, and it isn't so bad."

His grandfather clapped him on the back. "Well, you might be right, kiddo. But I gotta be honest. One thing doesn't change. Not ever."

"Hmm? What?"

"I'm still a mean, ornery son-of-a-bitch. Always will be."

Blake blinked, then laughed nervously. "Well, I kind of like you anyway."

"Why *thank* you, kiddo." Collins gave him another good-natured pat and pulled a corncob pipe from his back pocket. He sighed, packing it carefully with tobacco from a bag he produced from his shirt.

"I didn't know you smoked, Grandpa."

"This is the very first time since I was a young man. Bought the pipe and tobacco down at Stockton's just this morning."

"What's the occasion?"

Collins patted his pockets. "Where'd I leave my matches? Oh, here we go." He pulled a box from another pocket, struck a wooden match with his thumbnail, lit the pipe, and inhaled deeply.

The smell of burning cherries filled the air.

"That takes me back," he said through clenched teeth. "Smells are powerful when it comes to bringing back memories. You have any special smells that bring back memories, kiddo?"

Blake shook his head. "Nope. Can't say that I do, Grandpa."

"That's a hell of a shame. You know," Collins added abruptly, "Mrs. Gerts down the street is an old friend."

"Is that so?"

"Yep. I've known Myra Gerts for fifty years if a day. Small town, you know. And she tells the best damn stories. She hears things, you see, from here and there around town. Especially when she takes her supper at Maggie's Diner."

"Oh?" Blake looked distracted. He was squinting hard toward the distant townhouse frames.

"Oh, yeah. And one of those stories—one of her favorites, in fact—is about an uppity young man from Pittsburgh who talks too loud and...hey, but you look distracted, Blake. Why? It's a nice autumn day. Falling leaves, cherry tobacco...there's just one thing missing."

Blake blinked, took a step forward, stopped, eyes fixed on a spot in the distance. "Is that...is that *smoke?*"

"Hmmm?"

"*Smoke.* It...it is! Oh God! It's...*they're all—*"

"Well, would you look at that!" Collins opened the screen door and stepped out onto his back walk. Blake followed, mouth opening and closing like a shocked fish in cold air.

In the distance, flames licked higher as pine boards burned.

"Grandpa! Grandpa, call the fire de—"

The old man smiled. *"That's* what was missing, kiddo. Damn, but that's what it was."

"What? *What?"*

"That other smell," Collins said, removing the pipe from his mouth. "You can't have one without the other. It just wouldn't do."

"*Other* smell?" Blake had turned a deathly shade of pale.

"Wood smoke," Collins said, breathing deeply. "Don't you just love it? When I smell that and cherry tobacco mingling in the cool autumn air, it's like everything will always be all right and nothing will ever change. Oh, but I guess I told you that before. Here now, breathe deep. You'll *never* forget this day."

Blake ran around the house and into the street, screaming for help.

Collins shook his head, clamping the pipe between his teeth again. Cold, he stuffed his hands in his pockets. One of them found and shook the box of matches.

Half empty, it sounded like a rattlesnake.

The Return

Isabelle Benson lay under white sheets in the thin bed in the calm room and waited for someone to arrive. Someone always did. She never had to wait long. Everyone was very attentive. Everyone asked about her and how she was feeling. Today she thought she felt fine.

Some time later that felt like a little while but might have been longer, the door to her room opened inward. A figure entered. She had expected the door to open because someone always entered, but *this* visitor, this *man*...

She gasped, and in her thin wrist her pulse fluttered like a dove.

The man was middle-aged, dark-haired, chisel-chinned, kind-faced and tall. He wore a light spring sports coat that fit his good frame like a latex glove—every contour and angle cut to match what the cloth covered.

"You," Isabelle whispered. Then, as if reassured by her own voice, she said it again, louder.

The man said something in reply, something she didn't hear, so she continued, "It's been...oh, God, it's been so *long*. You look fine. You always did. Come and sit down by the bed. It's a comfy chair. Someone bought it for me."

The man did as she asked. He smiled and placed his hand on her arm, squeezing gently.

"Burton," she said firmly, and with the word out in the air, in the world, something clicked, a dam broke.

"You came back. They said you never would, but you did. Oh, sweet Jesus, you came *back!* How have you been? *Where* have you been? There's so much I have to tell you. The children, what they're doing and what they've done. And Mama and Papa. They...They..."

He said something. It was too soft, she couldn't hear, but the expression on his face conveyed it all.

"I know," Isabelle continued. "It was hard. Very hard. I think about them all the time. Mama went first some years back. Died while talking with Martha in the kitchen. Martha asked her a question and she didn't answer, and that was that. And Papa? He passed during a snowstorm. Crashed his truck trying to get home from the mill. And there's been others, Burton. Lots of others. Oh, you've been gone so *long*. They said you were gone for good..."

She paused, breath rasping in her lungs.

"And I believed them," she finished.

Again he said something, paused, then said something else. Still, his voice was too low, too faint.

"You murmur now," she said. "Always was a quiet one. Either you didn't talk or you talked soft. But don't worry." She scanned his face. "I can read you fine."

Isabelle stared at the familiar features for a long moment. The face seemed frustrated, confused, so she pulled it close and touched the smooth cheek. When she removed her palm he was calm again. Resolved like always. There was steel in him. She had always loved that.

"There now," she said. "And speak up so I can hear you."

"I said I've missed you, too," he said, voice slow and clear.

This time she heard him.

"There was so much to say that I never said," she said. "Things ended badly. It was my fault. I know it now, and I knew it then, but I couldn't do nothing about it because you left me." Rare tears filled her eyes. She wiped them away without thinking. "Burton, I always thought you wasn't ever coming back. I knew it like I know my own face. I was *certain*."

"I'm here now," he said. "I came back. For a little while."

"A *little* while?"

He nodded.

"But I don't want you to go away again."

"It's not up to me."

"What?"

He repeated himself.

Isabelle paused, considering. "I guess I won't question it. You're here now, and that's something. And here, now, there's something I've got to tell you."

He leaned forward, nodding his head.

She swallowed. Her mouth was dry. Her hand trembled as it touched the familiar head of dark hair. "Before you left, we fought. You remember. You couldn't possibly forget."

Again, he nodded.

"It wasn't about anything in particular. Something about the garden. You wanted tulips and I wanted white lilies. That night, when you left, the last thing I said was that you weren't good enough for me. That I should have looked ahead before we married and thought better of it. That you were a fool. And then...later that night...in the morning, you..."

He shook his head and touched a finger to his lips. Isabelle's agitation diminished.

"I wanted to say I'm sorry, Burton," she said. "All these years, these long years, and you were gone and I couldn't say it. Not so it counted. But now I can. Please. Oh, God, please forgive me."

A pause. Then, very clearly, he said, "I forgave you long ago. Remember that. Never forget it."

Isabelle sighed, old air rushing from her lungs like stale autumn wind.

And then she slept.

*****

"How was Grandma?"

Eric Benson poured himself a glass of lemonade and sat down across the kitchen table from his mother.

"Fine," he said, "but her hearing aids weren't working well. Hey, Mom?"

"Hmm?"

"How did Grandpa die? I know you were young."

The surprise showed on his mother's face. "Was Grandma talking about Daddy? She hardly ever mentions him. Keeps her grief buried deep."

Eric nodded.

"I was seven," his mother said. "They had a fight, and Daddy was upset and went to bed early. And he never woke up. Massive heart attack. He was only forty-one years old. Just five years older than you. God, that was over fifty years ago."

She looked up. "What did Grandma say about him?"

Eric took a big swallow of lemonade. "Nothing. She just said she'd been thinking about him."

A long silence.

"How was she?" his mother said finally. "Mentally, I mean? The staff at The Pines seem to think she's getting worse. Was it a good day or a bad day?"

Eric opened his mouth to speak, then paused, considering.

"A good day," he said at last. "It was a very good day."

The Subject

Halloween. Yeah, it's Halloween, imagine that! But if you look at it, that makes everything fit. Of course I don't know for sure. I mean, I wasn't around when it happened. But if it's not true, none of it makes any sense. So it's gotta be true, unless you can come up with something better. Yeah. Yeah, I'll tell you what I know. Then we'll see if you think what I think.

When I was a kid, Halloween was that perfect holiday. I mean, we got all dressed up, pretended to be what we weren't, flexed our imaginations. Monsters and myths and television characters. Yeah, we *pretended*. And I guess when you look at it, we were facing our fears, too. Don't you think? And the thing we fear worst of all is Death, isn't it? Sure it is. We fear what we don't understand, and that tops the list. And Halloween, it's a night for facing Death head-on, right? Staring it down and saying, "You don't scare me." And sure it did, but somehow Halloween made it all a bit easier. But that's not all there is to it. I know that now. After today, I know it. Halloween goes a lot deeper than that.

Where should I start? What he was like? OK. And how I knew him? And then what happened? I can do that.

Saul. He was a good guy. The best way to describe him was intelligent but easy-going, without that fake blasé attitude that usually comes to mind when you think of graduate-level arts majors. I mean, he wouldn't distance himself from those around him, and more than that, he usually went out of his way to be friendly. But when he painted, he unplugged the phone, locked himself in his house, and laid low for a few hours, sometimes six or seven at a stretch. He loved doing what he did. He never showed me anything he was doing until it was done, but that makes sense. I'm the same way with my graphics, and—

Yeah, I'm a grad student too. Study 3-D animation, same year as Saul. Nope, no classes together. We met as undergrads four years ago and continued on here 'cause the university has good programs in our subjects. So we've known each other a long time. *Knew*. We understood each other. Been good friends all along. Amazing. I mean—

What? Okay. Fine, I'll stick to it. In August, at the beginning of the semester, Saul began painting live models in his classes—some nudes, others clothed, and that really kept him on his toes, since I guess he hadn't worked in that area much before. He really enjoyed it, I could tell. Whenever I came over he was in his room with the door shut, sketching out hands, feet, necks, muscles. He told me once, maybe last month I guess it was, he said, "I'm capturing emotion like I never could with fruit." That really cracked me up, but I saw what he was getting at. I think he felt he'd found a new niche.

I didn't get to see him as much as I'd have liked, since we both had our classes and our studies and our side-jobs, and I had my girl-friend. That was a sore spot for Saul, the whole relationship thing. Why? Oh, that's kind of a long—well, 'cause we knew each other for over four years, and all during that whole time I was dating Suzie, but Saul, he couldn't find anyone who suited him. He must've gone through a good dozen relationships, not to mention one-night stands, most with women, even some with men. He said he tried homosexuality "just to see what it was like." That's Saul. Always trying something new. He'd do anything twice.

Anyway, around our senior year as undergrads, Saul started turning sour about what he called "the whole *love* thing." I mean, if I even brought *up* Suzie, that's all it took to set him off. And remember, Saul was usually easy-going…He was obviously having trouble, I guess because so many of his friends seemed happy with their partners and he was alone. He didn't believe in love, or claimed not to. Said not everyone was lucky enough to find a match suitable for both partners, or something like that. He always asked, "How do you know Suzie is the right girl?" or said, "Don't move too fast into marriage. You never know." It used to piss me off. And man, when he found out Suzie and I were *engaged?* You should have seen him. Speechless. Red-faced. I'd never seen him like that before, and never did again. Eventually he got over it, mainly because we'd been friends for so long, and I think because he realized one man's discontent isn't necessarily every man's, but it took a good while to smooth things over. He's passionate, and when he gets convinced he's right, it takes him a while to compromise, let alone admit that maybe not everyone sees things the same. Easy-going but a bit bull-headed. Yeah, that's Saul.

Was Saul. God. I mean, *was.*

Anyway, that's why I was so surprised when he came into The Easy on Thursday three weeks ago (that's when we always met for drinks, since it was almost the weekend and neither of us work on Thursdays) and, man, he *smiled* when conversation turned toward relationships and I brought up Suzie. What date exactly? Well…I guess it was October 12th. Yeah, since today is Halloween. Yeah, yeah I'm sure. October 12th.

So when he came in, it was almost like he was looking for an excuse to start talking, like he'd been waiting to say something but hadn't wanted to speak out of the blue. That's Saul for you. *Was.*

"Hey, guess what? I met someone last week," he said, and damn but his eyes didn't light up when he said it. That was strange. I hadn't seen him excited about a girl, or about *anyone*, for that matter, in over a year. Sure, he got laid sometimes, he didn't go without that, but to talk about it, and to talk about it like he was happy about it, that was something else.

Anyway, I asked him about this new girl of his, kind of amazed and all, and taking it slow and careful in case this turned out to be the start of one of those sarcastic rants of his, but he was for real. Very earnest, very serious. He said he'd met her the previous Saturday. Said she came to his door looking for someone else, got the wrong house or something, and 'cause it was raining outside he thought he'd at least invite her in since she looked cold and kinda wet. I mean, he was a considerate guy, and you know where his house is, all the way out in the country where the rent's cheap. It's pretty far off from any other place.

I guess she declined, said she'd drive on, but then the rain picked up. You remember how it was that night? Flooding all over the place, washed-out roads, and you couldn't see five feet in front of your face to drive. It lasted almost two hours before it began to calm down. So she stayed, and she and Saul got to talking.

Yeah, of course he told me her name. I already told you he said it was Lucy. Sorry that doesn't help much, but he never mentioned a last name. And that's another thing that should've bugged me. I'm not sure if even *he* ever found out what it was. In fact, I'd bet he didn't, considering. What did she look like? "Willowy," Saul told me. And long blonde hair. About our age.

No, I never met her. Not once. I always figured I would, you know. I always figured there would be plenty of times when we'd all go out together, me and Suzie and Saul and her. But now now, just the *thought*…

Gimme a minute, would you? Thanks. Just a minute.

Yeah. Yeah, I'm OK now. So they were talking, and then Saul said she started looking at some of his canvases, going from one to the next very slowly, very carefully examining each one. He kept the finished ones on the walls in the living room. They made him feel comfortable. Maybe it sounds vain, but I can understand why he did it. I'm the same way. Art's an expression of your feelings, your desires, what's important to you. It's an expression of yourself. Anytime I finish a rendering I'm proud of, up it goes.

He said she was really smitten with them, really smitten. That never did much for him, being complimented, since it was easy to be polite and easier to be insincere. That was one of his favorite phrases. But he said she seemed to know something about art, or about oil painting at least, and that her compliments were worded in technical terms. She even criticized a little, which *really* impressed Saul. And so they fell into some deep conversation—the kind of talk he couldn't get with almost anyone else. I could tell it excited him, having someone to talk to like that, someone who could keep up with his thoughts and theories and views, then insert her own and make him think. And finally, after three or four hours, he asked her to come back for lunch on Monday afternoon.

Yes, that would have been October 9th. I'd just bought pumpkins and decorated the apartment. I love Halloween. *Used* to. Not anymore. Not after today.

And so she did meet up with him again. She came back for lunch. And man, according to Saul, sparks *flew!* He said nothing physical took place, but when she left his house early that evening she'd already agreed to model for him, to be his subject for a series of paintings he was about to begin for his 538 class. Finding a good subject is tough, unless you want to use the people the class provides, and those aren't usually best. So that was good for him.

But Saul wasn't just happy, he was *thrilled.* She had a good mind *and* she was beautiful. I mean, it was as if after so long, after such a drawn-out period of building up a wall against a serious relationship, he was finally daring to peek over it and have a look around. He was attracted to her, and on more than one level. She meant something to him…connected with him. He was *interested* in Lucy. He *wanted* to know her better. She was good for him, that's the best way I can put it. Or I thought she was. I don't know, but there must've been something about her he'd been hoping to find for a long, long time—

Oh, God…oh, God…

Yes, thanks. Just…just…yeah, that's better. A cigarette beats caffeine any day. Calms the nerves when coffee riles them up.

So Saul was happy that night in The Easy, and we drank for a few hours, and talked about lots of things, but mainly about relationships. Saul also mentioned he'd met with Lucy at his house the day before—yes, the 11th—and started his sketches. He said she had no qualms about posing nude for him, no modesty. It was all for the sake of art, or so he claimed she said, although I bet he was hoping it was more than that. I could tell he thought it was.

And he said she had an absolutely beautiful body. "Stunning," he said. "Close to perfect."

I didn't hear from him again until the following Thursday— yeah, the 19th—when we met again, same time, same place, for our weekly thing. I'd had a rough few days, since classes were pressing with their deadlines, and my advisor was being a bear about my latest series of revisions. I didn't feel like talking much, or if I did, I wanted to talk about how much everything sucked. You know, to get it off my chest. That's what Saul and I usually talked about. Stuff like that. But Saul, he wanted to talk about Lucy instead.

He said he'd finished five oil paintings in four days. That he hadn't had more than four hours' sleep a night in the past week but felt great. Five paintings in four days? Man, that's output, especially on top of classes and everything else. And he said they were big canvases! That they were still drying but would set soon. He also claimed to be churning out charcoal sketches, and that Lucy never seemed to get tired of posing. That she was the perfect subject. Then he went on about all the great conversations they had, and how much they had in common, although he never mentioned what her major was, or even if she was in college. It was kind of funny, because, you know, I'd ask questions about her, and he said he didn't know the answers, as if that was completely natural. He said he didn't care.

Man, he even said he cooked for her, which I can hardly imagine, since Saul couldn't boil water without burning it. He went on about how close they were getting, and how he was hoping their relationship would turn into something bigger. Something even closer. He nudged me when he said that. God.

So I ended up listening to him instead of complaining about my week, and drinking more 'cause I wasn't doing most of the talking. I called it an early night, I guess since I was in kind of a bad mood and wasn't finding room to vent. Saul said he'd call me the following week about getting together again on Halloween. Yeah, today.

Saul called on Monday night. He said he'd finished another oil and was coming down the home stretch on plans for a few more. It was amazing. Those paintings can take *weeks*, especially the way Saul had always worked. He was still in a fine mood, although he sounded tired. Even so, since I was a bit perkier we chatted for a long time. He actually let me do most of the talking, so I went on and on about my workload, my Master's project, and stuff like that. We only touched on Lucy once, when he said she was coming over to see him again the next day, and he was going to try to "step up the pace with her," as he put it. I wished him luck. I truly hoped the relationship *would* move to the next level. He deserved some happiness, some contentment. And then we hung up. End of conversation.

Could I have another cigarette? Thanks. Sorry to bum, but I've really got a craving. Thought I was going to quit, but I guess not. Not for a while, anyway. I'll take the addiction for a bit longer. I think I'm going to need it.

Hmm? Last night. Do we have to talk about it right now? Can't I get something to eat? Fine, then. Yeah, I understand. It's just that it's been a bit of a...yeah.

Last night Saul called again, and this time, God, there was something wrong. I'd never heard him so upset.

"I pushed her away!" he said. "She's gone!"

"What happened?" I asked. "Why did she leave?"

Saul said, "I don't know, I put my arm around her, kissed her, and she kissed me back, was really getting into it, but then she just went cold—*so* cold—and she pulled away. I asked what I'd done, but she wouldn't talk about it. She just stood up, got her coat, and made for the damn door."

"She didn't say anything at all?" I asked. "No explanation?"

"She said she couldn't do it!" Saul said. "Said she didn't feel right about the whole thing and had to go. And that's all. That's all! I can't believe it. I didn't do anything wrong!"

"I'm sure that's true." And even if he had, I knew he sure hadn't meant to.

"No, no, I must have done *something*," he insisted. "I did something, and I drove her away, and now she might never come back. I couldn't handle that. I really couldn't."

And I said, "Well, maybe you could buy roses, stop by her house, see if you can talk it out together. Who knows what she's thinking? But if there's a connection, you need to go after her, to at least *try*. Sometimes there's something deeper at work—something in her past, some insecurity from way back. Like I said, you can't just assume it's something you did. And maybe if you put in the effort now, it'll show her things will be all right later on down the road; that she can feel comfortable with you, no matter what."

"But I *can't* go over to her house. Don't you get it? I just can't."

"Sure you can, Saul," I told him. "You just get up and go, and think about it later."

At that he just laughed. It was a desperate, flat, hopeless sound. And then he said, "But I don't know where she lives."

That brought me up short.

"You don't know where she *lives*?" I repeated.

"No, she never told me. She's shy, sometimes. Maybe she's poor. Ashamed of where she lives or what she does. That's the impression I always get. So I can't go find her... I can't."

Well, you've gotta admit, that's strange. Even then, I thought so. But I pushed all those thoughts away. Saul needed help.

He was devastated, crying with big, gulping sobs. Usually he was so calm about things that upset him, at least on the outside, but I guess Lucy really pushed his buttons the right way. She meant something to him. She was something special. Hearing him like that made me feel...well, you know. I hadn't heard him cry before, not even softly, but here he was, bawling his eyes out. It's hard to hear your friends in pain.

He calmed down after a while, though when I suggested he give her a call and talk about it, he said he didn't have her phone number. He didn't seem to think it was odd, but oh, man, isn't that the first thing you get when you want to see someone, even as a friend? And that's when I realized I knew virtually nothing about her. I wondered if he did, either—if he knew *anything about her at all*. But again, I didn't think much more about it until today.

So, after about an hour and a half, maybe around 10:30, we hung up. He'd promised me he was going to get some rest, take it easy, maybe watch a horror movie countdown on A&E. We were going to go over the whole thing again this evening at the bar and see if we couldn't find some way of fixing the damage. And then we planned on going to that Halloween party...

Could I have a break now? I really need a break. Thanks, ten minutes should do. Yeah, just to stretch. Water would be great. A Coke would be better. Sure, thanks.

I was asleep when Saul called back. No wonder. I mean, it was 3:30 in the morning. Today. Halloween. Oh, man, I'll never celebrate it again. No parties, no costumes, no candy, no movies…

Nothing. Not ever.

All I could hear was screaming. And distortion, because the screaming was so loud. I'd never heard anything like it. He sounded like a wild animal, like a dog howling and baying.

Finally he lowered his voice a little, but he kept repeating himself, over and over.

"She's *dead*," he said. "She's *dead*." He kept saying it, again and again: "She's *dead*, she's *dead*, she's *dead*…"

I talked to him. I don't know what I said, trying to get him to stop, and finally I ended up yelling at him to shut up, to just *shut up and tell me what happened*, but his voice raised with mine until we were both screaming at the top of our lungs, me telling him to shut up, and Saul just repeating, "She's *dead!* She's *dead!*" over and over. If I'd been there with him in person, I probably would have slapped him, like they do in the movies when someone's hysterical.

I need a glass of water. No, not another Coke, and definitely not coffee. Maybe another cigarette, too? God, look at my hands… Thanks.

He quieted down after five or six minutes. Maybe a little more or less, I don't know. Either way, it was a pretty long time to be screaming that loud. By then we were both hoarse, and I was afraid he was going to hang up, that I'd hear the *click* of the phone. And that would have scared me, because he was so upset, and you never know what a person could do when they're that upset…

But he stayed on the line. I could hear him gasping.

"What happened?" I asked again, trying hard to keep calm.

"Lucy's dead," Saul responded, almost in a whisper.

"Okay, okay, now I want you to listen…are you *sure* she's dead? I mean, absolutely *certain?*"

"Yes!" he said. "Yes, I'm sure of it! I've never been so sure of…"

That tone was creeping back into his voice, and his voice was rising again, getting louder. So I cut him off.

"How did it happen?" I asked. I just wanted to get the facts out of him, you see? And to keep him calm. Man, how I kept *my* voice calm, I'll never guess. Maybe I didn't believe it was true. Like I was in shock or denial, you know? It all seemed so crazy.

"I don't know how it happened," Saul said. "I don't know, I don't know, I don't know…"

"But you know she's dead?" I demanded. "I don't understand."

Then Saul, he just exploded again. "Neither do I! Neither do I!" And then he started shrieking, and he didn't stop for an awful long time.

I kept quiet, let him wear himself out, and finally, after a good while, he did. And he didn't hang up, either, although at one point he dropped the phone. Once he was calm again I asked, "Where is she?"

"I don't know!" he wailed. "God, she could be anywhere. Anywhere! *I've got to get out of here.*" That's what he said: that he had to get out of there. And he should've. He should've just gotten out and run.

Again and again I told him to tell me where she was, or where he thought she was. I told him I had to know, he had to tell. That the only way to get to the bottom of things, to make things better, would be to tell me, and that we could take it from there, we could work it all out.

And over and over, he said he didn't know. That he didn't *want* to know. His exact words? "I don't know, and I don't ever want to find out. Hopefully far away." That's what he said: "Hopefully far away." I didn't understand it. None of it made any sense.

Then I heard a muffled thumping on his end of the line, like a knocking, and his breath, it hitched in his throat, and then he started breathing real hard, real fast, like he was hyperventilating or having some sort of attack. And finally I heard a sobbing noise. Yeah, it was him. I'm sure of it. And I heard that knocking again, much louder this time. Yeah, like knocking on a door. I asked what was going on, who it was at the door, but he just sobbed one final time, and paused, and said, "I gotta go," and that's when he finally hung up. I yelled into the phone, but nothing. He was gone. I called back, over and over, but he didn't answer. So after 15 minutes more I called you guys, then I jumped in the car and beat it over to his place as fast as I damn well could.

When I showed up, two cop cars were already there, and three of you guys in uniform were standing around by the door, so I got out and went up to meet them, and they told me to stand back. I remember one started to call out Saul's name, over and over, louder and louder. The door? Hell, you saw it—splintered apart and ripped half off its hinges, forced open and inward.

They went inside, and I heard someone say "Shit," and then another said, "Holy Mary." That's when I said the hell with it, I'm going to find out what's going on, I have to know, and I rushed in past them before they had a chance to stop me. Of course, they weren't even thinking about me. Their attention was elsewhere.

And then they brought me here, to answer your questions and tell you what I know. And now I'm done, and I'd really like to go home, if that's OK.

...If I have to, I will. But if you're gonna ask what I think you are, then...yeah, good, please make them quick. Sorry, but...just make them quick.

Saul was...he was dead, of course. I knew that right away. He looked—I—God, this can't be happening, you know? This just doesn't happen. This can't happen. And it's Halloween. The jack o' lanterns were still burning on his porch. There's *no way*. It's supposed to be a *fun* holiday. All about using the imagination, you know? Not real. But this *is* real. I can't deny what I saw. Saul looked...there was no color in his face, and his hair was white...*fucking white!* And his eyes were wide, and his mouth was open, and he was slumped down beside the coffee table, looking up, his head against the base of the couch.

And then one of the officers ran out of the house, and I could hear him retching on the porch, and the smell mingled with the smell of burnt pumpkins.

And that's when I looked up.

I'll never forget it, those paintings. They were on every wall, some huge, as big as this table, others more traditional size. I'm sure you'll see them soon if you haven't already. You haven't? Fine. Yeah, I'll tell you. I don't want to, but...they were all labeled clearly in the bottom right corners, each one, and each label read "Lucy Series," followed by a number.

Don't you see? All that time she'd fooled him. He'd seen what she'd wanted him to see, even as he was unconsciously painting her as she really looked. I know that now, and don't try and tell me any different. I won't buy it.

But Halloween...On Halloween, I guess she decided to come clean, so to speak. There's a power to the day, like in all the old stories. That must be it. And so today he finally saw what she was, and somehow, I can't imagine, got her out of the house, and called me.

But she came back.

The paintings. Yeah, I'm getting there. I'm ready...

They were portraits of a skeleton. In some it was covered in a sort of white dress, or cloak, but the fabric looked mildewed, like it'd been exposed to the elements for a long time. Some were full-body paintings, nothing covering the subject, and the skeleton, God help me, it wasn't a *clean* skeleton, if you know what I mean, and on its head was a thin crown of matted blond hair. One of the paintings was a detail of just the head and shoulders. And yeah, that's when I lost it, and I guess they had to haul me out of there. I started screaming and couldn't stop...

Yeah, I'm sure she's dead. But he didn't kill her. You didn't find a body, did you? And you won't, either. She's out there. Walking the evening streets right now, as she really is. Among all the costumes, who would ever notice? And tomorrow maybe she'll look different again, *alive* again, and some other poor soul will find her attractive.

Attractive.

I can't say anything else. I'll lose it. But it all makes sense, doesn't it? What was it Hamlet said? "There are more things in heaven and earth, Horatio, than are dreamt of in your philosophy." That says it all.

No, no more questions. Please. Please, don't ask any more. That's all I know, and tons more than I want to. No. No more. *Enough.*

Par One

"Oh, for God's sake!" Livid, Charlie Neilson stared ahead, the smell of the Atlantic strong in his nose, his patient wife, Sarah, at his side.

Bethany Beach hummed around them: young parents led by restless children toward ice cream stands; bronzed teens loitering outside Beachfront Fries or strolling up the boardwalk, slick with suntan lotion, body boards attached to wrists with neon cord; and the elderly, a small but ever-present minority, quietly dining at outside cafés and sitting on boardwalk benches looking toward the horizon, thinking immutable thoughts.

Out of all these people, only Charlie stood stock-still, glaring intently and breathing hard, face a sunburned beet.

"Sarah," he said slowly.

"What, Charlie?"

"They tore the damn thing down and built a GAP over it!"

Sarah scrutinized the generic-looking chain store with mild disinterest. "What did they tear down?" she asked. "Which place? You've mentioned so many."

"The putt-putt golf course!" he replied, grinding his teeth. "It's been there fifty years, and sometime in the last few they tore it down, paved it over, and built *this* goddamned monstrosity. Hell, if they'd had room I bet they would have built a WalMart! It'd figure, it really would. And I guess this shouldn't surprise me, either."

Charlie and Sarah had been married two years. Charlie, a teacher, had saved up for this trip over six months, anxious to share his childhood vacation town with his new wife—to experience the old magic with someone new.

"What I wanted, what I really wanted, was to play that golf course with you," he said.

Sarah slid her hand into his. Without realizing, he gripped it hard and continued.

"An old man ran it. He owned half the town, did it for fun. Cost fifty cents to play, never more, no matter *what* year it was. And he had a little Scottie dog named Toto. There was a loop-the-loop, an old lighthouse with an eighty-watt bulb in the top, a rotating windmill, a mote bridge that rose and fell! And a metal ramp, a dozen sand traps, a stream you had to knock the ball over...and then, finally, Hole 18, a tiny bridge of wood with a hole at the end and a pit on either side. Get a Par One and you won a free game!"

"Did you ever win?" Sarah asked.

"Nope, never did. Mom, Dad, and me—we always missed, every single time. And when I was little I always figured next year would be the one, and then, that last year before high school when we moved too far away, I figured I'd come here again when I was older, married, maybe with children, and...but no." He shook his head. "Stupid of me to imagine, after all these years."

"Not stupid," said Sarah. "Sweet. But look around! This place is still full of life. Lots to do, lots to see, not too busy, not too lazy. We're going to have a great week."

"Hey," said Charlie, approaching a teenage clerk who had just emerged from the Gap for a cigarette. "Remember the old putt-putt golf course that used to be here? When did it close?"

The young man cupped a hand around his lighter and exhaled a plume of blue smoke. "Don't ask me," he said. "This is just my summer job. Live in Baltimore the rest of the year."

Sarah pulled at her husband's arm. "Dinner, Charlie. I'm hungry. There's a nice looking place around the corner. It's their Grand Opening Week. Bethany Bayou, it's called."

"No, no," said Charlie. "Suddenly I have a terrible headache. For me, a corndog and bed. Tomorrow will be better. You go out and have a good time."

*****

The evening passed, the night passed, and in the early pre-dawn morning Sarah, who *hadn't* had a good time the previous night, stole out of bed, left her husband snoring gently beneath sheets that smelled of sand and salt, and was back before he woke up.

After shutting the door with a slam, she shook Charlie's mattress, pinched his cheek, blew in his ear, and tugged his hair until he grumbled and snorted back to consciousness.

"Wha'?" he demanded groggily.

"Wake up, Sleeping Beauty, we have a game to play," she announced.

He sat up in the semi-darkness, rubbing his eyes. "Game?" he repeated. "What are you talking about?"

"Yesterday was a fiasco," she announced firmly.

Charlie cleared his throat and didn't meet her gaze.

"But I have a solution," she continued. "Get a shower, get dressed, and meet me out on the boardwalk in half an hour."

Without waiting for a reply, she walked out the door, slammed it again, and was gone.

*****

The sun, even at dawn, was a blinding beacon which shimmered water, heated air, and reflected sand like glass. Donning the $10 pair of sunglasses he'd bought the day before, Charlie scanned the boardwalk (new, he thought disapprovingly; *different*), and finally located his wife at the far end, where the last stairway down to the beach met a drift of white sand.

"What are those?" he asked, nodding at two somethings in his wife's hands.

"What do they look like?"

"Hey." Charlie leaned close. "These...how?"

"I went for a walk this morning," Sarah said. "All over town. Up streets, down lanes, between buildings, through alleys. And in one of the alleys, right behind the new Gap, in fact, I found an old pile of junk. Some fake green turf, an old model lighthouse...and a couple of beat-up golf clubs and two golf balls, one blue, one red."

"I remember these," he murmured.

Sarah nodded. "Here." She handed him a club. "And here." She handed him the red ball.

"How'd you know I always chose red?" he asked.

"You painted the outside of our house red," she said shortly. "The whole damn thing. Let's go down to the shore."

They walked out onto the beach until their feet touched damp sand.

"The 18th hole," said Sarah. She dropped her ball. "Par One. You ready?"

A slow, hesitant smile played across Charlie's face. He dropped his ball in the sand beside hers.

"Ready?" Sarah repeated.

"Yes. Yes! Ready."

They swung. The balls disappeared far out to sea, each plying a brief hole in the vast, golden expanse. Then they were gone.

"Hole in one!" exclaimed Sarah. "Two of them!"

Charlie looked out at the sea for a long, long time before turning to his wife.

"Breakfast?" he asked.

Sarah nodded. "If you're interested, there's this new restaurant called Bethany Bayou."

"Sounds great. You know, suddenly I could eat a *horse*."

A few hours later, the tide came in and took the two clubs.

Just Beneath

The day had been hot and humid, as most late-August days in central Maryland are, and with summer almost over and the smell of chalk and musty 8th grade textbooks haunting their future, the three boys looked for something to fill the evening that would remind them of the season all but done and past.

It was Scott Cleary who thought of going to the lake at Centennial Park, and Tim Wilson who agreed it was a good idea.

"We can get popsicles and go canoeing," said Tim. "I love canoeing. You can outrace other people and cut from one end of the lake to the other. Yeah, I'm in. Let's do it!"

That left Ron Atkins, who suddenly found himself under the scrutinizing gaze of his friends.

"You in, Ron?" Tim asked.

"Why don't we just go to the basketball courts?" said Ron. "There's a whole ton of stuff to do at the park besides splash around on the lake."

"We played basketball last night," said Scott.

"Rollerblading?"

"Boring," Tim said, voice flat. "And besides, my blades are busted."

Ron sighed, sensing a losing battle. Then genius struck. "I got a pack of Camels from my brother. We can go in the woods by the dock and smoke 'em. I just gotta run home first and sneak 'em out."

This did cause Scott and Tim to pause, but only for a moment. "No time," said Scott. "The sun's going down and they stop renting canoes at dusk. We'll smoke 'em tomorrow."

And that was that. Ron glanced around Scott's basement—at the flat-screen TV, the stack of Blu-ray discs, the paintball equipment carefully mounted on the far wall, the framed jersey worn by Cal Ripken at a game in 1992—then looked back to Scott and Tim, who were already pocketing money, iPhones, and keys for the walk.

And he suddenly realized, for the first time, that Scott's family had money, and Tim's didn't, and what that meant. He wondered if Scott knew why Tim always said "yes" to everything he suggested. Hell, he'd only just figured it out himself.

"Come on, Ron," said Scott. They were going with or without him. He could go to the lake or go home.

Bemused, he followed his old friends up the stairs.

*****

"Why you want to keep away from the lake, anyhow?" Tim asked, flipping Ron's baseball hat off his head and taking a bite of cherry Popsicle. They were sitting on the dock by the canoes, waiting for the attendant to bring oars.

"It's boring, that's all," said Ron, replacing his hat and slugging Tim's arm.

"I know," said Scott. "It's about the guy who drowned here last week. Isn't it?"

Scott knew Ron well. That had always been a strength in their friendship, but sometime, at some point—Ron couldn't tell exactly when, but recently—that strength had turned into something else.

"No, that's not it," Ron said flatly.

But Tim picked up the torch and said, "You don't like deep water, do you, Ron? I mean, you don't go swimming. I never seen you in the pool, only dangling your feet. You *ever* swim?"

"He doesn't know how," said Scott.

"I do," Ron retorted.

"Only the doggie-paddle."

The attendant handed each of them an oar, watched as they latched on their lifejackets, and helped them push off from the dock. "An hour 'til we close," she said, then walked back to the stand.

Tim threw his Popsicle stick over his shoulder. Ron watched as it landed in the water and floated, suspended on the surface. The lake, always muddy, had been the first thing to darken in the encroaching twilight, and he wondered how many feet of that darkness now wallowed and flowed beneath them.

"You're still thinking about the guy who drowned," Scott repeated. "Isn't that right? It's making you nervous?"

The oars cut through the water, causing slight ripples with every touch. Centennial Lake, wide, flat, expansive, spread out around them, reflecting the last fire of the dying day.

"It's sad," Ron said, sitting in the middle of the canoe, no oar, Tim before him and Scott behind him, both paddling strongly toward the center of the lake. "He was fishing in a little boat with friends, and he fell in and got tangled up in the lake weeds. That's what they think. As simple as that. Isn't it sad?"

Tim snorted. "What a dumbass. If he was that stupid, he deserved it."

Ron was silent.

"I know what you mean," Scott said, paddling as the canoe traveled farther from shore.

Ron was surprised. He turned around and stared at Scott, who was looking straight ahead. "You do?"

Scott nodded. "It's sad, all right. Just imagine. You're safe in a boat, surrounded by your friends. Maybe you just went out to relax, to get away from it all. The sun's bright and warm, and you're feeling pretty good, and maybe you feel a tug on your line, so you lean forward...and that's all it takes. You're up and over and into the water, and it's cold down there, cold and lonely, and you're all alone with everyone else safe up above. And you think to yourself, *I'll push up to the surface. I'll be back with everyone in just a second,* but then you try, and nothing happens, and you realize you're caught, and the more you pull, the tighter the vines hold on."

As Scott spoke, nothing interrupted him but the oars cutting through the water. Tim, besides his rhythmic rowing, was silent. Listening.

"And then you get it. You get that it's all over; that this is happening to *you,* not to someone else. That the cold and dark and loneliness is all you're ever going to have, and that the light and warmth belongs only to other people now. And then your lungs start to hurt, and the pain gets worse and worse, and you panic more and more, and everything starts to fade..."

"Stop it," said Ron. "Just stop." His voice was very small, very quiet.

And Scott did stop, and Ron knew it wasn't because he'd asked, but because Scott knew he had no need to say more. He'd said enough.

Then Tim laughed. Ron wanted to slug him, to shove him off the canoe into the dark water, but he didn't hate Tim enough for that. *No one* deserved that.

"I want to go back to shore," Ron said softly.

"I paid for the canoe, I'm getting my hour," Scott replied.

"I want to go back to shore," Ron repeated.

Tim laughed a second time—a rolling, high giggle. "Hear that, Scott? Ron wants to go back to shore. He's scared."

Ron once again looked back at Scott. Scott was smiling. Smirking, more like. And at that moment Ron realized Scott hated him, that the friendship had survived only as a remnant from a gone time, that it existed only as routine, that nothing deep or true remained behind it. He knew Scott and Scott knew him, and Scott, knowing him, now wanted him gone…and had all the ammunition he needed to make that desire a reality.

"There's no reason to be scared, Ron," Scott said, still paddling. "You've got a life jacket on, and the fisher guy didn't. You couldn't drown in this lake now if you tried. And as for the dead, they can't hurt you. Once he stopped breathing he became just another log. He'll turn up soon enough, I'll bet, and then—"

"Wait," Ron said. "Wait."

Scott waited.

"You mean…"

Scott waited some more.

"You mean he's…still down there?"

"Oh, c'mon, man, you knew that. They've been diving for the body over and over, and no luck. Probably stopped for the day just before we got here, come to think of it."

And suddenly Ron felt a creeping horror—a stealthy, sickening panic. He closed his eyes and grabbed both sides of the canoe. He breathed in, out, in, out, fast and faster, and then his gorge rose up in a big, hot rush, and over the side it all came out…

And as he vomited, he thought, *Scott knew that, too. How I got scared after seeing Grandma dead. About how ever since, thinking about seeing dead bodies makes me sick. I told him that at a birthday sleepover when we were nine, and I cried 'cause I was ashamed, and he cheered me up by getting me an extra piece of cake, though I didn't feel up to eating it…*

Scott turned the canoe around. Tim protested but they headed straight to shore. And the whole way, Ron kept his eyes firmly shut and his hands firmly clamped to either side of the canoe, even as Scott said, "Hey, I was only kiddin' around, Ron. There's no body still down there. They found him an hour later. I was only kiddin' around…" Even as Tim told puking stories of his own to try and make Ron feel better. Even as they both said that basketball sounded fine, just fine…a night game, maybe?

"Not tonight," said Ron, once they were back on the dock and his stomach had settled. "I'm just gonna go on home."

"All right," said Tim. "Maybe tomorrow."

"Hey, I'm sorry," added Scott. Ron couldn't make out his expression in the dark. "I didn't mean to freak you out so much."

"It's fine, I don't care," Ron said. But as he turned away and headed home in the muggy summer night, he felt very cold and very alone.

Come True

Jen was enjoying the Friday afternoon: the reprieve from students, the cheap merlot, the late-day autumn sunlight. Gloria's back deck was high up in the trees, and the bright leaves rustled in the cool, light wind. It was a time for thinking about nothing with any great passion; a time for unwinding and drinking wine and eating tortilla chips with mild salsa. October was a long month—no days off, a slew of papers to grade—and such breaks were to be cherished.

Then Tara said, "It's Jen's birthday next Tuesday, you know. We should do something."

Jen coughed. Gloria laughed.

"What's so funny?" Tara asked, crunching another chip.

"How did you find out about Jen's birthday?" Gloria asked. "She keeps that date pretty well guarded."

"It was on the faculty page of the school's website. They're all on there."

Jen smiled faintly.

"What's the big deal?" Tara prodded. "We don't have to cele-brate how *old* you are. It's just that it's your special day. And besides, you can't be more than…"

"Twenty-seven," Jen answered softly. "I'll be twenty-seven."

"This is your first year," Gloria said, shaking her head at Tara in mock consternation. "Otherwise you'd have known that birthdays make Jen nervous. She has a complex about them. Don't ask her to explain."

For Jen, all the color had drained from the autumn leaves, and the gentle wind, soothing up until a moment ago, now seemed tinged with menace and the sweet, pervasive scent of decay. One blink, and the afternoon was ruined. "Why not?" she said. "I can explain it very well, if I want to."

Gloria grunted, sipping her wine. "But in four years, you never have."

"You said you'd never bring it up."

Gloria swirled her wine in its glass. "I didn't," she said simply. "Tara did."

And then, for the first time in almost two decades, anger got the best of Jen's common sense. *Catty*, she thought, then turned to Tara. "Do you want to know why I don't like birthdays?"

"Um…yes. No. I mean, not if it's going to upset you. I didn't mean—"

"No, no, you didn't do anything." Jen cast a quick glance at Gloria, who met her gaze without blinking.

"It's very simple," Jen said.

*****

There was a party. A *great* party, all planned and orchestrated with meticulous care by Jenny's mother. She loved turning Jenny's birthday parties into immense, time-consuming projects, and the end-results of her efforts always met with success.

This year, the theme was *My Little Pony*—the current fad for seven year-old girls—and the house had been decorated accordingly. Jenny, dressed in her best, looked around, thrilled at the glittered floor paths, the sparkling pony banners, the pastel-colored pony doll at each place on every table. All of the other dozen girls were thrilled (but not Davy Perkins, it must be said; his mother had made him come), screaming and shrieking from one game to the next, but none more than Jenny herself.

It was a perfect day.

It was *her* day.

Even outside, even in October, the sun shone warm, compliant with the needs of the occasion. So eventually the party moved to the back porch, and then out to the back yard, where the great apple tree grew up to cover the cool grass and fallen, gently rotting apples in shifting shade and cascading leaves.

They raced around the trunk, all the girls and even Davy, holding their ponies, pretending to *be* ponies, running, then trotting, then galloping through the grass. And Jen felt free, and happy, and special, and thought of the presents waiting on the table inside, the ice cream, the cake, and everyone singing "Happy Birthday"…

And then Debbie Wilson, who lived three doors up, tripped her.

It was on purpose. Jenny saw Debbie's leg come out, felt Debbie's foot turn up to catch her ankle, and then she was falling, arms pinwheeling, to sprawl in a patch of rotten apples that left her white dress streaked with pulp, dirt, and grass stains and her left knee bloodied.

She didn't cry. Not yet. First she looked up, saw Debbie running away, saw Debbie laughing, saw Debbie glance back and continue on around the tree…

"Debbie did it," she told her parents moments later. But Debbie said no, no, she hadn't, she hadn't touched Jenny at all, and that's when Jenny started to cry—but Debbie started crying too, and she cried *louder* than Jenny, so Jenny's parents appeased her by saying it had all been a "big accident."

Ten minutes later, things were calm again—Jenny changed and cleaned up, Debbie smiling and laughing, all the girls (and even Davy) happily streaming back into the house for cake and ice cream.

But Jenny was still angry—*very* angry—despite her smile. And when her mother brought out the cake, candles a great wall of cheery light, she knew what she would wish for when she blew them out.

When the children finished singing, Jenny smiled, and it was genuine this time, and she was looking right at Debbie.

Then she blew out the candles. All seven of them. In one breath pulled from deep in her lungs.

And Debbie dropped dead.

*****

There was a pregnant silence.

It was Tara who finally laughed nervously. "You're joking!"

"No." Jen shook her head. "I wished that she would die, and she did. Five seconds later."

"Coincidence," Gloria whispered, then repeated the word louder, with more certainty. "Coincidence."

"Sure," agreed Tara. "Yes, of course it was."

"They said it was an aneurysm. A ticking time bomb just waiting to go off. No one could have known, and there were no symptoms." Jen shook her head and looked down into her wine glass.

Silence again. Then Tara cleared her throat. "Why did Debbie trip you?"

"Who can say? Children do things without thinking. They have flashes of meanness, same as adults. We'd always been good friends. For that matter, why did I wish her dead? Same reason, I guess."

"And all these years…" Tara trailed off.

Jen took up the line. "I've kind of blamed myself. At first, consciously. Then, as the years passed and I came to recognize how unlikely it all was, I knew on a rational level that I wasn't to blame, but I still felt guilty. Because deep down, I still believed I'd caused it to happen. Knowing and feeling are two different things, you see."

Gloria exhaled audibly. "Wow. What a story! No wonder. It must have been very hard, living with that. So no more parties, no more celebrations."

"Not since I was seven. Not a single one." Jen's lower lip quivered almost imperceptibly, then stilled. "But you know, I'm glad you brought it up, I really am."

Gloria arched her eyebrows. "Really?"

"Yes. I think talking about it made me realize how silly it is. And it would be a good, healing experience, to have a birthday party again...to help me put it behind me once and for all. Don't you think?"

"Oh, absolutely!" said Tara. "Sure it would!"

"Yes," agreed Gloria more quietly. "Yes, I agree."

"I can plan the whole thing," said Tara. "I'll get the cake, send out invitations. We can make it as large or small a party as you'd like! And I'll figure out who can bring what, and we'll throw you a 'Welcome back to Birthday Parties' birthday party. Oh, it'll be great!"

"That's so sweet of you," Jen said. "It really will help me put all this behind me. Of course," she added, almost as an afterthought, "it's hard to destroy *every* doubt. I think there will probably always be some small part of me that will wonder if I really had something to do with...no, but enough of that!" She sipped her wine and swallowed, enjoying the dry taste that somehow complimented the great spray of autumn colors that surged around them.

"What should I bring?" Gloria said. She didn't look at Jen as she spoke.

Tara opened her mouth to say something, but Jen beat her to it. "You've already done so much, Gloria. You made this possible by talking about it, even when you knew I didn't want you to. But it was for the best, and I thank you for that."

She pursed her lips, thinking.

"The *candles*," she said at last, snapping her fingers. "Gloria, you just bring the candles. That'll be plenty."

"Yes! A cake has to have candles," said Tara brightly.

Gloria fixed her gaze on Jen, who met it without blinking.

"That...that will be fine," she murmured.

"Great! And I know just what to wish for," Jen said, taking another sip of wine before reaching out and patting Gloria's cold, cold hand.

To Be

His name was Allan Eden, and he moved about in darkness absolute except for the stars.

As far as he could tell, the land before him had once supported his home. It was desolate now; charred, hard earth indistinguishable from the rest of the wasteland that extended for miles in every direction. He could see little in the blackness save the glint of mica chips and the outline of rough-hewn rock, but thought nothing of waiting the long hours until daybreak. He had plenty of time.

Allen Eden was lonely. He was also dead. Yet the loneliness was not that which most of the dead-and-left had felt since humanity's first tentative steps in the metaphorical garden that was his namesake. It was a loneliness the depth and breadth of which few had ever experienced, and none with any sense would wish to.

For the multitude, death was not so bad. Many enjoyed it, Eden thought with bitterness. But he had died under violent circumstances, and although the theories of the living rarely came close to approaching the true nature of life after death, some few individuals had embraced one during his lifetime that had turned out to be disconcertingly true: those who died unhappily, and under certain traumatic conditions, were bound indefinitely to the mortal plane: ghosts. And ghosts, in Eden's experience, were all unhappy. Some people who truly loved life remained partially behind after their body's demise to cherish the world a short time longer before moving on, but they weren't *true* ghosts: a healthy portion of their being had already achieved transcendence, and only a vague essence remained for a time before joining it. *True* ghosts, the "lifers" as one of his incorporeal companions once ironically termed it, were in the majority, and they all suffered.

To Eden, it seemed the time immediately following death was cheerless for ghosts, either because of the paths their lives had taken, or because of the way those paths had ended: a secret shame, a raging regret, murder, a car accident, drowning; any facet of life or death that made moving on seem more impossible than the suffering which thrust them into ghosthood to begin with. The instinctual need to *remain*, to make right, was very difficult for the Afterworld to reconcile; thus, it often did not. If strong enough, need could overwhelm the natural beck and call of higher dimensions, and Eden's need was very great.

Looking up at the bright, distant light of the stars and planets, he sighed, and the sigh was such that a thin wind sprang up in a cyclonic eddy before him and moved off down the barren plain. Unhappiness was not stationary: the range of its levels was great, and one manifestation could quickly take the place of another, or, even worse, join with it as two strong brothers often join up against a less fortunate only child.

He thought of the second manifestation of his sadness: how, gradually, once the sting of his own murder had worn off, the uneasy, hollow desire for revenge began to gnaw at his thoughts. Roughly two years after his death, Eden had visited his knife-handy wife for the first time since his funeral. Preparing for bed, Sarah had opened the bedroom closet to grab a bathrobe, and shaken hands with his cold, clammy hand instead. Her scream was music to his ears, and for the next fifty-seven years Eden enjoyed the various ranges Sarah's worn vocal chords could achieve when frightened. When she finally expired at the respectable age of ninety-three, having outlived the integrity of most of her vital organs by a number of years, his former wife had been near-catatonic for over a decade and raving mad for another before that, locked away in an asylum on the outskirts of Baltimore.

Yet following the conclusion of his vigorously-undertaken revenge, loneliness set in, as it does for all who don't belong where they are. Figuring eternity was a long time to deal with depression without Prozac, therapy, or even the option of suicide, Eden began devising ways to cheer himself.

*****

Eden struck a hard, pocked deposit that lay near the tips of his phantasmic tendrils. It clattered unevenly down the barren plain, kicking up sharp, orange sparks. He waited while the sound faded, the sparks went out, and the rock fell still again. He had been around so long, learned so much, that the ability to move physical objects was ingrained, like breathing had once been.

He thought again of Sarah, and how long it had been since their last post-death encounter. She had come to him just a few weeks after losing grip of her body, sane again and mad as hell. If looks could kill! Eden had never witnessed such concentrated vitriol. He attempted to flee but could think of no place to hide from another free-ranging ghost like himself. Sarah and her envenomed spirit-tongue followed him across the continental United States, over the Atlantic, and eventually caught up with him among the ancient-timbered buildings of London, in the famous Drury Lane Theatre, among the spirits of antiquity and during a somewhat under-produced production of *All's Well That Ends Well*. Then, as he stood before her blistering, withering onslaught of words, he realized something: it was good having her around again.

Upon seeing that her presence brought Eden happiness, however, Sarah quickly calmed and became one of the few purgatorial spirits to ascend to the Great Beyond, delayed peace serving as the key to her transcendence. In leaving him, she exacted the only form of retribution that could actually cause Eden pain. The loneliness began to bite harder.

Other spirits were difficult to talk to. The cynical and resentful generally tire of the happy and content, so Eden found the short-term "benevolent" presences not only boring, but often downright annoying. They kept trying to convince him to lighten up, sometimes quite eloquently, but simply didn't understand the nature of his situation. As for the other "lifers," for the most part all they did was complain, gossip, and sulk. He avoided almost all of them, save for a brief conversation now and again, and they him.

That left Eden with the living to toy around with. For years innumerable he haunted the darker avenues of the world, inhabiting everything from the undersides of Eastern-European stone bridges and the attics of campus dormitories in the American Mid-West, to cursed glades in the African wild and various unlucky passes in the Himalayas. For a time, he enjoyed the startled, fearful, and sometimes worshipful reactions that his moans, brief appearances, or icy touches invoked. But one day, after inadvertently causing the infant son of a young Queensland woman to burst into tears, the mother, bath-robed, face-creamed, and already well aware of his hauntings, actually *screamed* at him. Spinning around the room in circles, unable to see him yet obviously feeling his presence, she shrieked, "Jealous! Pathetic! That's what you are. Leave us alone and take it somewhere else!" Then, before leaving the room to calm the baby in the kitchen, she slowly, deliberately, *gave him the finger.*

Eden never bothered the living on purpose again. He was too offended.

He took, instead, to learning about the universe. For this task, Time, at least momentarily, was on his side. He read everything of scientific value that interested him. He visited museums, watched operations, looked over the shoulders of geniuses at work. He conducted as much field research as he could manage. He learned meditation and studied all the major philosophies. He immersed himself in theology (having an interesting personal perspective to aid him), numerology, and, for the hell of it, philology. His memory, improved by immateriality, acted as an information dump of almost limitless proportions. It took millennia, but by the time his lust for information was sated, Eden had proven the existence of no less than 26 dimensions; come to understand how a universe could exist without a beginning and without an end; expanded upon the theories of Einstein, Hawking, and two dozen others until discovering their ultimate cruxes; determined the logical meaning of life; discovered the logical meaning of death; debunked the concept of finity; and cured the common cold (imparting the cure to the living through automatic writing with a primary school mistress in Iceland).

Then, despite his labors toward enlightenment, a familiar darkness once again began to steal into Eden's sight, and this time it seemed to whisper, faintly, of an even greater darkness yet to come. Time, so integral to his studies, slowly, once again, became his curse.

*****

All those experiences, all those memories, were from years long ago, when the concept of years was still embraced by others besides himself. Now Eden, his presence permeating the site of his old home and ancient life, tried hard not to think about time. He felt the rare, yet growing fear of what a close review of his post-body existence would do to him. He knew his sanity, or at least its spiritual equivalent, had been growing increasingly fragile for ages, so he tried to avoid unnecessary provocations that might accelerate its decline.

Thinking too much about the present didn't help, either. Eden did not wish to consider how long it had been since he had seen a living man or woman. The last rocket had left for a better world eons ago, leaving him behind, trapped by the rules of the afterlife to haunt the globe the way some unlucky souls were confined to the site of a former building, lake, or forest. The strange animals that evolved as the sun aged and grew (vast beasts with skins of radiation-proof bone, tiny mammalian imps that chattered on the shores of the Great Sea) only perpetuated his loneliness. Their appearance, like the changes in the planet's geography, evoked within him a penetrating, profound sense of melancholy. Even most of the ghosts were now of species he didn't know or understand.

The weather, too, had shifted with the ages. Eden missed snow, and in the more recent past had often ascended the diminishing white-capped mountains or floated above the poles to relieve the tedium of hot weather. He missed the polarities of seasons. His favorite, autumn, was difficult to forget, despite the evolution or extinction of the trees that had once characterized it with falling leaves and colored brilliance, and despite that he had felt neither hot nor cold, wet nor dry, in a span of time that had seen half a dozen geologic ages come and go. He remembered pumpkins. Jack o' Lanterns. The smell of burning leaves and the decay of wet grass. The sound of costumed children giggling at doors. Not even photographs remained, but he remembered.

And last but not least, a final, bitter pill: the ghosts of his generation were beginning to lose their holds on reality.

Eden truly missed one of them, an old pirate named Charles Weary. Bound to the perimeter of the London tavern where he had tasted poison in the early sixteenth century, Weary had for a long while been something close to a friend. He had been a bitter soul but not as gloomy as the rest: a combination which attracted Eden. In fact, Weary hadn't even been above cracking a joke, although the old favorites had worn a bit thin after a few thousand years. Yet slowly, almost unnoticeably, his behavior had changed. On one memorable occasion Weary had called him "Father," and carried on an entire (one-sided) conversation with "Father" until Eden, dismayed, made some kind of excuse and fled across the world for a few centuries. On a much later encounter, when the progression had grown more pronounced, Charles had taken Eden by his vaporous shoulders, looked him in the eye, and asked, almost pleading, "Is this Heaven? Is this Heaven?"

Immortality was cruel; immortality with its own brand of spiritual Alzheimer's doubly so.

Best not to think of it, he reminded himself.

Eden blew upon the surface of the world with cold breath. Dust and sand rose, spiraled, and returned to earth with a whisper of contact. His home had been a simple, middle-class ranch house of red brick and white vinyl siding. The kitchen, the bedrooms, the living room, the dining area: all stages for fleeting emotions, some wonderful, others certainly not. Yet they had been *his* stages, places of ultimate shelter. Now, the land had risen six thousand feet, continents had shifted, everything had changed since it had belonged to him— and ultimately these results of time now brought to his attention, as they often had before, the inarguable fact that the small square of earth hadn't actually been his at all. He'd borrowed it long ago, and it had moved on.

Eden especially missed his tiny study, filled with the photographs of four generations, journals, prints, and books that had all served to mute and relieve the less agreeable aspects of his nature: impatience, anger, frustration, stubbornness.

His struggle to understand Sarah's ultimate acts of rejection, first adultery and then murder, had ended long ago. Which of his characteristics, if any, had driven her to such lengths? How much had he been to blame for her infidelity? For her hatred? How much had been her fault, how much his? It no longer mattered. His personal discoveries had taught him that the past, unlike almost everything else, could not be changed and was beyond manipulation.

As the wind blew cold over the rocky plain, Eden's thoughts turned, unexpectedly, to Sarah's garden. He had liked working it beside her during the first years of their marriage. Tomatoes, squash, lettuce, beans; all had grown ripe and strong under their careful tending. He missed the floppy straw hat Sarah had always worn when picking cherry tomatoes. He missed the tulip pattern on her garden gloves. Pulling the wisp of his form closer together against a chill he could not feel, Eden realized he even missed the ache of poison ivy blisters, always the only penalty for sharing such work with her.

The ink of night was lifting. Dawn was near, the once-pitch sky now a lightening ochre. Soon the red sun would rise, burning away the clouds to provide him an unobstructed view of its mighty, bloated majesty and the barren land beneath. The mold spoors that spread during the night withered, hissing, to die black and burnt, the meager remains leaving their cannibalistic descendants a form of shelter and sustenance in which to grow and reproduce when night came again.

"A new day," he muttered, thinking of poison ivy blisters, the lovely feel of the hurt and itch, and Sarah's careful administration of calamine lotion. "A new day."

Suddenly he paused, mind racing, scared. Poison ivy. Sarah's garden. Her hat. Sarah's gloves. Sarah's...

Sarah's face.

He couldn't remember it.

He stood motionless for a long time, the sun rising higher and higher in the white sky until it burned down directly overhead, scalding the land beneath him. Still he thought. Still no face came to him.

Finally, Eden looked at the sky, the ground, the horizon. Move on, he told himself. Move on and think later. To the south waited the tropics, lush jungles and warm rivers mocking paradise with visceral, dangerous life. To the north, desolation. East? The salt flats. West, the mountain ranges. And always waiting somewhere ahead and beyond, in every direction, was the sea.

Eden began to spin, fast, fast, faster, until he was oblivious to direction, the world a blur around him. When he stopped, he stopped suddenly, randomly. Everything was very quiet. Nothing living cried and there was no longer any wind. If he could have done so, he would have closed his eyes. If he could have done so, he would have slept. Instead, he began to move, not caring what lay ahead, the purpose of his thought like a vast, dark garden bearing fruit he knew, eventually, would have to be consumed.

The Key

"Again."

"Yes. Again."

The two men, both on the far side of middle age, stared at the abandoned house from the safety of the sidewalk. At their feet, on the edge of the overgrown front lawn, what had once been a cat lay rigid and desiccated, lips pulled back in a rictus sneer.

Richard Hawthorne spit.

Emil Braddock sighed.

"Something should be done," said Hawthorne.

"And what," said Braddock, "do you propose?"

Hawthorne stubbed the toe of his shoe against the cracked edge of the walk. "Well, Mayor, I have a couple ideas. Both involve demolition."

"Demolition involves people demolishing," Braddock said impatiently. "No one will do it. We've been *over* this. For years and *years*, we've been over this."

"We could hire people from out of town," Hawthorne continued. "They'll value the work."

"I can't have that on my conscience, Dick." Braddock looked up at the darkening sky. "Here, it's almost sunset. Let's go to Schooner's and grab a beer. I don't want to see her again."

"No. No, we can't have that. No. Me neither."

*****

For years, 101 Sycamore had been an unassuming house. Then, sometime during the course of its long history, things had taken a bad turn. The place was old and had been rented out as flats around the turn of the century, so the exact circumstances of the problem were hard to pinpoint. Too many people had lived there, and records were scarce. But shortly before half the men in town left for World War I, the house began to develop a reputation. By the time the surviving doughboys returned, it was abandoned.

And shunned.

Hawthorne took a pull of beer and sighed. "You know whose cat that was, Emil?"

Braddock nodded. "Your granddaughter's. Yes, I'm well aware. We've *all* lost pets to it, Dick. You can't take it personally."

Hawthorne leaned forward. "It's not about *taking it personally*, goddamn it. It's about taking care of this problem *once and for all*. The children of this town should be able to grow up without having to pay for therapy later! They should—"

"Lower your voice."

Hawthorne looked around. "Sorry," he said, addressing Schooner's few other patrons, then turned back to his drink. "It's just…this town is *dying*, Emil. When the kids grow up they move away and don't come back."

"That happens in lots of small towns, especially when the mines close."

"But we all know it happens more in Still Creek. And we all know why."

They were silent, both ruminating on encounters they wished to forget. After dark, the ghost that haunted 101 Sycamore was indiscriminate—it appeared to whoever happened to be passing by—staring out this window, leering out that, peering from the rotting cupola. One didn't forget the sight.

And then there were the animals.

The house, as anyone who chose to venture near quickly discovered, was invariably ringed with dead birds, squirrels, rabbits and chipmunks. Sometimes the bodies of fox, deer, dogs, and cats could also be seen, slowly putrefying in the brown, knee-high grass and weeds. And beneath them, like rotting strata, was layer after layer of desiccated skin, matted fur, and weather-stained bones.

"I saw it when I was seven." Hawthorne emptied the last of his pint and clunked the glass down on the scarred table. "That was the first time. I remember like it was yesterday. So many memories fade but that one doesn't. That says something, huh?"

Braddock grunted.

"I was walking home from Johnny Crane's. Remember him? Killed in the war? Well, he had a late birthday party. It was a *great* party. I'd won a goldfish. Dark had fallen and on I walked, poking at the bag, not heeding anything else, and before I knew it that damned house was on my left and I happened to glance up. And there she was, standing on the front porch. Her body glowed. She had on a mildewed white dress. Her arms were folded across her chest like a corpse in a coffin, and they were beastly thin, and her hair was all tangled and wet. And her eyes—"

"Oh shut up, Dick. I know about the eyes. We all do."

"There *were* no eyes, just huge, gaping sockets. And the lips were gone—her mouth a big, bloodless gash for her teeth to poke through."

Braddock shook his head. Once Hawthorne started, all you could do was be patient and let him finish.

"Well, I stood there a moment, thinking it was some kind of prank, then remembered the stories, all those horrible stories, and that's when she opened her mouth and shrieked.

"I dropped the goldfish. I remember the splat, the water gushing out on the sidewalk and the fish flapping around silently, pulling in air, dying, and then I ran. I ran like never before. I ran and I ran, on and on, until I slammed through the front door of my house and started hollering to wake the dead. Daddy had to throw a blanket over me and tackle me to the floor before I calmed.

"For weeks following I woke up screaming, night after night. Seeing her, it deadened the world for me. Every time I started enjoying something I remembered her, remembered that *shriek*, and all the fun went out of it. I wasn't the same for years. And Emil, little Barney Stover saw her just last week. He's only *five years old*, Emil. *Think* of it."

Braddock rubbed his eyes with his thumb and forefinger. "Maggie Stover was an idiot, taking her boy for a walk at dusk— never a brain in that pretty head of hers. I've always said so." He paused. "It doesn't do good to talk of it. Talk's cheap. There's nothing we can do."

"You're right. Talk *is* cheap. People want a man of action, and you're mayor of this town. Haven't you heard the grumbles? Unless I'm mistaken, there's an election coming up and Sam Kolbrenner's chomping at the bit for a piece of you. It'd pay to listen to me."

That silenced Braddock. Glowering, he sat back.

"No demolition," continued Hawthorne. "No out-of-town contractors. Fine. I understand. That leaves one option."

"What?" Braddock said, looking like he'd just sucked a lemon.

"Let's you and me head on down to the gas station."

*****

Wheezing and out of breath, Braddock and Hawthorne crouched behind a dead bush in the deepening twilight.

"I don't see how this is going to get me re-elected," Braddock growled. "I'm more likely to be arrested. Imagine what Kolbrenner would do with *that*."

"A good deed doesn't go unnoticed," Hawthorne replied, fiddling with the cap of his gas can. "Word spreads through odd channels. The town will thank you."

"Sure, sure. You take the front of the house. I'll take the back. And for God's sake, make it quick and keep your eyes down. If that thing appears on the porch, I'll shit myself."

"That'll make two of us."

"Go."

They went.

Ten minutes later, a warm, bright glow flickered all down Sycamore Street and outshone the full moon.

*****

"It's gone, Mayor. Every bit of it."

Emil Braddock stood on the sidewalk staring up at the smoldering ruins. A crowd milled around with him, over a hundred all told. *Like a nice day at the fair*, he thought. *Should I make a speech?*

Truth be told, he felt like it. He felt *good*. As he looked at the faces in the crowd—familiar, all of them—he saw nothing but relief, quiet pleasure…and approval. They couldn't know, could they? But like Hawthorne said, "Word spreads through odd channels."

"Yes, it's gone," he replied, turning to Mrs. Perkins, the old lady who'd had the misfortune of living in 103 Sycamore for over two decades. "You have nothing to worry about now, Dorothy. Nothing at all. You can pull the boards off your western windows and walk down the street on warm summer nights." He smiled. "This is one fire I can't feel too awfully bad about."

The relieved chuckle that went up from the crowd stayed with him all day and into the evening. It sustained him, lulled him, perked him up and pleased him.

Late in the evening, after a relaxing supper, he called Hawthorne to tell him about it—to tell him about how he'd been *right*—and to thank him.

He smiled, thinking how surprised Hawthorne would be. Braddock hardly ever said "Thank you," so people knew that when he did, it really meant something.

But Hawthorne didn't answer.

"Funny," he said, and stumped back down the hall to the living room as the sirens from the fire station began to wail. Hawthorne *always* answered his phone after dark; he never went out, unless with him. And the fire station? They never conducted drills after sundown. A real fire, just a day after the one he'd set? What were the odds?

His ruminations were cut short by a startled yell, then a scream, then a dog barking frantically before yelping and falling silent.

"Something," he murmured in his darkened house, "isn't right."

Another noise, persistent and severe: frantic pounding on the front door. Bemused, Braddock answered it.

"We never thought!" Hawthorne said, hair wild, eyes wilder.

"Get in here, dummy, and calm down."

"No! Not in there. Not *anywhere*. We have to leave!"

"What are you talking about? What's going on?"

Braddock stepped out onto his porch. The whole town seemed to be coming alive in what should have been a quiet, peaceful night: lights blinking on, doors slamming, a scream, a cry, the screeching of brakes…

"*Every animal dead in every house, every yard, every field!*"

"What! *What?*" Braddock dragged the frantic, protesting man inside and shut the door.

"It's loose," Hawthorne panted, hand over his heart. "Burning it? We were wrong, Braddock. All that smoke, all that ash. I didn't think! It landed…why, it landed *everywhere*."

Braddock's eyebrows furrowed. His lips pulled back. Then his face went slack.

"You mean—"

Hawthorne's eyes widened, focusing on something over Braddock's left shoulder. His lips turned blue. Silently, almost gracefully, he collapsed.

"You mean," Braddock continued, voice surprisingly calm, "that instead of destroying it, we gave it the Key to the Town."

He sighed. Something rustled behind him.

"This doesn't bode well for Election Day," he muttered.

Braddock turned around.

Seventeen

Seventeen years. He didn't know where to begin, so he began with Google, typing in her name and the last address he had. She and her family were long gone. Then the college she'd attended. Nothing. Then the city nearby. Still nothing, and God knew where she lived now. She was probably married, too. If so, her old name wouldn't be much help anyway.

Memories flood back at strange times. Michael knew that. Married six years, father to a three-month-old son, and suddenly, or perhaps slowly but insidiously, his thoughts had shifted back to the past. High school. The summer before he started college. And those first few months of new classes in a great, strange place where beginnings had ushered in endings and the future, quietly but irrevocably, had begun to narrow.

"You're online an awful lot now," Zola said, walking into the garage he'd converted into a den a few years before. "Want to come say goodnight to Danny and watch *Extreme Home Makeover* with me?"

He looked up from his laptop with a sigh, surprised by how much the interruption annoyed him.

"Sure. I'll be right up."

"Does that mean one minute or twenty?"

"I said I'll be right up."

The hunt hadn't started as an obsession, and he wasn't certain it had actually become one now, but certainly an urgency had crept into his searching since Danny's birth. Instead of merely checking his email and CNN.com when he went online, Michael often spent his rare free time searching old lists, class reunion bulletins, Facebook postings, and business profiles. Even as potential leads led nowhere, the memories that the hunt brought forward remained vivid for the first time in a generation—a catalyst between the years which left behind a dull, lasting ache that rose up throughout his busy days.

"Swenson," he typed into Facebook for the tenth time as the baby began to cry upstairs. "Mary Swenson."

Four dozen matches came up. A fourth of them had photographs, none of which were hers. The others were too young, too old, or had no information posted beside them. As before. As always.

Sighing again, he closed up the computer and went to change Jacob's diaper.

Afterward, he fell asleep on the chair across from his wife half an hour before Ty Pennington asked a happy, newly-saved family to yell out, "Move That Bus!" When he woke up, she was already in bed asleep.

Michael was grateful.

*****

Things took a downturn in the weeks that followed. Of that there could be no doubt, however much Michael and Zola tried to ignore it.

Finally, one evening after a silent dinner, Zola said, "You don't like the baby."

She might as well have slapped him in the face.

"That's ridiculous," he said sharply. "I can't believe you said that. Why? Why would you even *think* that?"

"Because you don't tuck him in. You let me hold him most of the time. You resent changing him or feeding him." Tears formed in her eyes but her anger kept them from falling. "For years you talked about how much you wanted this, and now that you have it, you don't."

"That's ridiculous," he repeated. "Simply ridiculous. And malicious, too. I can't believe you have the *nerve...*"

Zola left the room, leaving him with racing thoughts and a profound silence.

In that silence, Michael realized that despite his denial, Zola had a point. There was something about the baby that bothered him. Not the baby itself, but in *having* one. Something that had caught him off guard and left him without the faintest idea of what to do.

Going to the bathroom and pressing a damp washcloth to his face, Michael looked in the mirror. What he saw shocked him: thinning hair, beginning to gray at the temples, and the start of a sagging double-chin. It made him think of something—some*one*.

He knocked on the locked bedroom door. "I'm going to see my father," he said. He waited for an answer, but none came.

*****

"Calling me out for a beer at ten o'clock at night? What you do, lock yourself out of the house?"

Michael smiled in spite of himself. "No, just looking for some answers."

"No one ever found them in the bottom of a glass," the old man said, lifting his mug. "But as the barflies all say, it never hurts to look."

For several minutes they drank in silence. Michael tapped his fingernail against his glass until his father reached out a hand to stop him.

"OK, what gives?"

"Dad," said Michael. That was all that came. He tried again. "Dad."

"That's me."

"Did you ever…I mean, have you…oh, it's all so damned stupid. I don't even know what to ask. I'm wasting your time."

His father polished off his Yuengling and asked for another. "Yeah, you really know how to ruin my night. *Dateline* was on. I don't know how I'll get over missing *that* again." He grunted. "OK, don't ask questions, just tell me what's happened."

Michael nodded. "The baby. He's three months old. I should be happy, and I *am*, but instead of wanting to spend time with him, I find myself trying to get away. And I spend all my free time on the Internet, trying to track down someone I haven't seen in years."

His father raised his eyebrows. "Who?"

He sighed. "Mary Swenson."

"Mary Swenson? Hmm…oh yeah, the girl you dated your senior year in high school? *That* Mary Swenson?"

"Yeah. That Mary Swenson."

"What's she up to?"

"I have no idea. I can't find out a thing about her. But I keep trying and I don't know why."

His father nodded, rubbing his gray beard. "Let me ask you three questions. The first two are 'yes' or 'no' questions, so they're not hard. But you have to be honest. Got it?"

Michael nodded.

"Question One: do you love your wife?"

"Of *course* I do."

"Yes or no, please."

"Yes."

"All right, then." His father took a swig of his second beer. "Question Two: do you like your job?"

"Teaching? Sure, most of the time."

"That's a 'yes.' OK, Question Three, and this is the toughie: *why* do you want to find Mary Swenson?"

Michael grunted into his mug and shook his head. "I don't know, Dad. I guess that's what I wanted to ask you."

"Just do your best."

"Because…because, well, I want to see her. I want to know what she's up to. See what she looks like. See what she's done with her life."

"Bonus question, then. When you think of Mary Swenson, what comes to mind?"

"I don't get what you mean."

His father grunted. "I mean just what I said."

Michael gazed at the scarred surface of the bar for a long time. "The Fourth of July," he said at last. "When we sat on the hill at the top of the street and watched the fireworks. And Senior Prom. And the dress she wore. And the smell of her favorite perfume. And me giving her a ten-dollar locket with a rose. And us walking by the stream in Spring Creek Park. And, oh, God, that whole *summer*. And she was *beautiful*. It was all so new. Anything was possible. It was all perfect."

He fell silent.

His father looked at him steadily. "And then, at the end of that summer, you broke up. You went away to college and she stayed behind, and you started dating someone else and so did she."

"That's right."

"And you never saw her again."

"That's right."

His father leaned in close. "I'm sixty-seven years old. I've done some stupid things, but I've learned a bit along the way, too. So here's what I'll do, for what it's worth. I'm going to give you two quotes by two of my favorite writers. You can take them or leave them, and then I want you to go home to your loving wife and cute little kiddo. Got it?"

Michael nodded.

"Then listen close…"

And the older man spoke, paused, and spoke some more.

*****

There was a sleepless night, a restless morning, then late afternoon gave way to evening again.

After a tense dinner, Michael clomped downstairs, plopped down in front of the computer, and checked his email.

No new messages, save one.

The note was from an old high school friend, Andy Collins. Michael faintly remembered sending him a brief line a few weeks before. The reply read,

Hi, Mikey!

It's good to hear from you. So you're trying to track down Mary, huh? Believe it or not, my wife works with her in Sagaponak. She gave me Mary's email address to pass along to you. So here you go. Hope this helps and that all's well.

Andy

Below the note was the email address. Michael, cold sweat beading his brow, clicked it. A blank email opened, addressed to Mary. He could write anything he wanted. Anything. And then seventeen years of silence would be broken by a thunderclap click of the mouse.

He paused, fingers hovering over the keyboard.

"'You can't go home again,'" his father had told him. "Thomas Wolfe. Ever read him?"

Slowly, his fingertips descended. They rested lightly on the keys. *I can try*, he thought.

His father's voice again: "Remember, 'This moment and all moments last forever.' Kurt Vonnegut."

Michael closed his eyes. His fingers trembled, knuckles white. Electric fire flowed through his nerve endings.

Time slowed.

"You can't go home again," he murmured, the words measured and cadenced, "but all moments last forever."

With a deep push, he exhaled.

His hands drew away from the keyboard.

He leaned down and turned off the computer.

"She is seventeen," he said softly. Upstairs, the baby began to cry. He headed up to help Zola tend him.

"And somewhere, to someone," he added, clicking off the light and closing the door, "so am I."

Miss Riley's Lot

How 'bout when my big brother Chris took me up on Uncanny Hill during hunting season and let me watch while he and his buds shot a woman?

I was fifteen, and it was the day after Thanksgiving, and Chris, he was nineteen that year, a real bruiser who liked to drink and get in brawls around town, but he got along with me bettern most.

Well, he and Jim and Dale, that's his friends, they took me up in the woods above town, and further in, deep in, until Uncanny Hill reared up, and then Chris ran up ahead to the clearing, he had us wait, and came back and said, all breathless, "She's there, OK."

And I said, "Who's that?"

And he said, "You'll see," and nudged his pals.

We went on up the hill together until it broke clear from the woods and there was wheat all over on the top, and there was an old woman sittin on a rotten stump. She was all wrapped up in a shabby black-knit shawl and had on black stockings, and a black bonnet, a natty old black dress, and a tattered, dirty pair of black old wooden clogs. It was like she was in mournin or something, dressed up so. White hair streamed out from 'neath her shawl in long, thin strands. Her face, oh, it was like lookin at one of them maps with mountains on it, the kind that stick up a little. And her eyes, I remember when we got close thinkin how they musta once been green, but now was all faded, kinda olive-colored, and red round the edges.

"Well, Chris, that's Miss Riley!" I shouted.

All the other fellas laughed long and loud at that, but I can't say as I knew why, 'cept we wasn't supposed to say a word to her cause she was 'touched,' like they put it, and she had always kinda skeered me. She liked to clump around town now and again, but 'specially out in the woods and through the fields, and she muttered and laughed and smiled like there was somethin real sad and unspeakable behind those four black teeth of hers.

"You ain't frightened, now, are you Jeff?" Chris asked, nudging Dale.

"No, no, I ain't a bit."

"That's a good whelp. Now you follow close and watch real good."

So they moseyed on down to Miss Riley, me followin behind, and Miss Riley came clumpin up the hill aways to meet 'em, and Jim, he said, "How's it goin, Miss Riley?" And Miss Riley, she stopped and smiled that smile, then laughed, and it sounded like a squalling baby. And she said, "I'll show you a thing or two!" then turned and walked on down the hill agin to her dead ol stump and took a seat.

"Here now, whose turn is it?" Jim asked.

"I thought we said it was mine," Chris said.

"No, I don't remember that," Dale said.

"Three's better'n one!" Miss Riley piped up, and I thought to myself, *What's she runnin her gums about?* And then I found out.

"You say so," Chris said, and set his .30 caliber against her chest, just as Jim and Dale did the same.

And then I'll be damned if they didn't lift up the safeties, pull the triggers, and the world went up in smoke and thunder.

What I felt, it's kinda hard to put in words. All time, it seemed to hang on edge, and I let out a whoop and a cry and fell on my knees as Miss Riley, she blowed backwards, knocked straight outta her shoes, and a fine red mist sprayed the ground, my brother, his buds, my face. Then Miss Riley just lay all still, her chest pretty well gone to glory, and her bones and innards all on view, and I closed my eyes and pinched my arm and tried to wake myself up, but acourse I couldn't cause I was waked already.

That then is what happened to begin with, and it's bad enough. But with my eyes still clamped shut so tight I saw stars, I next heard a rustling and a whispering and a grunt from one of the boys, and then high above it all, shrill and clear as winter water, Miss Riley's laughter.

I opened my eyes real slow, 'cause I didn't want to see no more, but there's no way I could keep 'em shut after hearing *that*. And what did I see but Miss Riley standing there in the knee-high wheat, puttin her shoes back on, balancin from one leg to another. Her hair, it was all wild cause her bonnet was knocked clean off by the blast, and her face was covered in blood, but she was alive, though I could still see her innards, and they was waving as she moved.

There's no point lyin, I passed out cold on the ground at that, and when I came to Chris was lookin down at me and shakin his head.

"Sorry 'bout that, fry. We didn't figure you'd take it so ruff, though it *is* a bit of a trial when you don't see it coming. But that's always been the best way to let a newbie know what's goin on with Miss Riley, since no one'd believe otherwise."

I wiped my mouth and sat up. Jim and Dale were outta sight, but Miss Riley was sittin on her stump again and starin at me with those faded olive eyes of hers, smiling that hoary black-toothed grin.

"You're dead," I said, and pointed at her. "You gotta be."

"Ha!" she spat.

"You saw her chest," Chris said. "Look agin."

I peeked over, and that big old hole was still there in her gullet, but it didn't look too bad from what it was before.

"She'll get better," Chris said. "She always do."

"Come on by an do the same any time!" Miss Riley cackled at me, but I couldn't look at her again, an didn't feel too steady on my legs.

Chris put a hand on my shoulder. "Come on, let's get back to the house and go for a drive. You'll get your answers. It's time."

*****

We got back to the house and didn't even go inside at all, but went straight for the old Model A Chris'd bought from Doc Weaver for twenty clams. And when we was inside and rolling down the road toward nowheres, Chris started talking.

"Here's the thing about Miss Riley," Chris said, staring ahead. "How old you say she is?"

"Eighty-five," I said, cause that was the oldest I could imagine.

Chris shook his head. "That end of town she lives in? Back when Grampa was a boy there was a big flood, and a heap of people died. You know that, don't you? You better, the way Gramma keeps on about it. OK, so most everything from there was either warshed away or left to rot, so nobody'd have to think about all the people that got kilt, and so they wouldn't disrespect nobody's memory by building it all up again. Except Miss Riley stayed, because she was there then, and already old, and she lived through it even though she was swept away more'n a mile. She came back when no one else did."

"That flood was almost a hundred years ago!"

Chris nodded, keeping his eyes on the road. "I ain't saying anyone gets it. And I guess you're wondering how she does it? Well she doesn't do much of nothing, as fur as I can tell. She just can't damn well lay herself down and die.

"Before Grampa passed on when you was little, he took me out for my first hunt and showed me what I showed you today. Miss Riley, she goads hunters into doin it, and finally long ago one of 'em did it for the first time, and ever since it's been kinda traditional-like for some of them to take a shot at her every year at the start of the season. Good luck, they say.

"But Miss Riley, I know why she keeps at 'em. She keeps at 'em cause she keeps hopin one of 'em will do her in right and kill her. It don't happen, though. Sometimes it takes longer and sometimes it takes shorter, but she always gets better. Even so, she won't never give up."

We was both quiet for a bit, and I watched the blue November sky meet the road as Chris kept drivin.

"How come she don't die?" I finally asked.

Chris sighed, then shook his head and wrinkled his nose. "There was talk of great sadfulness and all the kind of things you'd think'd go along with such a queer situ'ation. Somethin 'bout her son gettin kilt and her swearin to stay until he got back, and him not gettin back, so her stayin on and on. But now she's ready to go, and been ready for a long bit now."

"You think that's true?"

"Mebbe. But one thing I know is when folks don't get the ins and outs about any given thing, they make up somethin so they think they do. And that's what happened, I guess. But ya know what I think? I think there *ain't* always no reason for everythin. I think she don't die cause she don't die. That's her lot, jus like it's some's lot to die young. She's durn tired, has been since anyone alive's knowed her, but that's her lot."

That stuck like glue, and I come to think maybe Chris was right bout a story makin people feel better. I like to think the tales was true, meself. They give what happened to her some reason, bad or crazy besides. Better than none, for sure. But I'll never know one way or t'other, and so be it.

Chris snuck a glance at me. "So you're probably wonderin why the hell you ever need know bout all this business. Well, you've heard stories told, and at your age you'd be hearin more shortly as all that talk begins to take hold in you. And that'd be a damn shame, 'cause privacy's a right few don't deserve. So most of you boys need to be told, and have it all out in the open, and understand how things is, and that way you won't need to talk bout it ever agin unless you're careful who with and when. You see how things stand?"

I guess I was starin out ahead at me and didn't say nothin fast enough, cause Chris reached over and punched my arm real hard. "You see how things stand?" he repeated.

"Yeah, I guess I see how things stand."

He nodded. "That's what I wanna hear. Now, she's harmless, I'll swear by that. She's odd but she won't hurt you. So if you wanna take a shot—"

"No!"

"That's your good choice, either way. But if you wanna keep away from her, there's a couple things you should know. First, next time you go swimming down at Uncanny's deep hole on a hot summer day, better be careful not to go too far underwater. I've heard it told she sets herself at the bottom of the pool with a rock tied to her ankle. It's her way of keepin cool, since drowning's death, and she can't die. So if you feel someone grab you, that's what it is. And if you don't want to get grabbed, use the hole downstream by the hill.

"Second, if you ever walk in the woods and see her hangin from the old oak tree over on the edge of Mr. Scot's, don't get scared. She do that sometimes, too. You just ain't ever seen it yet, but you will, if you keep on huntin.

"And third? Once in a while, usually at night, she'll climb up the library tower and take a leap. It's the highest buildin in town. She don't do that often any more, not since Sheriff Rogers had the borough add on that grate. And she usually only does it when she's been hittin the bottle, and no one in town's allowed to sell her any hard stuff anymore, neither. But you might see that, too, so it's best to keep one eye out and the other open." He paused and chuckled real dry. "That way she won't land on you."

We drove back home just in time for Ma's supper, and it was good but I didn't have much stomach for it. And Chris and me, we never spoke of Miss Riley again.

*****

What happened after that? you might well ask. Well, time fades old frights. I had a good group of friends back then, Philip and John and Drake, and as we growed up we hunted together. Now we was good boys for the most part, even if we got in our share of trouble.

Still, good or no, we was also of the age that liked to walk the line with things, and death is the biggest line of all. And so one early Saturday we was back in the woods hunting, and came up Uncanny Hill, and Miss Riley was there all right, settin on her stump, and she came up on us like she came up on my brother, and said, "You wanna go? I'll show you a thing or two!"

And so we talked a fair bit about it, then Drake went up and shot her right in the gullet.

The old woman staggered back a step, and her face screwed up in pain, and she let out a wollop of a holler, almost as loud as Drake's, but she didn't drop, and when she looked down and saw her stomach, she started laughin, then walked off like nothing much was the matter. Just as before.

"Now you's a man!" she crowed, hobbling away. "Now you's a man."

I gotta admit I shot her too when I saw her next, and the scary thing is, it felt *good* in a way I don't understand. But I can't say as I felt like a man. In fact, I kinda scared myself, doing that thing.

And so we'd see her around, and got used to the idea that she couldn't die, and life went on. She was crazy and not worth talkin to, otherwise I guess I'da tried to get a better thing goin with her. Knowing someone like that? Couldn't help but be interestin, but she never had nothing to say. And she was a bit of a creep, stalking around in woods and hiding in lakes and hangin from trees and laughing and smiling with those rotten teeth. And that's all there'd be to the story, 'cept for one more thing that happened a few years later.

There was a house up on Barnaby Street, about three blocks from my family's little place, empty about fifteen years. Well, fifteen years is a long time, and it started fallin down in places, but us boys used it for all kindsa things. We went even though we knowed it wasn't a safe place. There was wires and electrical fixins and rotten wood all about.

Shortly after I turned seventeen, me and my friends was up there one afternoon with some young ladies, and we was havin our own party in a way, and someone dropped a match in the wrong place. A bunch of old heavy yellow curtains caught fire, and before we knowed it we was runnin for our lives out into the open air. It was December, so I remember the cold of the day and the heat of the fire hittin each other, and then I heard the screams, but they warn't like those of us who was runnin. They was of pain, and they was from inside that house.

I was in quite a state, and my lungs was all filled with smoke, but I looked around and took in who was missing, and it was Drake. He was still inside. But I looked at the house, and knew I couldn't do a flat thing. There wasn't no way I could get back in there. The whole doorframe was blazin. All I could do was cover my ears, and cry, and watch, and wait for what I felt sure would happ'n.

And then Miss Riley showed up.

She came striding up the walk in her old black clogs, and she handed one of the cryin girls her tatty ol shawl, and there was a look in her faded eyes I never saw in nobody's before or since. "Here's sumpin I haven't tried!" she said, and she didn't stop walkin, just strode on in through the flaming door.

There was a long moment when nothin happened, except Drake's screams stopped, and we all feared the worst. But then out comes Miss Riley, and the fringe of her dress was burning, and her face was all smudged and black, but she had Drake slung over her back like a cord of wood, his legs held tight in her wiry old arms.

She dropped him down on the sidewalk, and I caught his head in my hands, and he was breathin. His face was black but it was only soot, and I guessed right it was the smoke that got him mostly, and that he'd fainted dead away. And sure enough he got better with only a few bitty burns and some black in his lungs.

But Miss Riley, she had plans. She took a deep breath, and my *lan* she looked so sad. And she looked us up and down, and then suddenly her eyes blazed bright, and they didn't look so old, and with a wide smile and a screech she ran back toward the smoking front door. A big lick of fire reached out to meet her, an a second later her white hair was nothin but burnin light, and the light wreathed around her head, and then she was gone.

We could hear her laughin for a long time, and her shadow flitted by the windows, and we could see her burnin in the flames, and then the whole house, it come down and she warn't laughin no more.

I figgered Miss Riley would come out chucklin again soon enough. She'd taken worse in her day, I thought. But when the ambulance came I was taken away to the hospital in Plumville, and didn't see no more of it. But I heard the fire department got there right fast, and it took ages to put out all the smolder, and the next mornin they dug under all the mess and rubble, and there she was, but there warn't much left, and she wasn't movin a whit. And I heard it said a great winter wind came up ahead of a storm not far behind, and it scattered her ashes all over town and beyond.

Well, it looked like the tired ol lady'd found her rest at last, and I must say I felt mighty good about it, even if town was a little less *interestin* without her in it. And Drake? He went on talkin to everyone who asked bout how she saved his life, which a course she had.

That said, I guess I was twenty when I first heard it.

Sure, it kept away for a good few years, but then there it was, and there was no hidin from it, and there still ain't. Not in town, and not in the woods, neither.

It was laughter, and it came from nowhere but the wind. Sometimes it came on fast and left quick, sometimes it seemed to circle 'bout the house or down the street and back and stay awhile. And sometimes it was cryin I heard, high and hard one time, soft and tired-like another. Course, it coulda been just the wind, and not sumpin else carried on it, say like ashes. The wind can be funny sometimes, soundin like a person. But how many times you ever recognize the voice? How many times it sound like it's singin through the dust of four black teeth?

So that's old Miss Riley's lot, and I guess some kinds of livin can be just as scary as dyin. Truth be told, I ain't half as scared of droppin dead now as I once was. No, not half as scared.

Time to Go Home

The movers took the last furniture out of his grandparents' house before nightfall, and then it was empty for the first time in seventy years. People had lived and died full lives, and the house had not known silence. Now it knew that, and it knew darkness.

John Haggerty shivered, feeling both on the back of his neck.

He stalked the empty halls and rooms. They didn't echo because of the worn carpets. To him, they did. But the emptiness, however it sounded, was necessary. Only now, vacant, could he gauge the true condition of the house and decide whether or not to keep it.

What he found did not please him.

A great crack ran across the archway between the living and dining rooms. The corners of the carpeted floors in the study sponged beneath prodding fingers. Dank basement timbers hosted termite borings. Reams of wallpaper sloughed off walls, freed from behind bookshelves and cabinets, the air a catalyst for dead glue to give way.

John surveyed these problems and a score of others in silence, pausing occasionally to make a note on his Blackberry or mop his face. Once finished, he stepped out into the gathering shadows of a late-June afternoon and flipped open his cell phone.

No signal. In Still Creek, there never was.

*****

He went for a walk. He knew the streets and side-streets well, and there weren't many. A walk around Still Creek, through all byways and alleys, took only an hour. During that hour he thought, and the more he thought the more hardened his resolve became.

No one in the family felt he should buy his grandparents' house. His uncle thought the idea "sentimental nonsense," his mother "a money pit," his father "a waste"—and his wife, more bluntly, "the hallmark of a true idiot."

But as John turned onto Church Street off Main, then down to Pugh from Church, breathing in the smell of mown grass and late-afternoon backyard bonfires, he made up his mind: the house, regardless of how much it cost, would remain in the family.

He turned back onto Main Street and walked until the house came into view again. In the long-shadowed light, he half-expected to see his grandmother framed in the screen door, waiting for him like she always had, before Alzheimer's, then death had taken her away.

The sun reflected off the door's window glass.

John squinted.

The door opened.

And there she was.

*****

"Come on in, supper's almost ready!"

Light-headed, throat dry, he stumbled up the front steps and into the house.

His grandmother stood before him, a paragon of health. Black hair, flower-print dress, apron and glasses, light hazel eyes. Seeing her now, four feet in front of him, was like finding something familiar that had been lost for years—sight and memory had to reconcile the object—the *person*—before mind and reality could meet.

They did so now, and John stepped forward. *A ghost.* He touched her arm. *No. Real!*

"What's the matter, John?"

"Nothing," he said slowly. She looked a quarter-century younger than the last time he'd seen her. "Just…you had some flour on your arm."

His grandmother smiled. "Here now, shut the door. It's cold outside."

He turned back, surprised. Night had come, and snow fell steadily upon a sea of drifting white. Smoke rose from chimneys all down the street. Luminaria lit every driveway. Golden Christmas stars shone through tinsel on every telephone pole.

Numbly, he shut the door on the winter night.

"All day you've wanted to open presents, and now you're stalling! We have to eat if we want the strength to tackle that mountain beneath the tree." Grandma bustled off to the kitchen. "Your place is all ready," she called over her shoulder. "You can sit next to your Grandpa. And remember, don't give Sandy any turkey!"

Mouth working silently, John stepped into the living room.

Sandy, his dog, dead twenty years, lifted her head from its place of rest beneath the piano bench and eyed him drowsily before flopping back down again. On that bench sat his mother, twenty-five years younger, playing "O Holy Night"—fingers nimble, no arthritis. On a nearby couch his father talked with Great-Uncle Tom, who'd died of heart failure when John was 21. And listening quietly from the overstuffed armchair by the reading lamp—

"Grandpa," John mouthed.

The old man listened quietly to the conversations around him, saying little, but his presence filled the room like that of a benign king: John's hero of heroes, who had died of a heart attack in the February snow a week before John's tenth birthday.

Before anyone except Sandy and his grandmother noticed he was there, John stepped quickly up the stairs and raced down the hallway to the bathroom. Breathing fast and heavily, he sank to his knees by the eagle-clawed tub.

It was the carpet that brought him back to himself—the fuzzy yellow strands, so familiar, that he ran through his clutching fingers.

Gingerly, he got to his feet. Ever so slowly the world stopped spinning. He looked in the bathroom mirror.

The face of a nine-year-old boy met his gaze.

He looked down at his hands. Big, worn, and glazed with years of work and living, he turned his palms up, then let them fall limply to his sides.

Through all his tumbling thoughts, one broke out louder than the rest. *Dinner's waiting*, it reminded him.

Dinner's waiting.

Five minutes later, John stepped down the stairs and joined his family at the table.

It was a table surrounded by a dozen faces, its surface warm and breathing with the good smells he'd forgotten or half-forgotten, and he ate like he never had as a real child—two helpings, then two slices of pie washed down with milk and orange pop. He sat on the wooden bench pulled in from the kitchen, wedged between his grandparents, his dog beneath his feet, his young parents laughing about distant memories still recent to them, to everyone except him, and soon all his panic and disorientation fell away, lulled to sleep by his grandfather's beloved voice and the smell of his great aunt's green bean casserole. The frosted windowpanes fogged with steam. Uncles laughed. Cousins argued. And he, now the youngest again, thought of what he should say—all the things he'd wanted to tell these people which had come to mind far, far too late; all the questions that, through the years, he'd wanted to ask yet hadn't... What had they *been?*

He remained silent. But in the ebb and flow of the meal John was aware, from time to time, of his grandfather's gaze upon him.

After dinner, it was back to the living room and the Christmas tree, all white tinsel and red bulbs, angel decorations and gold lights. And presents piled beneath it. And he, the youngest, to hand them out.

He did, enjoying the old job like no other.

Then, sitting in a giant circle, everyone took turns opening them. For John that meant clothes offset by a baseball glove and a fossil kit, a new pencil case for school and half a dozen *Star Wars* figures.

I still have these somewhere, he thought. *Packed away, battle-damaged, accessories lost. And the baseball glove—stolen in sixth grade by Bert Winger!*

After all the presents had been opened and a second round of desserts eaten, cousins began to trickle off home and the house took on a drowsy feel. His parents spoke softly with Grandma and a few remaining uncles and aunts in the living room. Sandy, a bow on her head, slept once again beneath the piano bench. And John, forgotten for the moment, stole out to the back porch, dark but for the lights shining through the kitchen windows, and took a deep breath of cold winter air.

"Hi, Grandpa," he said.

"Hello yourself!" The old man, tall even when sitting, waved him over to the wicker chair beside him. His breath, raspy from the Black Lung that eventually killed him, sawed through the silence of the night in a quiet rhythm. They sat side by side for a long time, there in his grandfather's favorite place, until Grandpa finally spoke again.

"Tell me, John, what's on your mind?"

John turned to look at him. The old man gazed back intently.

"I..." He stopped, started again, fell silent.

"Let me help," his grandfather continued. "All day you've been different. Your mannerisms, your smile, even your appetite!" He chuckled at John's expression. "Surprised I noticed?"

"No," John said immediately. "You always saw everything."

"*Saw.* Past-tense." His grandfather nodded. "There's the rub. Eyes, John. A famous dead writer once said eyes are windows to the soul. And your eyes? They, too, are different this evening."

John looked out into the darkened back yard, clear moonlight shining down on a perfect blanket of glittering snow. In the middle of the yard he could just make out the shadow of the old maple tree that lightning had struck down when he was nineteen.

"Grandpa, can I ask you something?"

"You know you can."

John licked his lips. "What if I told you that a man, thirty-five years old, was cleaning up his grandparents' former home and deciding whether or not to sell it. And that after taking a walk around the block to clear his head, his grandmother, who...who..." He cast a sideways glance at his grandfather. The old man looked back at him steadily.

"...who was no longer around, *answered the door*. And that he walked out of a June afternoon in 2008 and into a winter evening in—"

"1983," Grandpa finished, leaning forward and smiling faintly. "And what if I told you that when a certain old man looked at his nine year-old grandson a quarter-hour to midnight on Christmas Night, 1983, he saw a thirty-five year-old man looking back at him from behind his face?"

John swallowed. "I'd say he was a very perceptive old man whose grandson still loves him very much."

Another long silence, save for the old man's breathing and a slight rocking of the chairs. Then:

"Grandpa, why am I here?"

The old man coughed, a great racking cough that shook his body. John winced.

"I'm fine," said his grandfather. "But I don't have all the answers. Why am *I* here? Either of us? Brought together out of time. No, no answers."

John sighed.

"But if I had to *guess*?"

Now it was John's turn to lean forward.

"I'd guess you're here to say goodbye."

The breath kicked out of John's body. "*No.*"

His grandfather nodded. "John, I've always said I want to live to see you graduate high school. From the look in your eyes tonight, that doesn't—*didn't* —work out." He paused. "There were so many things I could have told you during those later years," he said. "So much advice, some of it even good."

He smiled, and John, after an unsteady moment, did likewise.

Grandpa glanced at the white face of his gold watch. "Ten minutes to midnight," he mused. "So I have to choose my advice carefully. Something tells me that at midnight, this gift will have run its course. So here."

He cleared his throat and stood up. He opened the screen door. Together they walked around to the front sidewalk, where they could take in the whole panorama of the house.

"When I was in college, working nights in the mines and taking classes by day, I took an acting course. Did you know that?"

John shook his head.

"Well, I wasn't any good. Instead, happily, a teacher's life for me."

"And me," John added.

Grandpa nodded approvingly. "Well, in this acting class we learned that an actor can only return for so many bows, no matter how successful the show. I think this is my last bow to you, John. And you, in the audience, must likewise go home, leave the theater, and continue on. There's nothing more depressing than an empty theater, seats folded, lights up, then off, and all the people who gave it life gone elsewhere."

A strong hand squeezed John's shoulder. He grabbed it, and the house full of warmth and light blurred until he wiped his eyes.

"Now Christmas is almost over, and I want to give you one final gift," said Grandpa. "I want you to go back in, take a good look around, give everyone a hug, and sneak Sandy a piece of turkey. And when you do, tell each of them you love them. I'd trade almost anything to go back and do that to the people I loved. And you can."

"And *then*?"

"Then go up to your bedroom, slide under the quilt your grandmother made you, and go to sleep. And, sleeping, dream of all the good things the future will bring. Then, when you wake at dawn, leave this house and never come back."

John took one final look at the half-dozen cars in the driveway, at the orange Christmas candles in each window, at the well-lit living room from which muffled laughter touched the otherwise silent night. Then together, hand in hand, John and his grandfather walked up the steps to the front door and into the waiting warmth.

*****

And in another year, a bright, sunny June morning, John woke on the bare floor of his old room, oddly refreshed. Quickly he descended the stairs, shut the front door behind him, and locked it. He pulled his car out of the weed-choked driveway, and, humming, clicked the gear into drive.

Looking back at the house through his rearview mirror, he thought he caught a glimpse of someone—*two* people—waving from the open front doorway.

He blinked and looked again. Now the door was shut, just as he'd left it.

Still humming, he drove toward home.

The Character

Every day Wilfred Colson sat at a corner table in the café area of the bookstore, and every day he observed the people who sat around him. At first, head to his computer, he tried to block them out. They were an enormous distraction, especially the women with their occasional high-pitched giggles and the old men who felt the need to scream into the cell phones their children had bought them. But then, slowly, he came around. They were *characters* in their way, and hadn't Dickens mastered his art of dialect and description by staring out at the London streets while working as a clerk in a lawyer's office?

So he began paying attention. Every so often, taking a break from his newest story or novel, he would allow the outside world fully in. The results were extraordinary—as were the regulars who arrived at their tables with clockwork routine: the wild-haired old man who wore the same blue shirt every day, grimaced at anyone who looked at him, and nursed the same cup of tepid coffee for two hours without once reaching for a book or magazine; the "Doll Ladies," who met every third Thursday of the month, with their gastrointestinal complaints, creepy three-foot-tall dolls, disturbingly detailed back stories for the "babies," and brightly-colored muumuus; and, of course, the towering giant who ate five doughnuts with colored sprinkles, told startled strangers about his brother's unexpected murder, then invariably exited through the fire escape, setting off all the alarms in the building.

There were others, too. People passing through with their quirks, eccentricities, and foibles. These he never saw more than once or twice, but there was always *someone* interesting and worthy of a couple pages of notes. And before he knew it, they began to enter into his short stories fully-formed. Colson had turned a nuisance into art and was suitably pleased with himself. Soon he began a series of stories based entirely upon people he observed in the café. The project promised to be an interesting character study that, Colson hoped, might end up as something of a post-modern *Winesburg, Ohio*.

He first noticed the new guy several months after starting the collection. Unusually diminutive and tiny (no more than four-feet, ten inches tall), unusually expressive (he smiled at virtually everyone in sight, though never engaged anyone beyond that), and also possessing the uncanny ability to sense when someone was staring at him, the "Little Fellow" (as Colson named him) quickly became a regular.

This made Colson's observations difficult but entertaining. He liked a challenge, and the struggle to take notes on the man while sparring with his apparent sixth sense enlivened more than a few dull days.

Everything was going fine until three weeks after the Little Fellow first caught his attention. Colson, hard at work and in "The Zone," reached for his cooling cup of Chai and touched, instead, a clammy, thin-fingered hand.

Startled, he looked up. The Little Fellow stood just inches away, smiling at him. "Hello," the man said, and sat down at Colson's table.

Bemused, Colson cleared his throat. "Yes, hello there. May I ask what you're doing?"

"I could ask you the same question, Mr. Colson."

He blinked. "How do you know my name?"

"I'm a reader, Mr. Colson. Along with the works of many other authors, I also read *yours*. Because of that, I know what you look like and I know you're local. Makes sense."

Colson nodded. "Yes, it does." He didn't like meeting fans in informal settings. They took up too much of his time, and disentangling himself from their questions and requests was distracting and tiring. He hoped he could shoo the man away quickly by being as terse as possible.

He opened his mouth to say something curt, but the Little Fellow interrupted. "You've been watching me, Mr. Colson." He wagged a thin finger in mock admonition. "Now don't try and deny it!"

Colson thought fast. Perhaps honesty would be best. It wouldn't do to have a short story appear with the Little Fellow in it (such as the one he was writing now), then have to deal with a resentful source of inspiration after the fact. He would turn on the charm and see if that worked.

"Yes," he said, "I have to admit you've got me there, Mr…."

"Bagby. Burt Bagby."

(*Better than Little Fellow,* Colson thought.)

"Ah. Mr. Bagby."

"Ever heard of me?"

Colson shook his head. "Sorry."

Bagby looked hurt. "I've been published in *Merry Times, Hard Rain*, and *Lost Stars*. I write stories too, you see."

"Oh! Well, congratulations. You see, Mr.... um..."

"*Bag*by," said the little man, smiling again.

"Mr. Bagby. Yes. You see, I've recently started using my surroundings as inspiration. Particularly, ah, *people* in my surroundings."

"Hey, like Dickens!"

Colson was surprised and somewhat pleased. "Yes, exactly like Dickens. And I'm afraid, Mr. Bagby, that you caught my eye. I'm sorry if this is unacceptable. If so, I can tear up the story I've started, and—"

Bagby gripped his arm. "Not on your life!" he said, mouth suddenly tight, eyes wide and gleaming. Perhaps feeling he had overstepped, he released Colson's sleeve, leaned back, and mopped his brow. "How fortuitous. How positively lovely. I'm honored, Mr. Colson."

Colson smoothed his sleeve. "Well, I thank you, Mr. Bagby. I'm a bit embarrassed to be *caught* like this, but you have good eyes. And I appreciate your understanding."

"A character in one of your stories! Wonderful."

"Yes, indeed. A minor character, but a character nonetheless. Well, I must be going." The whole tenor of his work day had been thrown off. Colson was finished for the afternoon.

*****

And that, he thought, was that.

Except it wasn't.

In the weeks that followed, little Burt Bagby seemed to be everywhere, at all times. At Starbucks. At Wash & Go. At Giant Eagle. And at the bookstore, of course. Always at the bookstore.

It took Colson some time to realize what was happening. When he did, he was more annoyed than worried. Finally, a month later, during a break in his writing at the bookstore café, Colson looked up, and there was Bagby again. It was too much. This latest appearance had toppled the stack.

Colson caught Bagby's eye and motioned to him. Smile wide as always, Bagby jumped up and scampered over.

"Look here," Colson said, tapping the table top with a bony index finger. "You've got to stop this. It isn't proper and it isn't dignified. You say you admire my work? Then do it and me the favor of allowing me to continue it. I can't write when I'm distracted, and you, Mr. Bagby, are becoming a distraction."

Obviously wounded, Mr. Bagby looked around the café. "This is a public place, Mr. Colson," he said. "We live in the same town. We go out in public. It's bound to happen, that we see each other."

"Not eleven times in two weeks!"

"Hmm! Well, perhaps you've got me there. But you have to admit, all this makes for an interesting character, doesn't it? Perhaps a somewhat *important* character?"

Before Colson could get over his shock, Bagby rose to his feet, tipped his hat, and sauntered off.

And Colson couldn't be sure, but the one time Bagby looked back, he thought he caught a wink.

*****

Two months passed. In December, in the middle of the night, Colson woke from a fretful sleep, crossed to his window, scraped away the frost, and blinked out at the silver nightscape.

Burt Bagby, bald head reflecting moonlight, was kneeling by Colson's car, letting the air out of his tires.

Colson couldn't believe it. He'd seen less of Bagby over the previous few weeks and figured his pep talk had served its purpose.

He threw open the window. "Hey, there! You! Bagby! I'm coming down! I'm calling the police!"

"Good! Wonderful!" Bagby called back. "Aren't I *eccentric*, though? Aren't I *unpredictable*?"

"No! Now clear off!"

Without another word, Bagby scampered away.

*****

After that, Colson didn't see Bagby for close to three months. He hadn't bothered calling the police on him; Colson hated distractions, and since the vandalism went unrepeated, he decided to let the matter drop.

But the incident had bothered him; his whole sense of peaceful routine had been compromised, and his writing had suffered as a result. Bagby could be *any*where, doing *any*thing, at *any time*. His absence, if anything, made Colson more disconcerted than his constant appearances. Because of that, Colson's writing had fallen behind schedule for the first time in nearly fifteen years, the quality had likely suffered too, and that simply wouldn't do.

Happily, he had chosen a solution, should the day come when Mr. Burt Bagby dared show his face again.

That day came late in March, when Colson, sitting at his usual table, swatting away at his slacks in the bookstore after dumping some caramel latte on them, looked up to find Bagby's pallid, lightly sweating face just inches from his own.

"Hello there, old chum! Miss me?" Bagby cried.

"Ack!" Colson choked, slopping more latte on himself.

Bagby pulled up a chair. "How've you been?" he asked. "Lots of good ideas? Lots of *character* development?" He pantomimed elbowing Colson in the ribs. "I thought I'd give you some uninterrupted time to think about me, but I figured I'd given you long enough. Now I'm back!"

A cold fury awoke in Colson. The tips of his fingers turned to ice. A vein pumped alarmingly in his temple.

"Mr. Bagby," he said in a low voice—flat, calm, and dangerous. "You are an annoyance, Mr. Bagby. A burr in my sock, quickly removed and just as quickly forgotten. Additionally you strike me as somewhat pitiful—*pathetic* might be a better adjective. I assume you are single and are likely to remain so not by choice, but by circumstance. You are also a failure. A failure as a writer, and, by proxy, a failure as a person; a late-middle aged sycophant. And I hate to break this to you, Mr. Bagby, but I don't write about pathetic, annoying, sycophantic failures. You will *never* be a character in any work of mine. Not even a minor one. The story I was writing didn't pan out with you in it…because, simply, you're a *bore*."

Mr. Bagby's face lost a great deal of color during Colson's controlled explosion. Surprisingly, he regained it fairly quickly.

"I see," he said. "Well, that leaves me just one option, then. Since *you* won't write about *me*, *I* will have to write about *you*. Because you are, as I'm sure most of your millions of readers would readily confirm, an 'interesting character,' Mr. Colson."

Colson chuckled. "By all means! If it makes you happy, turn me into a character for one of your stories. Publish it in one of your little 'zines. Good luck to you! Now *goodbye*."

Bagby shook his head. "I wasn't talking about fiction, Mr. Colson. No, I thought I'd try my hand at something else. A memoir, perhaps."

Colson snorted. "Nonsense. Who would want to read what *you* have to say about *me*?"

"Oh, I think a great many people will," Bagby said, smiling faintly. "Many, many people indeed."

And without so much as another word between them, Bagby reached out and cut Colson's throat.

The Leasehold of His Days

The ultrasound showed it and there could be no doubt. His wife was pregnant. Two years of trying and it had finally happened.

Jason Emery walked out of the hospital in a startled daze, numbed by a strange sense of unreality.

"Whatcha thinking?" asked Susan.

"I...I don't really know."

"That's a first."

He stopped walking. So did Susan.

"My mind's a rush," he said. "It doesn't know what to focus on. What...how..." He paused, breathing heavily. "What does being a father *mean*? Most of all. In one simple sentence. I need something to hold on to, or I'm never going to know how to feel or what to do. I've wanted this so long, but now..."

Susan laughed and continued walking. He fell in step beside her. "I don't think there *is* one simple sentence that sums up what it means to be a parent. If there was, life would be simpler to understand." She pinched his arm. "You're thinking too much. That's the problem. Parenting isn't just in the head—it's in the glands, too."

"Maybe," he said.

*****

Was it true?

Late that night he sat in his study, surrounded by his books. They were a constant source of comfort and always had been, even back in college when he'd owned only a couple of dozen battered paperbacks. Now he was a school librarian, and surrounding himself with the subjects of his love kept him grounded and safe. So when he wanted to think, when he was lost, this, his *own* library, was where he went. Answers, if they were to come, came to him here.

He scanned the shelves. *The Great Gatsby, The Scarlet Letter, Dandelion Wine, Adventures of Huckleberry Finn, The Canterbury Tales, In Our Time...*

More: *The Collected Poems of Dylan Thomas, The Secret Histories, Wind in the Willows, Memoirs of Ulysses S. Grant, Idylls of the King, The Iliad, Beowulf...*

He stopped, pulled *Beowulf* from the shelf, opened to a random page, and read,

> ...*Beowulf was foiled*
> *of a glorious victory. The glittering sword,*
> *infallible before that day,*
> *failed when he unsheathed it, as it never should have.*
> *For the son of Ecgtheow, it was no easy thing*
> *to have to give ground like that and go*
> *unwillingly to inhabit another home*
> *in a place beyond; so every man must yield*
> *the leasehold of his days.*

Jason sighed.

At the beginning of every year he started the first day of school with a little speech to the classes visiting the library. "Remember," he told them, "the greatest thing about writing is that it lets you communicate with someone from another time, another place. When you open *The Odyssey*, Homer speaks to you across the seas and across the millennia. The Greeks roar through his blind lines. You read, he breathes. You turn a page, his voice is carried on its whisper."

He looked down at his battered copy of *Beowulf*, written by an unknown poet 1300 years before.

"But he *is* known," Jason murmured. "Each line is a thought, each stanza a bellow across time. That nameless scop will never die."

On certain rare occasions, always late at night, a despair, also nameless, would wake him from sleep, toss and turn his thoughts, and spin him downstairs to sit beneath the neon kitchen light for long hours before exhaustion drove him back to bed. He didn't think of such times often, but he did now.

And, thinking, Jason realized the root of his despair was the certain, heartbreaking realization that *he* would not be among those who spoke across time. He tended books but did not create them. His own writing had never amounted to anything. When he died, his voice would be silenced forever.

His hands went cold. A shiver of incredible sadness etched his spine. He gasped, the backs of his beloved books spinning. *Beowulf* fell from his hands to the carpet, pages crumpling, spine splaying wide. He cried out—

Then fell silent.

Only the pounding of his heart, a deep metronome of seconds, thumped in the darkened house. Upstairs, his wife continued sleeping. No dogs barked outside.

His frantic eyes had caused his quiet, for they had alighted upon the open page of the broken book. With a mind of their own, they had read the words of Beowulf's dying moment. With more than his mind, he understood them:

> *Now is the time when I would have wanted*
> *to bestow this armour on my own son,*
> *had it been my fortune to have fathered an heir*
> *and live on in his flesh…*

And Jason suddenly remembered why he was here, what had brought him down to his books in the middle of the night, why his racing mind had been unable to sleep.

His heartbeat slowed.

Suddenly very tired, he replaced *Beowulf* carefully on its shelf, rested his hand on it for a long moment, then went back upstairs.

At the top of the landing he paused, brought up short by a photograph hooked on the wall. Young eyes gazed out at him from across the years—his own. And his small, young hand held that of another—his father, dead three years.

Jason took a deep breath. The day of that photo had been a fine one. He and his dad had gone fishing, and he'd caught a five-inch trout; barely a minnow, but his first, and his father had made him feel like he'd single-handedly landed Moby Dick.

He looked at the small, young hand, tightly clutching his father's reassuringly large one, then turned away. He held out his hand and examined it closely in the moonlight—the little hairs, the worn ridges. His eyes widened, as if seeing it, *really* seeing it, for the first time.

Two minutes later, back in bed, he fell instantly asleep.

*****

The next morning Jason tripped lightly down the hall and poured himself a cup of coffee.

GREGORY MILLER

"You slept in!" Susan exclaimed, spreading grape jam on a piece of toast.

"It was a topsy-turvy night."

"Coffee?"

"You bet." He surveyed the kitchen and smiled, then picked up the newspaper and scanned the headlines.

"You're awfully chipper this morning," she said. "After all that stress yesterday, I'm surprised."

"Some friends helped me find the answers I was looking for."

"No more crises about the nature of fatherhood?"

"None."

Susan set down her piece of toast. She gave Jason a long, appraising look.

"You have good friends," she said.

Jason smiled. "It's a beautiful day. I'm going for a walk. Wanna come?"

On their way out the door Jason paused by a small mirror. He looked at himself closely.

"Hi, Dad," he said quietly. "It's good to see you."

266

A Quick Break

B rian Lumley knew how important it was to get away from the books for a few hours every week or so. Penn State, for all its possible avenues of growth, could become a stifling place, especially with final exams approaching. But without money, car, or time, even getting out for a haircut and a cup of coffee was difficult—and the best he could do.

He shook rain from his coat as he pushed open the glass doors to the Nittany Mall. Just inside, he encountered a contest in full swing.

SHOW YOUR PATRIOTISM FOR A CHANCE TO WIN BIG! a giant banner read. Beneath it, a least a hundred people had surrounded a particleboard stage by the big fountain. On it, above a line of perhaps two dozen other hopefuls, a pimply teen with braces and corn-shuck hair stood awkwardly, belting out the national anthem for all she was worth.

Brian winced as she veered off key, stumbled, resumed, then finished to a smattering of applause. He ducked into Holiday Haircuts, signed in, and took a seat. Flipping through a well-thumbed *Newsweek*, he tried to read, but found himself distracted as more contestants took their turns. The din of the noise coupled with the neon lights of the salon left him feeling slightly anxious.

"Hello there."

He looked up.

A plump, smiling old lady took a seat. Brian noticed that although the waiting area was empty, she'd chosen the seat directly beside him. He could smell her perfume—lilacs—and see a tiny smudge of makeup caked in the crease between her ear and face, just beneath the closely-permed white hair.

"Goodness, but I'm glad to see it isn't crowded. I didn't even have an appointment!"

He smiled. "Oh, you don't need one here. They're never very busy this early in the morning."

"That's good to know. Thank heavens for that!"

Brian liked the look of her. She seemed down-home, agreeable, and relaxed... quite different from most of the people he knew on campus. It felt good to get away for a quick break, even if it *was* for a mundane reason.

269

"You have a busy day planned?" he ventured.

"Oh, yes. Yes, indeed! I'm here visiting my son, and I can't be late."

"You're from out of town?"

She nodded. "Pittsburgh. But while I was driving up, I happened to look in the mirror, and my *land*, what a sight! I thought, 'You can't be seeing your son like *that*, can you?' And I knew the answer was no. So I stopped off here. I still have an hour to spare before I'm expected."

Brian nodded. Behind him, out in the mall, a small child wailed about "the land of the free" so shrilly the sound system gave off an earsplitting shriek of reverb. He winced.

"Well, I hope you have a good day together," he said, determined to drown out the noise. "Does your son live in State College? Or Bellefonte, maybe?"

The old lady looked at him with eyes suddenly wide and glassy. "Oh, no, no, I'm off to Blairsville to see a psychic! Just five miles down the road."

"Hmm?" He furrowed his brow. "I don't understand. Didn't you say you were going to visit your son?"

"Oh, yes, dear!" she exclaimed, grasping his wrist in a firm, clammy grip, giving it a hard squeeze, then releasing it. "My son is dead, you see. They found his body next to his car on Route 26 three years ago. Not a drop of blood left in it."

Brian blinked rapidly. Finally, he cleared his throat.

"I'm...I'm sorry," he said lamely. His lips worked silently a bit longer before he added, "Um...what are you going to ask him? The psychic, I mean. Or, you know, your son *through* the psychic. Or...or whatever."

"Oh, that's simple!" The woman threw back her head and cackled. "I'm going to ask what happened to his head! They never found it!"

"I see." Brian's vision blurred.

The lights, the singing, the perfume, the laughter...

"Well, ma'am, I think I'm going to go out and watch the contest while I wait," he announced as brightly as he could. "I love the national anthem."

"Oh, good idea!" She squeezed his wrist again, pumping it hard with her damp, cool palm. "Isn't that precious?"

Brian felt nauseated as he staggered out into the mall.

On stage, a fat man with a tobacco-stained beard and jean overalls was belting out the part about the "dawn's early light."

Brian walked quickly back to the glass doors and pushed through them, stepping out into the cold, wet day again. He hoped the bus to campus would come early. He needed to get back there, he really did. He no longer wanted a haircut. He no longer wanted to get away.

"A break," he muttered, pacing back and forth in the rain, letting the cold drops numb his skin. "It was just a quick break."

Graduation Day

It was 1996, it was May, it was a Friday, and evening was already coming on. As always, Patrick Hughes wanted to go out. His mother had given him the Corolla, the loan good until his eleven o'clock curfew, so after dinner he escaped into the fading sunlight and warm twilight air, buckled himself in, and had already dialed the first number on his new cell phone before even clearing the driveway.

He called Bill Plourde, his best friend, as he headed, without really thinking, toward the Columbia Mall.

No answer.

Strange. He'd said he would be around. Well…

Charlie Karavlan, then. Charlie was always up for anything. And wherever he was, others were too.

"Charlie?"

"Sorry, Pat," said Charlie's father. "He's away for the weekend."

"What? Really?" Charlie hadn't mentioned that in school.

"Sorry," Mr. Karavlan repeated, and hung up.

Shaking his head, Patrick dialed his girlfriend, Lisa. The phone rang ten times. He frowned, hung up, dialed again. Nothing. Not even her voice mail. Same with her home number…it just rang and rang, no answering machine message, nothing.

Two stoplights from the mall, he abruptly took a right turn, cut through the neighborhood of Thunder Hill, and continued calling numbers, now systematically going down the list of his friends. Dave Turnbull? No answer. Brian Sheets? Out. Rich York?

Someone strange answered the phone when he called Rich's home number.

"Who?" It sounded like an old lady. Was his grandmother visiting?

"Rich. Rich York. This is his number."

"I don't know no Rich York."

He paused. Maybe the old lady was senile.

"Are you visiting family?" he asked. "Is this the York house?"

Click.

Maybe he'd misdialed. But no, he was pulling the numbers from his contact list. The dialing was automated.

With a sign of relief he pulled into Lisa's driveway. He honked the horn. No one came out.

"Jesus. *Someone* has to be home. Mrs. Horowitz never leaves the damned house."

He got out of the car and slammed the door. The night—*full* night now—was dark, a deep ebony. No streetlamps, and Lisa's front door lamps weren't lit. Patrick felt the hair on the back of his neck and rubbed away a shiver. He rang the doorbell.

Flower, Lisa's German Shepherd, didn't bark on the other side. She *always* barked.

No lights came on.

He peered in the garage windows, cupping his hands to ward off reflections.

No cars.

"What the *hell* is going on?" His voice sounded weak and thin in the thick, late-spring air.

Ten miles away and fifteen minutes later, he pulled into VIPs, his favorite pool hall. Every other Friday night for three years he'd gone there, usually with half a dozen friends, to play eight-ball, smoke, cuss, and eat frozen candy bars from the freezer behind the counter, fifty cents each, before turning to the old arcade games along the far wall, then heading out to the Double-T Diner for late-night dinner.

He pushed open the broken glass door and entered fast, scanning the cool darkness, the whispering fans, the muted yellow lights over each threadbare table.

It was too quiet. A couple of old men played billiards nearby, but the rest of the tables were clear and empty, and so were the arcade stools.

"Evening," said the attendant behind the counter—an old man missing his top front teeth. "How many hours you want?"

Patrick took another look around.

"Kind of dead tonight, huh?"

The attendant laughed dryly. "When is it ever not?"

"Last Friday there were fifty people in here. Hey, I never saw you before. Where's Carl?"

The attendant pushed his tongue through the gap in his teeth and whistled. "Son, you been drinkin'?"

"No."

"Then you'd know I own this place. And I can't remember seeing you before in all my days."

Patrick lit a cigarette with a trembling match.

"No smoking, kiddo."

"What?"

"Get gone. You make me nervous."

He didn't want to go anywhere else. In just an hour and a half the night had taken a bad turn, a surreal tinge, and all he wanted now was for it to end. But he couldn't just go home. Not on this night. And he needed to see one more place...

Patrick pulled into the parking lot of the Double-T Diner and was immensely reassured by the bright lights, the busy parking lot, the other kids milling around outside...it was all familiar. It was all *right*.

But he didn't know anyone. He always knew at least a handful of the kids who milled around out front or talked loudly at the tables, sucking up milkshakes through straws and picking at limp fries. And there was always, *always* someone he could sit with, a table he could join.

Not this time. Not now.

And he realized, with a cold shock, that he didn't belong here, that he needed to find another place to go. He just didn't know where.

So he went home.

When he arrived, Patrick half-expected the house to be dark, or to find a strange car parked in the driveway, or even for the whole place to be gone, only an empty lot left in its place.

But it was there, lights reassuringly on, cars in the driveway reassuringly familiar.

He let himself in, and there were his parents watching television, his dog asleep at his father's feet.

"Hey, you're home early, kiddo!" his father exclaimed. "Only ten o' clock!"

"I'm glad," said his mother. "Tomorrow's a big day."

"A bunch of people called for you," his father added. "Bill and Charlie and Lisa. Lisa was angry she couldn't get a hold of you. Isn't your phone working?"

"It was acting up," said Patrick faintly.

"So where did you *go* then, if you couldn't find your friends?" his mother asked.

"All over, but there wasn't..." He paused. "I couldn't find them tonight. Because...because of my phone. So I came home."

"Well, just as well, like your mother said." His father smiled. "In case you forgot, tomorrow afternoon you'll be a high school grad! You'd better be rested for the ceremony."

Patrick nodded, did his best to smile, and went up to bed.

"Graduation," he said to himself as he walked up the stairs. "Did they really think I could forget?"

And for long, long hours, after everyone else had gone to sleep, he thought about all the things from which he was graduating.

Dead End

C utting his parents' lawn just wasn't enough anymore. Summer wouldn't last forever and James needed more money. He wanted that iPhone, *had to have* that iPhone, and time was ticking by.

Taking his incentive from Harry Larkin, an older boy who always seemed to be mowing a lawn somewhere in the neighborhood, he set to work. After several hours with paste, pencil, and marker he headed out to post two dozen signs around the neighborhood. They read,

> Lawn need mowed??
> Leaves need raked??
> Dog need sat??
> CALL JAMES BROCK!
> 1-814-555-8927
> 109 Sycamore
> CHEAP RATES!!

That done, James sat back and waited for the money to roll in.

He waited a long time. Rain streaked the signs. Wind blew some of them away. No one called, no one came by.

"Why?" he asked his mother.

"Maybe Harry Larkin's got the market cornered," she answered.

"Why?" he asked his father.

"The economy," the old man answered, but didn't elaborate.

Then, just when everything seemed positively hopeless, Mrs. Wentworth knocked on the door.

The old lady was a piece of work. James had never spoken two words to her before. She chased children off her property on Halloween and scowled at them from her living room window while they waited for the bus. She walked around the block every evening, humming a strange tune, but never said hello to anyone and grumbled when they made any overture. Once a year, on Christmas Eve, she attended church, but never stayed for the reception afterward.

So James was amazed to find her standing there, clutching one of his faded signs in a skeletal, blue-veined hand.

"You sit dogs?" she demanded abruptly. "The sign says you sit dogs."

"Er," James replied.

"You an idiot, boy? I don't have the time of day for idiots." She pursed her lips.

"Uh…that is, no ma'am. And yeah, I sit dogs." He'd added that job to his signs as an afterthought. To the best of his knowledge, Harry Larkin didn't sit dogs. Not that James knew much about how to do it himself.

"Well, I need my dog taken care of. His name's Riley, and he's a sweet fellow. Kinda big. No trouble, though. He's too old for trouble. What do you charge?"

"Ten dollars a day," he said promptly, rattling off his spiel. "That gets you two feedings and two walks, plus all messes cleaned up. Should there be any. And it's two dollars a day extra if I have to give him any medicine."

The old woman signed impatiently. "Highway robbery. I'll give you eight. No walks needed. Riley's too old. And no medicine, either. Deal?" She stuck out her hand.

James shook it. Her hand was cold and dry. Later, he brushed some hair from his eyes and happened to smell the fingers that had touched hers. They stank like something gone rotten, covered over with talc.

"You begin tomorrow morning," she said, clearly ready to be on her way. "Eight. Then again at four. The key is under the mat. The food is on the counter. I'll pay you when I get back from my sister's next Sunday. She's got arthritis real bad, but it's a pain for both of us, let me tell you."

And then she was gone.

James stood in the doorway blinking.

"Mom!" he shouted. "Mom, I've got a job!"

*****

He was curious about Mrs. Wentworth's house. Entering it was like entering enemy territory, except that suddenly it was OK, he was allowed, and that made it even stranger.

But what James found left him disappointed: a slightly musty, perfume-laden home filled with faded photographs, a broken record player, old prayer books, frilly curtains, and the kind of precious knick-knacks the five-and-dime sold at the back of the store for 75% off. It was exactly like Great-Aunt Irene's house: a place that bored him to tears the three times a year his parents forced him to go there.

James sighed. Where was Riley?

He remembered the dog vaguely: a brown Great Dane, paws the size of a bear's, with lanky strides and a droopy muzzle. He hadn't seen it outside in a long time. Too old, he supposed, like Mrs. Wentworth had said.

He sneezed. Really, he'd never been in a place so covered in perfume. Like funeral flowers, he thought fleetingly. The old lady must drench herself in it. And everything she owned.

Riley. He walked slowly through the living room and back into the foyer, then started down the hall.

James hated empty houses. He didn't like being alone, didn't like it when his parents went to dinner or parties or the movies and wouldn't let him come. Didn't like the way every sound amplified, every piece of furniture loomed when only he was there. Didn't like the pregnant, waiting darkness as he moved from room to room, or the cold, impersonal light when he flicked the switches on.

He had never been alone in a stranger's home before. Somehow that was much worse. And maybe it was the strangeness of the place, sure, but there was something else he couldn't quite put his finger on…a hostile, bleak feeling. Later, when he was older, he would recognize it for what it was: the knowledge that he had entered a part of the world that didn't know him, that he hadn't touched and which didn't need his presence, that didn't care if he lived or died.

Moving down the hallway, steps slow and unsteady, he marveled as the heady, stifling air grew denser and more saturated. Roses and lilies, wild gardenias. His stomach lurched. He swallowed. Lilac. Tulips and chrysanthemums…

Where was Riley?

"Here, boy," he called in the thick stillness. No sound of the dog. James entered the kitchen and caught a whiff of something else, something buried beneath the flowers. It made him remember shaking hands with Mrs. Wentworth, of the bad smell on her fingers.

He flicked on the light switch. The smell, the stench, gained identity.

Riley lay in a huge wicker basket. Both it and the dog were covered with flies. They streamed over the body, rose disturbed and buzzing to resettle, and beneath them James caught sight of things white and wriggling, things he'd only seen before on dead birds and rabbits left on hot, blacktopped roads. Everything about the basket and the body seemed in motion—two things made one by a seething, boiling sea.

As he ran from the house, sleeve over his mouth, eyes streaming, he thought, *I hate the cold light in empty houses. Hate it, hate it, hate it...*

Then he was home, back where he belonged, in a part of the world where people lived who cared about him, where things made sense, where he felt safe.

But not as safe as he once had been.

*****

A week passed. Mrs. Wentworth hadn't left a number where she could be reached and didn't call. James' father buried the dog in Mrs. Wentworth's side yard and returned home sweaty and pale. His mother helped clean out the kitchen.

Both his parents spoke words of comfort to James, trying to shrug off what had happened, to joke about it, to let him know *it wasn't his fault.*

Well, no kidding, he thought.

But at night they talked, and James, sitting half-way down on the stairs, heard.

"That dog had been dead for weeks," his father said, folding the newspaper.

"James mustn't see her again," his mother replied over the sound of Johnny Carson. "When she comes over, I'll talk to her."

But Mrs. Wentworth didn't come over.

*****

"What did you do with Riley?"

The words were a shriek, barely language.

"I...I..." said James.

He'd been expecting Brooke Newcomb to call with help on his math homework. Instead, it was Mrs. Wentworth.

"You *buried* him*?*"

"I...yes!" he blurted. "Yes, he was *dead*. He was...there were flies, and—"

"Well of *course* he was dead, but *you buried him*?"

James held the phone, still and silent, not daring to suck air.

"That means you didn't *feed* him. All week *without food*!" Mrs. Wentworth was breathing heavily. Then, seeming to calm herself, she took one big, deep breath and said, more evenly, "Well, I think you can see why I won't be paying you, young man."

And with that, she hung up.

*****

James took the long way around the block for weeks, all to avoid passing Mrs. Wentworth's house on foot. He didn't mind, except that the longer walks gave him more time to think. Sometimes, he discovered, thinking too much wasn't a good thing.

For instance, he often found himself thinking about the newly-dug hole in Mrs. Wentworth's side yard—the hole his father had dug and filled, and which was now empty again, dirt piled up alongside it. He could see it every time the bus passed her house to and from school.

And invariably, when he thought of that, he also thought of his father's comment after he'd told him about Mrs. Wentworth's phone call. His father was a man of few words. But when he spoke, James usually listened.

"I suppose," his father had told him, handing him a new iPhone, "that you'd best take down those signs. That business venture of yours was kind of a dead end, don't you think?"

Yes, he did, but he didn't want to think *too* much. Not about that. No, he didn't want that at all.

And looking at his new iPhone, a gateway to the homes of a billion strangers, James suddenly felt as though he were holding a part of the world that didn't know him, that he hadn't touched and which didn't need his presence, that didn't care if he lived or died.

Comfortable Silence

He was on an airplane, wearing an uncomfortable suit, book untouched on his lap, plastic cup empty on his tray, when the older woman next to him leaned over and asked, "Where from?"

He didn't roll his eyes—he was too polite—but he wanted to. He had no interest in talking, or at least engaging in idle chatter, but courtesy won the day.

"Pittsburgh," he said, then added, two moments later, "and yourself?"

"Cleveland. I'm going to my high school reunion." A chuckle. "My *fiftieth*."

"Hmm! Well, that's nice. I hope you have a good time." He eyed his book.

"I'm not so sure I will," she said, and the blandly affable smile often afforded strangers faded.

She wanted him to ask why.

"Why?" he asked.

"Well, you know, it's been so long. I haven't lived in Aurora for thirty-six years. And all my old friends…"

She didn't finish the sentence, so he simply nodded.

"It's not the old clichés that worry me," she went on. "You know… 'Oh, what if Sally Henderson's career went better than mine did? Oh, what if everyone aged better than I did?' I'm past all that. None of it matters."

"So what's worrying you?"

She shook her head. "It's silly, but what's kept me up these last few nights is just one question: what are we all going to talk about?"

"That's it?"

"Good heavens, isn't that *enough*? Think about it! Fifty years since we graduated. It was a small high school and we all knew each other. But after graduation we went our separate ways, and now we're all spread out across the country. A few of us even live abroad! It was easy to know each other and get along when we all had geography in common—the same town, the same classes and school hallways—but when you're thrust back into a room with people and that common ground is gone, what then?" She paused. "I'm Grace, by the way."

"Adam." He extended a hand. Grace took it.

"It was wonderful to know them," she said, sighing. "But I have a fear that's all it will ever be now—a past-tense relationship."

"So you didn't keep in touch with *any* of them?" Adam asked, surprised the conversation had pulled him out of himself a bit; he was interested in spite of everything. "I mean, a good friend that's lasted all the years?"

"Ah." Grace quieted, fiddling with the ice in her empty cup of water. She did this for quite some time, until Adam thought she wasn't going to respond at all. Then, quite suddenly, she said, "One of *those*."

"Yes. Is there one?"

"There was," she said. "Dorothy Price. A dear friend."

"*Was?*" he said. "I'm sorry...I don't mean to pry."

"No, no, not at all. Dorothy died three years ago. Heart attack. Quite unexpected."

"I'm sorry."

"Me too."

There was an awkward silence. Then Grace said, "That's funny. Looking back on it, you know what really defines a true friendship? One that lasts the years?"

"What?" He really wanted to know. He'd been thinking a good deal about friendship over the last few days.

"It's the *silences*. Do you know what I mean?"

Adam shook his head.

"You're still a young man," she said, "but as you get older, you'll see for yourself. A friend, a *true* friend—the kind you keep for life— is someone you can sit in the same room with for a minute, an hour, even *three*, without saying a word...and not feel uncomfortable that whole time. Not needing to fill the gaps with idle chatter. Comfortable silence. That's the test."

He thought about it for a long time. "Yes," he said finally, "I see what you mean. That makes good sense. I...I have someone like that in my life, in fact, although I never thought of it quite that way."

"Well do me a favor, Adam, if you don't mind."

He looked up. Grace was gazing at him steadily, earnestly, without blinking.

"Hang on to that person. Keep them in your life always."

"I will," he said firmly. "I promise."

*****

Adam disembarked, stretched, got his luggage, took the shuttle from O'Hare to his rental car, and drove straight to the funeral home. Once there, he checked his watch. Two hours early.

He went inside. An attendant greeted him. Adam asked if he could have some time alone with the deceased.

"Are you a relative, sir?" the man inquired, his tone a perfect blend of somber empathy and professional detachment.

"A friend," he said simply. "A good friend."

The man smiled understandingly—Adam was grateful for that smile; it seemed more real than the tone—and invited him into a small anteroom.

The coffin, closed, gleamed in the half-light, a sideways monolith of polished brass. Far different from the elderly man whose remains it contained: Adam's dear old friend, a professor from long ago whose lessons spanned all the years. Someone who had listened in college when his family was far away, given advice, and helped do what he could to set him on the right path. The man inside the coffin had been a powerhouse of humor, good stories, energy and dynamism. A kind man. A kindred spirit.

He thought of silence—the silence of eight years, when his life had taken him away from that old friend and sent him off to start a career, a family, a life far removed from those college days.

Adam should have sent a card. Many cards. And letters. And called him every month, especially during the years after the old man had been forced to retire, victim of the degenerative illness that eventually killed him.

But he hadn't.

Silence. What kind of silence had it been? He wondered. Grace had spoken of hours without speaking, of comfortable silence.

Could a comfortable silence last eight years?

If he'd sent cards, written letters, called, would they have picked up right where they'd left off? Would his friend have understood?

Adam sat for a long, long time in the dim room, and the silence drew out, lengthened, like shadows in a late afternoon.

Then he started talking.

On the Edge of Twilight

A t least half the time, when the young man walked briskly through the park at twilight, he saw the old man sitting on the bench beneath the oak tree. And every time the old man was there, he called out to the young man and asked him a question.

And the young man sometimes stopped and sometimes continued on without bothering to answer, but the question, and the answer (when it came), were always the same:

"Have you seen the ghost?"

"No."

And then the young man was gone, gone to meet the girl he loved at their special spot. Or they were already together, walking hand in hand, to sit for a moment before going on to dinner, a movie, or someplace private to explore their love in new, breathless ways.

Neither knew what happened when they left the old man, and neither thought much of him; when their thoughts strayed to him and his strange question, they only focused on those things for a little while before excitement or happiness or a combination of both drew their attention away.

Both attended high school across the river. Both were seniors. They had been together, inseparable, for a year and a half. And in that time their routine on weekends, when the weather allowed, always included the park.

When they came together in the fading half-light she always slid her hand into his, either before they began to walk or when they met at their bench—always empty, as if waiting for them. The path to their bench led through the fields bordered by hedges and trees, past the old man's spot, through a gate, then finally down to the edge of the river, its shifting waters reflecting distant lights of houses on the far shore.

And when they chose to remain there instead of venturing out for the evening, they sat for hours, sometimes talking, often in murmurs, and night fell upon them and they came to life, focusing on each other with words and without, while staring at the river and the moonlight, and feeling rain and wind or stillness against their skin. Fireflies blazed around them in the summer-scented air. They rarely saw other people besides the old man; the park was old and difficult to find, and perhaps no one wanted it anyway. And then she would take his left hand again, threading her fingers through his, and he would put his right arm around her and pull her close, settling his cheek against the side of her head so he could smell her perfume and shampoo.

Every so often he would kiss her neck, and she would rub his knee, and they would shift their bodies so they touched in different ways. Then eventually, always, they found the rhythm of the night, and were lulled by it, and closed their eyes, drifting into a doze through the comfort of their attraction and the culmination of their surroundings.

And sometimes shortly after midnight, often not until several hours past, they would rouse each other, move into each other, run their hands over each other, whispering, kissing, sighing, before finally standing, walking, leaving their spot and returning to the world where other people lived and their love continued, but in the ebb and flow of an active world.

And the young man often thought, by day and at night, that he was fortunate, so fortunate, to have found someone who cared about him like she did, who understood him like she did, who loved him like she did.

Early on in their final year of high school, they spoke of attending the same university, and applied to several local schools together. But then, as the autumn progressed, they came to an obstacle. She was accepted to a university in California. He was accepted to a college in Maine. They were good schools, *excellent* schools—perfect for their interests and far better than those they might attend together. So they accepted the invitations, figuring a long-distance relationship would work, that they would *make* it work. And so they settled back into the comfort of their routine and didn't think of it.

Or said they didn't. For as the young man ticked off the days on his calendar and their 18th summer approached, he began to worry they would eventually be swept apart by time and circumstance and the need for something more—swept out of each others' lives forever, never to return, because perfection is fleeting, and elusive, and always becomes a thing of the past.

So he lived in the present more than he ever had in his life. Instead of looking to the future, he embraced where he was, when he was, who he was with and how he felt. *Healthy*, he thought. *It's healthy to do that.*

He told her that once, when the future weighed heavily upon them and she, too, suddenly became sad. And she agreed with him, and her mood brightened, and that was the last they ever spoke of it.

Once, out of the blue, when they were holding hands and looking out over the river, the bench warm and comfortable beneath them, she said abruptly, "I will never meet anyone else like you. And if I meet someone who is half the man you are with me, I think I could be content."

He nodded, took it only as a compliment, and chose to ignore the deeper implications.

Until suddenly the future became the present, and they were done with high school, graduation two months a memory, the cross-country moves in opposite directions just a day away.

At their spot, sitting on their bench, they said they would write, and keep in close touch, and see each other several times a year, but he knew it was all over, and he knew she knew it, too. And when true night fell and midnight knelled, the dark beginning of a new day, everything they shared retreated into the past.

They stood up from the bench for the last time.

She left quickly. He lingered a long while.

Eventually he walked slowly back toward the street, where his car waited in the shadows of the trees.

But he didn't go to his car. At the last moment he changed direction, instead approaching a second bench, the distant bench where the old man often sat in silence. He was there now, still awake; his watery eyes gleamed in the faint sliver of moonlight.

"I've seen you many times," he told the old man. "Why do you always come here?"

The old man looked up at him. "I wait for the ghost," he said simply.

"Is this place haunted?"

A nod.

"What does the ghost look like?"

"Different things to different people."

He gazed at the old man, then peered toward the dew-covered fields, the lengthening moonlight shadows, the cold river.

"Have you ever seen it?"

The old man nodded.

"How many times?"

"Every night."

The young man paused, blinking rapidly. "Mind if I join you?" he asked.

The old man looked surprised. "No…but why would you want to?"

The bench creaked under new weight. The old man slid over a fraction of an inch.

"Because I want to see it, too."

And the sliver of moon began its inevitable descent.

Supper-Time

"**G**et in here, Hank. No use turning my hallway into a wind tunnel."

Henry McMurran limped in with a grunt and shut the door behind him with a tremulous hand, cutting off the frost-flecked breeze and stomping slush from his galoshes.

Simon Farber led the way back to his kitchen, cane tapping the worn linoleum. "One lump or two?" he asked over his shoulder.

"In all my years, have I ever taken sugar?"

"Always a first time."

"And don't ask if I want milk, neither."

Strong coffee met chipped mugs, and the two old widowers creaked down in their chairs at the scarred kitchen table, fixtures in the room as much as the decades-old stove, hand-cut cabinets, and fly-specked overhead light.

Farber observed, simply, "Cold outside."

"How would you know? You got to go *out* to see what the day's like, you old recluse. You even know what month it is? What *season?*" Hank grinned, then grimaced. "Damn, this coffee's hot! Make the devil himself wince."

"Stop your whining. Mine's better than yours and you know it. And I don't go out because there's no good point."

Silence followed—the quiet of old friends who, after 75 years, don't need to talk in order to feel comfortable in one another's company.

Finally: "I had a dream last night, Simon."

Farber set down his cup. "I guess you'll have to tell me all about it, then. You always do."

McMurran leaned forward, elbows on the table. "This was an odd one. Left me feeling...strange."

Farber raised his eyebrows, waiting.

"I was here, in Still Creek, but the old Carnegie Library was still standing and Main Street was still dirt. The cars? Model-Ts. And the great old oak tree that stood in the square...remember it? Struck down by lightning in 1951? Yeah, that was there, too."

The mildly amused gleam in Farber's faded gray eyes disappeared.

"Hank," he said softly. "Was it summertime?"

McMurran looked up sharply. "Sure was. *Middle* of summer, I'd guess. Maybe a week shy or a week late of Independence Day."

"And," continued Farber, his whisper now just the faintest breath of stale air, "was *I* there, too?"

McMurran took a fast, deep swig of scalding coffee. This time he didn't even wince. His answer came as if blown into the room on a far-away wind. "Yes."

"And we were young."

"Twelve, I guess."

Farber nodded. "And we went fishing with our split-bamboo rods down at Cobblestone Creek outside town, in the hollow where the water's deep and the swinging rope used to hang from the willow tree."

McMurran's mug dropped from his hand to shatter, unnoticed, on the table. "What else?"

Without hesitating, Farber replied, "Margaret Pendergast was there, and so was Bud Collins, and his little brother Jake…Oh, and…"

"Johnny Saxon," McMurran finished. "Jesus, Simon, what's *happening?*"

Farber flashed an odd smile. "I haven't the foggiest idea, you nutty old coot. But I *like* it. Now clean up your damn mess."

*****

That night, with the wind howling through the eaves and snow falling thick and heavy on every rooftop, road, and lawn across town, Simon Farber lay beneath crisp, clean sheets and his favorite old quilt and tried to sleep.

Across the street, he knew, Hank McMurran was already unconscious, probably in his overstuffed chair by the fireplace. The man could fall asleep during an earthquake, nod off in a flood. Anticipation didn't faze him and neither did novelty. Only death scared him, and so he avoided beds, icons of hospitals and illness, diminishment and frailty.

And Farber himself? The only thing that scared him was the world outside his house—the looming, teeming world that had struck down his wife with a car four years before, then continued spinning, as constant and oblivious as ever, toward other destructions.

He sighed, and his thoughts shifted back to the dream.

Would it come again?

Farber moved slightly. Arthritis shot pain through his knee and into his hip, where it remained, pulsing to the beat of his heart.

I want to run, he thought, *but that's a luxury I haven't had in forty years.*

The thought a mantra in his mind, he rolled over, settled, finally closed his eyes...

...and awoke in a field of tall grass, warm sun blazing overhead, the sound of bumblebees and cicadas a constant, rhythmic drone.

He sat up, looked down at his body, then leapt to his feet.

He ran.

Dandelions exploded beneath his sneakers. Milkweed pods broke against his legs. "Hey!" he cried, spreading his arms. "Hey, I'm a bird, I'm an *airplane!* Hey!*"

"You're a nut."

He turned.

"Hank! *Look* at you!"

"Look at *you!*"

"I...It's...I'd *forgotten what I looked like!* It was like a movie, like another person, like something in a *book.*"

"What?"

"My childhood."

Hank smiled, his two front teeth still ridged nubs. "We were here yesterday."

Simon's mouth worked for a moment before he could speak. "I didn't *know* then," he said finally.

"Know what?"

"That it wasn't only in my mind."

Hank nodded. "You remember this place?"

"Blaze Field, past the fishing hole on the other side of the creek!" Simon motioned with a lean, tanned arm. "Town's that way!"

And Still Creek was just as it had always been—before the mines closed, the sinkholes opened, the strip malls shut the shops, and half the town moved away. The Model-Ts, the good brick buildings with lead-glass windows, the plank sidewalks, and Quigley's wooden-floored drug store...

And it was there that they found Margaret Pendergast sitting on a tall stool at the counter, sharing a root beer float with Johnny Saxon.

"No one here to help us, guys," said Johnny. "So we helped ourselves. C'mon, have a malt!"

Simon scratched his head. "Yeah, where is everyone, anyway? It's a ghost town! Just us and the empty streets."

At that moment Bud Collins stumbled in. He looked eagerly at the other children, then his face fell. "I can't find my brother," he said, slumping into a booth. "I thought he might be with you."

They clustered around him. "Maybe Jake's not asleep yet," said Margaret.

Bud shook his head. "You don't know?"

"Know what?"

"What, Bud?"

"He died yesterday afternoon. Cancer. Had it for years. And I thought, you know, that maybe he'd still be *here*."

Silence. No one could think of anything to say. Then Bud got up, went behind the counter where Mr. Quigley used to serve ice cream and malts, and made himself a banana split; the icebox was frosted and fully stocked.

"I'm sorry," Hank said at last. "He was a great fella."

Bud nodded. "It's strange…I *feel* him near, but I can't find him." He took a bite of ice cream and banana, then another, until the whole thing was gone. At last he smiled. "Well, Jake never liked too much mourning and maudlin talk, so I'm done. Wanna go swimming in the quarry?"

They did.

*****

Every night for the next two months, Simon joined his friends in the young town, in an old time, but they never saw Jake. While awake, it was winter and he felt it in his bones. Asleep? Summer. Every evening as his wispy hair touched the cool, white pillow, he anticipated it. And every night he played in the empty town of his youth with his four old/young friends in the blazing sun of an early-July day.

"Strange," Hank said in Simon's kitchen one icy morning in mid-February.

"Hmm?"

Hank eyed his coffee disdainfully. "This is awful. Strange, I said. We always wake up when it's getting on toward evening in our dream, right? Just as the fireflies are coming out?"

Simon nodded.

"Well, last night, as the sun began to set and the dream began to fade, I *swear* I heard a voice calling my name."

"A voice?"

"Yep. And what's more, I *knew* it."

"Who was it?"

"I'll give you a hint. When it came, we were five doors down from my old house."

Simon paused, thought, then said, "But Hank, we were *in* your folks' house earlier. No one there! Just like everywhere else. Food in the pantry, lemon pie on the windowsill, toys in your room, but no people."

"Doesn't matter. It was my mother. I haven't heard her voice in sixty years, but I'd know it anywhere."

"What did she say?"

Hank cleared his throat. "She was calling me home for supper."

"I don't understand." Simon sighed. "An empty town, phantom voices…"

"Simon."

He looked up. Hank's face was set, like he had something he wanted to say. Then it relaxed. "Gimme some more of that rotten coffee, huh?"

*****

They were catching the first fireflies in the growing dark with Margaret, Johnny, and Bud when it happened. Hank snapped his head up, eyes wide, and dropped the Mason jar. Two-dozen glowing pinpricks rose up in the air around them and flooded the sky.

"You hear it?" Hank demanded.

Everyone stopped. Margaret shook her head.

"None of you? Clear as a bell!"

Hank started for home.

"We'll wake up soon," said Simon, trotting along beside him. "We always do before full dark. You won't make it."

"Yes, I will."

"But—"

"Simon," Hank said, his young face very serious, "there's something for you under your welcome mat. I put it there before I went to sleep."

"But Hank, I don't—"

And then the world began to spin, time shifted, one season intruded upon another, and Simon woke to another dark winter morning in his still, quiet house.

He breathed deeply, cocooned in his quilt, then remembered, limped downstairs, opened the front door, hissed as the cold air hit his face and legs, and stuck his hand under the mat.

The note was short. It read,

> No more bad coffee, Simon. Heart's been aching for a week, and worse tonight.
>
> These last few months have been a gift. Why, or from whom, doesn't matter. And we both know the same gift means different things to different people. For me, it was the chance to get ready for what I knew was coming. For you, it's something else entirely. I'm sure of it.
>
> Ain't that grand?
>
> I'll be waiting to play Kick-the-Can when the time comes. Always was better at it than you.
>
> Call Blake's Funeral Home if you get this.

The breath woofed from his lungs. Numb hands dialed 911.

*****

"I'm sorry, Simon."

They sat beneath the old oak tree in Still Creek Square. Margaret placed a gentle hand on his shoulder. Johnny blew his nose. Bud remained silent, brooding.

"He said he'd be here," Simon said. "He said he'd be waiting to play."

But he wasn't. And in the days that followed, Simon Farber turned further in upon himself, by day a quiet old figure in his cold winter house, by night a boy who thought more and played less in the warm summer sun.

"I wonder," Bud said some weeks later, light reflecting off their favorite fishing hole in a shimmering veil, "why we're always here by

day? Never night. Night was my favorite time during the summer."
He laughed. "Still *is*. And it was Jake's, too."

Simon nodded. A trout nibbled his line but didn't bite. "I guess
we all felt that way." Off in the distance, Johnny was teaching Margaret how to throw a football.

Bud, always the quiet one, continued, mouth a rare fount of
words: "Remember? We'd go in for supper, eat as fast as we could,
then meet by the baseball diamond at the end of the street. Half a
dozen, ten, a dozen of us! You and me and Jake and Johnny and
Hank and Bill and Travis and Davy...even the Moeller twins! And if
we didn't want to play, we'd race downtown and all the stores would
still be open, the street lamps blazing, and Preston's barber pole all lit
up, and we'd go to Quigley's for a malt and some penny candy then
rush off to the State for the late-night feature. The whole town would
be alive—young couples courting, old folks on porches, dogs in the
park, little children chalk-drawing on sidewalks. Or sometimes, if we
didn't have money, we'd eat homemade ice cream and head outside
for a game of—"

"Kick the Can," Simon finished. He looked up at Bud and
smiled. "That was always Hank's idea...his favorite. It was a game for
the evening, when our dads could join us if they were feeling young
and we could see the glint of tin in the dark. Always late in the day.
Always..." He paused.

"Always after supper," he finished slowly.

Bud nodded. "Jake heard someone calling, too. The day before
he died. Just like Hank. Know what I think? We're the last living
people from the town of our childhood. And you know what else?"

Simon looked at him closely. Suddenly, surprisingly, he thought
he did. Bud didn't even need to say it.

Hours later, in the early evening half-light, he stood before his
old home—long demolished but now whole again, wrap-around
porch freshly painted, wicker swing creaking softly in a warm wind—
and waited.

Nothing. No voice. No feminine hand and summer-green sleeve
pushing the screen door open to venture out into the heat. No familiar but long-lost face to look first up the street, then down, before
calling, calling, calling so that wherever he was, he'd hear, then
come...

"A bit longer, I guess," he said softly. "Sometime soon. But for
now..."

He looked up at the sky. "Fifteen minutes of daylight left. Still enough for a little fun."

*****

And when he woke up to the bright sunshine of an early March morning, Simon Farber went downstairs, wincing as his arthritis complained, and stepped out on his front porch, surprised to find the snow melting and a warm breeze heating the air.

"A good day to go out," he murmured.

Stepping carefully down onto the sidewalk, he began to whistle. His young neighbor, Dan Preston, called out, "Good to see you about, Mr. Farber! What's up?"

"Oh, just enjoying the day," he replied. "They go so fast, you see. And then, before you know it, it's supper-time."

"My favorite meal!" Preston exclaimed.

"Mine, too. It's nice to know it's always there, waiting for us. But in the meantime…what a beautiful day for a walk."

Simon Farber tipped his hat. Whistling again, he continued on down the street.

Acknowledgments

These stories from *Scaring the Crows: 21 Tales for Noon or Midnight* were first published in the following venues, and are reprinted with permission:

"Steel" in *Rosebud*, Issue 41. Spring 2008.

"Without Power" in *Don't Turn the Lights On*. StoneGarden.net Publishing, 2008.

These stories from *On the Edge of Twilight: 22 Tales to Follow You Home* were first published in the following venues, and are reprinted with permission:

"The Forest and the Trees," "Time to Go Home," "The Leasehold of His Days," and "Supper-Time" in *The Sounding of the Sea: Five Tales of Loss and Redemption*. Lame Goat Press, 2010.

"The Saver" in *Potter's Field 4*. Sam's Dot Publishing, 2011.

"Shells" in *Three Stories (Vol. 1, No. 2)*. OmicronWorld Entertainment, 2009.

"Par One" and "A Quick Break" in *Flash!* Static Movement, 2010.

"The Subject" in *Halloween Frights II*. Static Movement, 2011.

"The Return" in *Cup of Joe: Coffee House Flash*. Wicked East Press, 2011.

"The Key" in *Caught by Darkness*. Static Movement, 2010.

"Miss Riley's Lot" in *Day Terrors*. The Harrow Press, 2011.

"Wood Smoke" in *Don't Tread on Me: Tales of Revenge and Retribution*. Static Movement, 2010.

All others are original to the two collections reprinted herein.

Finally, many thanks to Laury Egan, Tracy Fabre, and Anne Hardin for their thoughtful and painstaking editorial work and suggestions, and to Kristofer Stamp for first publishing these books through StoneGarden.net Publishing.

About the Author

Gregory Miller was born in State College, Pennsylvania in 1978. His short stories, poetry, and essays have appeared in over 60 publications. In addition to the two collections of stories gathered in this book, he is also the author of *The Uncanny Valley: Tales from a Lost Town*, two chapters of which made Ellen Datlow's "Best Horror of the Year" list. A high school English teacher for over a decade, he lives in Pittsburgh with his family, where he is currently working on a prequel to *The Uncanny Valley*. Miller's website/blog is: http://author gregorymiller.wordpress.com/.

About the Illustrator

John Randall York was born in Tyler, Texas and grew up playing and working in a small zoo where his father was the director. He loves ghost stories, old horror movies, and illustrations from the middle 20th century. He also enjoys writing songs and playing guitar.

In addition to *Crows at Twilight*, John has illustrated *On the Edge of Twilight: 22 Tales to Follow You Home*, *The Uncanny Valley: Tales from a Lost Town*, *Scaring the Crows: 21 Tales for Noon or Midnight*, and the cover of *The Sounding of the Sea: Five Tales of Loss and Redemption*, all by Gregory Miller. He also recently wrote and illustrated his first children's book, *King Bronty*, published by StoneGarden.net. His artwork is available on his website, johnrandallyork.com.

He currently lives in Tyler, Texas with his wife and three cats.